Praise for Matt Bronleewe's Novels

Matt Bronleewe mixes the thrills of James Rollins and the history of Steve Berry into an explosive combination. *House of Wolves* takes everything up a notch from Bronleewe's first thriller, and peels back layers of secrets, conspiracies, and family betrayal. What a fun ride! I can't wait to see where intrepid August Adams leads us next.

> — Eric Wilson,
> author of *Field of Blood* and
> *A Shred of Truth*

I think we're going to have to invent a new genre to describe Matt Bronleewe's "theological thriller," *Illuminated*. Obsessively detailed and so fast-paced it could outrun a freight train, Bronleewe's debut is a taut, intelligent ride that will induce finger cramps from how tightly you'll be clutching the pages.

> — Robin Parrish,
> author of *Relentless* and *Fearless*

Matt Bronleewe's ability to take something and turn it into an opportunity for innovative expression is one of the very reasons I choose to work with him so often and respect him so much. And *Illuminated* is no different. I was educated while I was entertained. This is not your every day read, but such an intelligent escape from it. Loved it.

> — Tiffany Arbuckle Lee a.k.a. Plumb,
> Songwriter and Curb Records
> recording artist

Illuminated is a riveting debut from a fresh new voice in thriller fiction.

> — Chris Well,
> author of *Tribulation House*

Illuminated is a wonderful work that shows Matt Bronleewe is simply warming up.

> — Dan Haseltine
> (reader of some books, and writer of
> essays), Jars of Clay

Multi-talented is a vast understatement when used to describe Matt Bronleewe! I have worked with Matt in his songwriting and producing capacity for many years now and have long been impressed with his creativity. Now we add novelist to the list! This book reads like a movie. With drama and realism combined, Matt takes his readers on an unforgettable and thought-provoking journey. Rock on Matt!

— Rebecca St. James

Illuminated flickers with past secrets, present puzzles and a future that could fade to black at any moment.

— *In the Library Reviews*

HOUSE OF WOLVES

HOUSE OF WOLVES

MATT BRONLEEWE

THOMAS NELSON
Since 1798

NASHVILLE   DALLAS   MEXICO CITY   RIO DE JANEIRO   BEIJING

Published in Nashville, Tennessee, by Thomas Nelson. Thomas Nelson is a registered trademark of Thomas Nelson, Inc.

Author is represented by the literary agency of Alive Communications, Inc., 7680 Goddard Street, Suite 200, Colorado Springs, CO, 80920. www.alivecommunications.com.

Thomas Nelson, Inc. books may be purchased in bulk for educational, business, fund-raising, or sales promotional use. For information, please e-mail SpecialMarkets@ThomasNelson.com.

Herzog August Bibliothek Wolfenbüttel:

Cod. Guelf. 105 Noviss 2°, 19r
Cod. Guelf. 105 Noviss 2°, 169v
Cod. Guelf. 105 Noviss 2°, 171v
Cod. Guelf. 105 Noviss 2°, 111r
Cod. Guelf. 105 Noviss 2°, 170v

Scripture quotations are from the King James Version of the Bible.

Quotation from *Art at Auction: The Year at Sotheby's 1983–84* used by permission of Sotheby's Publications. By Tim Ayers, © 1984.

Publisher's Note: This novel is a work of fiction. Names, characters, places, and incidents are either products of the author's imagination or used fictitiously. All characters are fictional, and any similarity to people living or dead is purely coincidental.

Page Design by Casey Hooper

Library of Congress Cataloging-in-Publication Data

Bronleewe, Matt.
    House of wolves / Matt Bronleewe.
      p. cm.
    ISBN 978-1-59554-250-2 (hardcover)
    1. Antiquarian booksellers—Fiction. 2. Booksellers and bookselling—Fiction. 3. Manuscripts, Medieval—Fiction. 4. Suspense fiction. I. Title.
PS3602.R64266H68 2008
813'.6—dc22   2008015744

Printed in the United States of America

04 05 06 07 08 QW 6 5 4 3 2 1

For my parents, Tom and Bev Bronleewe,
who raised me in a house filled with love

ZERO

AD 1181

WESTPHALIA, GERMANY

Henry the Lion could feel their eyes digging into his skull. The blindfold held fast, but the theater of his mind played out the scene—the golden statue of the Virgin before him, and around him, cloaked from head to toe in robes the color of coal, the members of the Black Vehm. His ears filled with the sound of their breathing in unison, like the bellows of hell sighing in eternal lament. The dank-smelling subterranean room bore no other sound—no one was allowed to speak, save the Lord of the Tribunal.

"What say you, *Lion*?"

Henry recognized the booming voice immediately. A chill rippled through his body.

The blindfold was torn from his face. Through blinking eyes he watched the giant approach, inching so close that his flame-red beard scoured Henry's face.

"Are you surprised by my presence?" Barbarossa asked.

Henry answered, "Your presence is of no importance to me. I am simply dismayed by my position here. I have stood before this court many times, but never from this foul vantage point."

It was true. The red-bearded giant occupied Henry's usual position of authority. Apparently he had missed the message that there had been a change in leadership. How unfortunate. It would not be long before they killed him. That was the only purpose the court seemed to serve— to vanquish from society those who abused the Ten Commandments. Of course, over time the court had found the commandments to be too narrow a constraint and had drawn up its own long list of amendments to God's holy law, including six sins held to be the worst of all offenses.

1. Heresy
2. Perjury
3. Paganism
4. Witchcraft
5. Revealing the secrets of the Holy Vehm
6. Revealing the secrets of Charlemagne

Sixteen years earlier Barbarossa had canonized Charlemagne, the first emperor of the Holy Roman Empire. Barbarossa seemed obsessed with continuing the great king's legacy. Henry knew that his own ascent to power put that goal squarely in jeopardy.

"Why have I been brought before this court, Duke of Swabia?" Henry asked. The name was a deliberate stab at the giant's authority— an undercutting of his title as the new emperor of the Holy Roman Empire. He immediately felt the needle-sharp point of a sword creep under his chin.

"You will call me Emperor, as the commoners do," Barbarossa said, pressing the sword tip ever so slightly into the soft flesh of Henry's neck.

"You have persuaded me, Emperor," Henry said, filling the word with as much disdain as he dared. He backed away from the sword, which Barbarossa lowered—but not before flashing the insignia stamped upon its blade. *SSGG.* The hideous initials made Henry's blood run cold. He cleared his throat, gathering his nerve. "I demand to know why I have been brought here."

"You *demand?*" Barbarossa said, turning and walking toward the statue of the Virgin Mary, which glowed with the mirrored flames of the surrounding torchlight. "Well . . . if you *demand . . .*" He motioned for another blindfolded victim to be brought from the back of the chamber. The lamenting prisoner was dragged to Barbarossa's feet by two of the deputy judges, known as the *Freischoffen.* "Do you recognize this man?"

"I do," Henry the Lion said. "His name is Burkhard. He is a faithful servant, a worker in one of my stables. What could you possibly want with him? He has broken none of the Vehmic laws."

"I will ask him the same question I plan to ask you, Lion," Barbarossa said. He leaned over until he was face-to-face with the prisoner. "Where is the relic?"

The man's mouth fell open. He shook his head. "I don't know what you mean," he said, pleading for his life.

"Where is the relic?" Barbarossa asked a second time.

"Please, Emperor, I beg of you. I do not know!" The two Freischoffen held the poor man fixed as he fought against his restraints.

"Let him go!" Henry the Lion said.

"Silence!" Barbarossa roared. He turned back to the prisoner, ripping the blindfold away from the man's eyes. "I will ask you only one more time: *Where is the relic?*"

The prisoner closed his eyes, a visible wish for the blindfold to return. "I do not know, your lordship."

Barbarossa stepped aside. "Liar! You are commanded by the Holy Court to approach the Virgin and kiss her feet."

The prisoner seemed stunned. "I will be allowed to live?"

"Kiss the Virgin's feet," Barbarossa said. "Your fate is hers to decide."

The prisoner trembled as he knelt before the Virgin. He glanced around nervously, as if expecting a blade to promptly deliver his head from his body. But no blade came. The man smiled and wept, bowing to kiss the Virgin's feet. As his lips touched the cold metal he felt a deep groan from within her frame. He shrieked and jumped back, his face contorted with fear. He would have bolted from the cave if the Freischoffen hadn't stopped him.

"The Virgin does not sound pleased," Barbarossa said. He nodded to the Freischoffen.

Suddenly, through some unseen magic, a fissure running down the front of the Virgin opened. Her two sides split wide, exposing the horror within: an iron maiden—thick spikes, set at even intervals for maximum penetration.

"This man is innocent!" Henry the Lion cried.

"No man is innocent," Barbarossa said. "Your turn will come soon enough."

The Freischoffen dragged the thrashing prisoner forward and threw him inside the terrible chamber. Before he could protest further, the Freischoffen closed the statue. The prisoner could be heard screaming from within.

Barbarossa turned to face the members of the Holy Court. "The Virgin has declared her judgment! Let any man who opposes her speak now!"

The cavern fell silent, save for the cries of the pierced prisoner.

"So be it!" Barbarossa said. He advanced to the Virgin, head lowered, and placed his hand upon the heart carved into her chest. He pressed the blessed symbol, and a grinding rumble emanated from beneath the floor. A moment later the cries of the prisoner vanished. Barbarossa turned and raised his arms. "Behold! The Virgin's judgment has come swiftly today, my brothers!"

The Freischoffen threw open the Virgin. The interior was empty. The flickering firelight revealed the only evidence of Burkhard's short tenure there—a dark, glistening stain of red.

"You will pay dearly for this," Henry the Lion said as he watched the hulking form of Barbarossa draw near.

"His life could have been spared," Barbarossa growled under his breath. "As could yours. Now, I ask you the same question: Where is the relic?"

Henry the Lion peered around at his brethren, hoping to find some measure of support in their shadowy faces. But there was nothing save their cold condemnation.

Barbarossa's serpentine fingers curled around Henry's neck. "Tell me where you have hidden it, or I will spare you the Virgin's wrath and choke the life from you myself!"

Henry the Lion didn't flinch. His countenance was as calm as the evening waters of the Dead Sea, which he had viewed during his crusade to the Holy Land almost a decade earlier. It was there that he first heard about the relic the red giant now desired. But the relic was far more dangerous than Barbarossa realized.

"Death would be too great a reward for the burden I carry," Henry the Lion said, his voice strained but steady. "Generations will pass before the relic is found again. And to the one whose hand finally discovers its holy power—*God save him.*"

ONE

August Adams could feel their eyes digging into his skull. He was on their turf, and they wanted answers.

"Mr. Adams?"

August massaged his temples with his fingers, trying to kick-start his mind. He hadn't slept a wink the night before. Now his brain felt like the bowl of cold oatmeal he'd left lying on his kitchen counter.

"Mr. Adams, do you plan on saying anything?"

He glanced at the clock on the wall. Only five minutes had expired. Could that be right? Five minutes? He could feel his heart pounding. Another twenty-five minutes of this torture would kill him.

"Mr. Adams?"

August squeezed his eyes shut and tried to focus, to forget the news he'd heard last night, that horrible phone call he'd received just before midnight. *August, I've got something I need to tell you*. Nothing good started with those words. Especially coming from his ex-wife, April.

"Dad?"

August opened his eyes and stared into the quizzical face of his nine-year-old son, Charlie. *Sorry*, he telepathed to him, wrinkling the small expanse between his eyebrows for effect.

The boy shook his head, like a coach witnessing his star batter strike out in the final game.

"Mr. Adams, would you mind explaining to the class exactly what a bibliopaleontologist does?"

August stared blankly at Charlie's fourth-grade teacher. Her stern expression reminded him of the reason he was here—Career Day. Originally, Charlie had asked April's boyfriend, Alex Pierson, to come speak. But that arrangement changed in a hurry due to last night's news.

"The term is *archeobibliologist*," August said, snapping to attention. "But I gave that up a long time ago." He turned to his son. "I guess Charlie forgot to tell you that."

The class giggled. Was it funny? Not really. But the fact that he was having a nervous meltdown right in front of them probably was. What kid wouldn't be amused by the sight of a grown-up completely losing it?

The teacher squatted down until she was level with August, who was sitting on a pint-sized plastic chair. "Well, since you're not an archeo-*whatever* anymore, maybe you can tell the class what you do for a living now?" she said. "Please?"

August cleared his throat and adjusted his tie, which displayed the thinner underneath tail extending two inches beyond the wider top layer. He loosed it in an attempt to even things out, then finally took it off altogether. The children giggled again. He considered telling them that he was a clown. At least that would seem believable.

He scratched at the thick stubble that spread like a dark moss across his chin. "I buy and sell rare books," he explained. "Emphasis on the *sell* part." This usually brought a chuckle from an adult audience. Instead, the class looked bored.

"Do you buy and sell comic books?" one boy asked, brushing aside the dark, straight hair that covered his eyes.

"Occasionally," August said, his musical crescendo in the middle of the word implying that special circumstances had to surround the notion.

"'Cause my dad has a comic book that he says is worth a lot of money."

August pondered this. "What comic book is it?"

The boy shrugged his husky shoulders. "I don't know."

"Have you seen it?"

"Yes."

"And you don't remember?"

The teacher stepped in. "Mr. Adams, maybe it's time you—"

"I remember!" the boy said, his smile pushing his face into a perfect oval. "It had a picture of a guy like Superman. But it wasn't Superman."

August stood up. The entire class followed him with their eyes as he approached the boy. "Think hard. Was it Captain Thunder?"

The boy's jaw dropped, amazed at the mind reader. "I think that's it!"

"You're telling me your dad has a Flash Comics #1 ashcan?"

The boy's face went blank.

"Never mind," August said, letting him off the hook. He plucked a business card from his pocket and jotted his private cell phone number on the back. "Give this to your father. Tell him to talk to no one before he talks to me. *No one.* Got it?"

The boy nodded emphatically.

"Good." August returned to his undersized chair and nearly missed it altogether, forgetting its humble height. The class laughed uncontrollably.

"Everyone!" the teacher said. "Let's give Mr. Adams a big thank-you before he leaves."

"Seems a little early," August said.

"We'll fill the extra time," the teacher said.

The kids were already clapping and saying their good-byes.

"I've got one more thing to show them before I go," August pleaded with the teacher. He looked over at Charlie, who had his head buried under his hands. "Please?"

The teacher sighed. "You're not going to try and sell someone a book, are you?"

August set his briefcase on his lap and unclasped the front. He opened the lid and lifted a large volume from the titanium-framed vessel, setting it on his lap. "This isn't a genuine rare book, but it's an exact copy of one," he said. He slipped a thumb between two pages in the middle and slowly pried the book open.

The children, seeing a brilliant glimmer emanating from the pages, stood at their desks to get a better look. *Ooohs* and *ahhhs* fell from their lips.

"Charlie," August said. "Think you could help me out up here?"

Charlie rose from his seat, apprehensive at first, until he saw the looks of envy that marred his classmates' faces. He tried to keep from breaking a smile as he joined his father at the front of the room.

"Thanks," August said, putting a hand on his son's back. "I want you to hold up the book so everyone can see it."

Charlie held out his arms, and August propped the book against his chest like a human easel.

"It's really heavy," Charlie said.

August put a supporting hand on the underside of the book. "I've got you covered," he whispered. He turned to the class. "Has anyone here ever heard of a guy named Henry the Lion?"

A pigtailed girl in the front row waved her hand. "He's on Nickelodeon, right?"

"I don't think so," August said. "Anyone else?"

The comic-book boy raised his hand.

"Just to warn you," August said. "He's not a superhero."

The boy's hand went back down.

"Henry the Lion," August began, "was a famous warrior duke who lived in the late 1100s. He was part of a powerful family known as the Welf dynasty. Does anyone have a guess what *Welf* means?"

The pigtailed girl raised her hand again. She didn't wait to be acknowledged. "Is it like *Belf*?"

"Belf?" August repeated, not sure that he had heard her correctly.

"Like . . . like when a . . . um . . ."

August could tell she was clueless. Just a girl looking for some attention. "Sorry, it's not a *belf*. Anyone belf? I mean . . . anyone *else*?"

The class chuckled. The teacher chuckled too. He was beginning to figure this crowd out.

A wafer-thin boy in the back raised his hand, but only halfway.

"You think you know the answer?" August asked.

"Is it an *elf*?" the boy asked, his voice shaking.

August smiled. It must have taken every fiber of the boy's being to venture an answer. "Not quite. But you're on the right track playing with some of the letters . . . you just chose the wrong ones."

The timid little boy put his hands over his face. August thought he was about to slip underneath his desk when he suddenly reappeared. "Wolf!"

"You're exactly right!" August said. "Welf means wolf!" He thought the revelation would elicit a response. It didn't. Fearing he'd lost their attention altogether, August howled like he was baying at the moon. The class erupted in delight.

The teacher calmed them down. "Mr. Adams," she said. "Maybe you can tell us about Henry the Lion's relation to the book we're all looking at?"

"This book," August said, flipping through the pages, "is called The Gospels of Henry the Lion. Prince Henry and his wife, Matilda, ordered its creation in the late 1100s. As you can see from the elaborate pictures inside, it's more than a book: It's an amazing work of art. So amazing, in fact, that Sotheby's of London sold it at auction in 1983 for nearly twelve million dollars. It would easily be worth three times that today. And probably a lot more."

Tiny sparks of astonishment could be heard exploding among the students.

August held his palm up to them. "This is just a copy!" he said, quelling their enthusiasm. "You think I'd let you even *look* at this if it were the real thing? No way! But don't worry. You can look at this replica all day."

The kids gathered en masse before the luminous book.

The teacher disrupted the chaos, ordering them to line up. She then bent down for a closer look herself. "It's a remarkable copy," she said, inspecting the pages.

"I agree. The best I've ever seen."

"Are you sure it's not real?"

August laughed. "That's not possible. The real book is under high surveillance, half a world away in Wolfenbuttel, Germany."

"So where did you get this copy?"

"From my father," August said. "He sent it to me for my birthday yesterday. It was a great birthday. At least for the first twenty-three hours and fifty-five minutes."

TWO

August tried to push the events of last night out of his mind. If only he hadn't answered the phone. Why did he have to pick up? He knew the minute he saw April's number that he should let it go through to voice mail. But that's exactly what she wanted. A nonconfrontational communication. That's why she called late, probably hoping he was out celebrating, cell phone forgotten, drowned out by the noise of some loud uptown party. And so to spite her, he had picked up. A mistake.

"Mr. Adams?"

"Yes," August said, gazing at the teacher with the same blank look he had given her earlier.

"Thanks for your time. You're free to go."

"Sure," August said. He took the book from Charlie's arms and put it back in the briefcase, thanking his son for his help by ruffling his hair.

"Dad?"

"Yeah, I know, not in front of everyone . . ."

"No, it's not that," Charlie said. "You got that book from Grandpa Adams?"

"Yes."

"But I thought you weren't talking to Grandpa Adams."

August sighed. "I'm not. In fact, to be honest, I don't even know for sure that he was the one who sent it. There wasn't a card or a phone call, or anything like that. But your grandpa and I have what you might call a mutual fascination for the book. No one else would have sent it to me."

The teacher was giving instructions to the class to put away their things. The end of the school day had arrived.

"So does that mean you're talking again?"

"I don't know what it means," August said. He put a hand on Charlie's shoulder. "But don't think for a minute that that could ever happen to us. Is that what you're wondering?"

"Maybe."

"Don't think about it for another second," August said. "Your grandpa has a lot of problems, and those problems are why we're not talking."

"But what if I have problems? What if you won't talk to me either?"

The kids put on their jackets and placed their books and homework in their backpacks. The teacher turned out a few of the lights. The bell rang.

"I promise that won't ever happen," August said.

Charlie pulled away, retreating to his desk. "You're not very good at keeping your promises."

August glanced over at the teacher, hoping she hadn't heard their conversation. She seemed busy gathering up some pencils that had strayed from her desk. "We can talk more about this later," August said.

"Later? I thought Mom was picking me up."

"No," August said. "I'm taking you. Your mom is going to be busy with Dr. Pierson tonight."

"Why?"

"Because . . ." August sputtered to a stop. "Hold on a second," he said. He pulled out his cell phone and asked the teacher if she could keep an eye on Charlie. He pressed a speed-dial button and stepped out of the room.

Three rings.

"Hello?"

"April, it's me. I think you know why I'm calling. I was talking to Charlie about why he was coming home with me tonight, and I realized he had no idea—*no idea!*—what's going on. Is that possible?"

There was no answer.

"Are you there?"

"Yes, I'm here. But I'm not going to talk to you if you aren't going to be reasonable."

"Reasonable? You just got *engaged* last night, and you haven't even told your own son?"

"I wanted to wait until I had the ring."

"Is that what you're doing tonight with Alex? Ring shopping? Isn't it traditional to have the ring before you propose?"

"He said it was spontaneous. And he wanted me to get exactly what I want."

August fought the rage welling up inside him. Grade-schoolers swarmed around him in a race for the exit, their grins infuriating him even more. "April, listen to me. I've known Alex longer than you, and he's *never* spontaneous. The reason he didn't pick out the ring ahead of time is because it would kill him to choose the wrong one."

"I'm not speaking to you like this."

"Just tell me what I'm supposed to tell Charlie."

"Tell him . . . just tell him . . ."

August could tell she was holding back tears.

". . . tell him I'll have a surprise for him when I see him tomorrow. Tell him that." She hung up.

August tucked the phone away and reentered the classroom. The teacher was talking to Charlie about the colorful fish that filled the small aquarium behind her desk. He walked up and gently interrupted her. "I'm sorry I was a little off balance today, Mrs.—" He blanked.

"Mrs. *Walters*," she said. She pointed to the front of her desk. There, in giant capital letters, was printed M-R-S-W-A-L-T-E-R-S.

August slapped his forehead. "I'll understand if you never ask me back," he said. He looked down at Charlie, who was still mesmerized by the swirling aquatic life.

"From what Charlie says, you're a very busy man, so don't worry about it. I forget my name some days too." She handed Charlie his backpack and began marching him toward the door. "Now, if you two don't mind, I need to get ready for tomorrow's class."

"Never ends, does it?" August asked. He picked up his briefcase.

"Never," Mrs. Walters replied.

August and Charlie exited the classroom into the hallway, which reverberated with the sounds of children anxious to leave.

"You still haven't told me why Mom is with Dr. Pierson tonight," Charlie said.

"It's a surprise," August said, his tone flat. "She'll explain everything tomorrow."

"A surprise?"

"Don't get your hopes up," August said. "Now, c'mon. Let's get out of here." They walked down the hallway toward the rear parking lot, where August had stowed his car.

"Charlie?"

"Yeah, Dad?"

It was wrong for April to keep their son in the dark like this. Should he tell him? April would never forgive him, but did it matter? It would only be one more grievance upon a stack of a million more. The camel's back had already broken, so what was a little more straw?

"Dad?"

"Never mind."

He pushed open the door at the end of the hallway. Across the parking lot, he could see his car. There was a young man leaning against it. He was swathed in black, with raven-feather hair cropped in a lopsided V over his face, a dark trench coat with a variety of foreign symbols stitched across the arms, a mesh shirt, leather pants, and boots strapped halfway up his legs.

August's first thought was that perhaps this was the school's art teacher. He'd heard stories. But when their eyes met he knew that the Goth-garbed punk didn't have finger painting in mind.

"Dad?" Charlie asked. "Were you going to tell me something?"

"Hold on," August said. He watched as the punk crossed the parking lot. He didn't run, but he didn't exactly stroll either. August pulled Charlie back inside the school and closed the door, checking to make sure it was locked.

"What's going on?"

August swiveled and locked arms with Charlie, keeping him close by his side. "I forgot something," he said.

"What?"

"My keys."

"I saw them in your hand."

"Wrong keys. I need the other ones."

August heard the door rattle. The hallway was disturbingly empty. He hoped Mrs. Walters was still around so he could alert security. Maybe he was being paranoid, but only a year earlier he had paid a high price for being careless. He wasn't about to let it happen again.

August opened the classroom door and hustled Charlie inside. Mrs. Walters was still there. He locked the door behind him.

"What's going on?" Mrs. Walters asked.

"I need you to call security," August said. "There's a guy in the rear parking lot that looks like trouble."

"You mean the teachers' parking lot?"

"I guess."

"Mr. Adams, only teachers are allowed to—"

August cut her off. "I was late! There's no time to argue. This guy . . . I just have a feeling he's dangerous. Please, could you call security?"

Mrs. Walters picked up her phone. "They're going to have some questions for you too, Mr. Adams. For parking in the teachers' lot."

August wasn't listening. He set his briefcase up on Charlie's small desk and opened it. He stared at the book inside. "Can't be," he whispered.

"Can't be what?" Charlie asked.

August pulled out his cell phone and punched in a long series of digits. A woman's voice answered.

"Hello," August said. "I'm looking for a Dr. Cleveland Adams. Is he available?"

"I'm sorry," the woman said, "but he left unexpectedly. Do you want to leave a message?"

"No, that's all right."

"And your name is—"

August hung up. The question might have been innocent, but there was something in her voice that bothered him. He stared at the keypad, then dialed a set of numbers he'd memorized but never expected to use. There was a ring tone. And then he heard it. His father's voice. He expected it to be shocking, but it wasn't. It wasn't at all. It was worse. It was comforting. The sound of his childhood, alive once more.

"Dad. It's me."

"August?"

He listened to see if he could detect any aging in his father's voice. But if anything, the voice sounded younger than August remembered. Maybe it was his memory that had tarnished, maybe his father had always sounded that way. "Yeah. It's me."

"Ah! You must have received your birthday present."

August feathered his fingers against the cover of the book. "I need you to tell me exactly what you sent."

"It should be quite obvious what I sent! It's your favorite book! At least, it used to be."

Mrs. Walters spoke up. "Mr. Adams, a security guard has been sent to go check things out in the teachers' parking lot. And he would like to talk with you afterwards about why your car was there in the first place."

August ignored her. His father was the bigger problem right now. "It's a *copy* of The Gospels of Henry the Lion, right?"

His father didn't respond.

"Dad?"

"We can't talk about this over the phone."

"We have to talk about this over the phone, because Death's errand boy is waiting for me outside, and I need to know *why*."

"Meet me at Times Square in an hour, and I'll explain everything."

"Times Square?" August asked. He tried to keep his emotions in check. "Are you in New York?"

"I just got here."

"Are you in trouble?"

His father's voice shifted from light to dark. "Son, you're the only one I can trust. Guard that book with your life. I'll tell you everything when I see you. One hour! Don't forget! And don't let anyone follow you!"

Then, like a ghost receding into August's memory, his father disappeared.

THREE

Lukas Daraul pounded his fist on the school door, leaving an impression on its weathered metal exterior. He closed his eyes and slowed his erratic breathing. *Careful*, he told himself. *No need to lose control. Focus on the solution, not the problem.* He would never admit to any of his friends online that he relied on such spongy self-helps, but the truth was, some of what his high school counselor had told him really worked.

Some.

The rest was junk.

He was on his way back to August's car when he heard the door open behind him. He turned and flipped the cords of hair out of his line of sight. It was a teacher making a quick exit to her car. Her bouncing stride reminded him of a prancing forest fawn or an African gazelle, probably a memory of some stupid nature show his mom forced him to watch as a kid.

The teacher was very young. Maybe only a year or two older than he was. And hot too. Why hadn't he had teachers like her? He moved toward her slowly like a jungle cat.

She spotted him, and her hand impulsively plunged into the top of her purse. Her eyes darted between her car and the school door. She was obviously contemplating her best method of escape.

"I'm not going to do anything," he said. Why was she passing judgment on him? Maybe he wasn't going to hurt her at all! How could she know?

She put up a hand, still fumbling in her purse. "Just stay away," she said. "If you want money—"

"I don't want money," Lukas said, palms up in surrender, still inching toward her. "I just need to get into the school."

"Why?"

"I left something inside."

"Do you have a student here?"

Lukas hadn't considered this option. "Yeah," he said. "Got a boy in kindergarten."

"What's his name?" she asked.

"Lukas." The name fell out of his mouth like a giant boulder, tied to his foot, dragging him to the bottom of an ocean. The name was death. It was an instant mistake, one he couldn't take back. If he left her alive, she would surely remember the name, and they would eventually put together the fact that he didn't have a kid at the school and that the name was, in fact, his own. His fate—and thus hers—was sealed.

"Lukas?" she said, as if struggling to find it on some invisible list. "Who is his—"

He sprang on her. His speed surprised them both. Lukas had always suspected he possessed powers that he hadn't tapped into yet, that he would find when the moment was right, like Neo in *The Matrix* or Buster Casey in *Rant*.

She screamed.

"Stop it," he said, feeling the power of her shriek beneath his fingers, which were stretched across her mouth like a wide strip of duct tape. He pushed her head against the pavement, watching the tears build in her eyes until they were dual pools spilling over the sides of their tiny enclosures, creating rivers of mascara that cut trails down her makeup-caked cheeks. "You're older than I thought," he said. The attraction he had felt for her dissipated. She had to be at least thirty.

His free hand fished inside his trench coat for the appropriate blade for the job. Thirteen of them traveled with him today, chosen specifically from his collection. It was an outrageous collection, one he had amassed through a battery of eBay transactions and knife-show trades. Not to mention the plundering of a dozen museum storage spaces.

The thefts didn't bother him. Knives were created for a purpose—to defend and destroy—not to hang in a display box. Lukas was simply saving the knives from a meaningless existence. He contemplated which blade would find its destiny first:

Blade One—a Kommando Spezialkrafte Gerber "Mark II"

Blade Two—a nineteenth-century Will & Fink push dagger

Blade Three—an Ostblock Spetsnaz ballistic-model

Blade Four—an Emerson CQC-7B with G-10 Handle

Blade Five—a seventeenth-century Italian stiletto

Blade Six—a Microtech OTF "Nemesis"

Blade Seven—a CRKT Serengeti hunter

Blade Eight—a WWI Fliegerkappmesser M

Blade Nine—a seventeenth-century German triple-blade dagger

Blade Ten—a nineteenth-century American naval dirk

Blade Eleven—a Moeller "Viper I"

Blade Twelve—an Emerson CQC-T "Hawk"

Blade Thirteen—a Boker "Specialist" with MCS

"Blade Five," he said aloud, as if this would somehow convey the necessary information to the girl in his grip. He wondered what her name was. He wished he could ask her. Groping about her person for identification would only confuse her, as well as give her the opportunity to escape.

He drew the Italian stiletto out from the thin sheath he had woven into his jacket. It had a slim, sexy edge, the perfect knife for killing a woman. He imagined Juliet would have pierced her breast with such a blade. It was a romantic thought, one he immediately extinguished.

Suddenly a voice spoke behind him. He swiveled his head but couldn't see who it was through the sheaf of hair covering his eyes. Another reason to switch to a Mohawk, he thought.

"What's going on over there?"

Lukas returned the stiletto to its hiding place, replacing the emptiness in his hand with Blade Three. He stood to his feet, and the teacher tore away from his grip. He saw the speaker, a security guard—graying at the temples, swelling at the midsection—probably late to a job where nothing usually happened anyway. The guard reached for the walkie-talkie hanging on his belt.

"Don't," Lukas said, holding out his knife.

If the guard was worried, he didn't show it. "Put it down," he said calmly.

Lukas replied by flicking a trigger on the side of the knife handle. The blade flew out, landing with a foul *thunk* in the middle of the guard's chest. The guard hadn't anticipated this: a spring-loaded weapon, created in the Soviet Union during the 1980s for a special division of the KGB. Before today, Lukas had played this moment out with store mannequins. It didn't surprise him that the death-play's real-life counter-part was immensely more gratifying.

The guard fell to the ground, blood foaming at the corners of his mouth. Lukas rushed over to greet him, laying him flat on his back to pry the knife from his quivering form. He contemplated using a second blade to slit his throat, but as soon as the thought entered his mind the guard kissed the world good-bye.

Lukas cleaned the blood from the knife, paying special attention to the section in the middle where the letters were imprinted: *SSGG.*

The Black Vehm promised him that upon his return with The Gospels of Henry the Lion they would fully explain the meaning of the letters. *Every blade must bear the SSGG*, he had been told. He didn't argue. He would have been killed on the spot if he had.

Just as instructed, he placed the blade underneath the guard. If it had been dirt and not pavement, he would have stuck the knife into the ground and then propped the body on top of the short hilt. But this would have to do. It was allowable by the rules of the Holy Court.

FOUR

He still couldn't believe he had found them—the Black Vehm. Of course, the truth was that they had found *him*. In their twelve-hundred-year history, not a single member had ever disclosed his membership to the fraternity. What was known about them had been gathered from the journals of dead men.

Lukas had always wanted to belong to a secret society. For some reason they didn't exactly advertise their whereabouts. But an online friend of his had had an idea: *Have you tried joining the Belegarth Medieval Combat Society?*

MED13VALMAN: THE WHAT?

MARAUDER1492: THE BELEGARTH MEDIEVAL COMBAT SOCIETY.
    YOU NEVER HEARD OF THEM???!!!

MED13VALMAN: STOP YELLING. NO, I'VE NEVER HEARD OF THEM.

MARAUDER1492: YOU KIDDING?

MED13VALMAN: WHO ARE THEY?!?

MARAUDER1492: YOU EVER GO TO A NEW YORK DRAGONS GAME?

MED13VALMAN: I HATE FOOTBALL. ESPECIALLY ARENA FOOTBALL.

MARAUDER1492: ME TOO. BUT AT HALFTIME THE COMBAT SOCIETY
TAKES OVER.

MED13VALMAN: ???

MARAUDER1492: THE WEAPONS AREN'T REAL, BUT IT'S PRETTY
COOL. ALL THESE HARD-CORE DUDES IN CHAIN MAIL. THEY
FREAKING POUND ON EACH OTHER. IT'S ABSOLUTELY WICKED.

MED13VALMAN: YOU SERIOUS? THAT'S COOL!!!!!

MARAUDER1492: I KNOW. I CAN'T BELIEVE YOU DIDN'T KNOW
ABOUT IT.

MED13VALMAN: PROBABLY 'CAUSE IT'S AT A FREAKING FOOTBALL
GAME! HOW LAME IS THAT?

MARAUDER1492: IT'S 'CAUSE OF THE FIELD. IT'S PERFECT FOR
BATTLING.

MED13VALMAN: YEAH. I GET IT. CAN I JOIN ON THEIR WEB SITE?

MARAUDER1492: I THINK SO. FUNNY THAT A MEDIEVAL SOCIETY
HAS A WEB SITE!

MED13VALMAN: NO LIE! TALK L8R MAN . . . I GOTTA CHECK THIS
OUT!

He did more than check it out. He became leader of the local realm—
the WelfLanders. It took a lot of hard work: entering as a peon, advancing as a pawn, and rising as a knight before finally becoming a war leader.
He became an expert foam-smither, learning how to construct the vari-
ous weapons of the sport. Bows, arrows, daggers, glaives, javelins, bag-
head flails, pommels, and punch shields—all of them took exhausting

hours to create, something the watchers of their sport never seemed to appreciate.

But it was all worth it, because it led him to the Black Vehm. Lukas vividly remembered his first encounter.

It was a night like many others, waiting backstage for the halftime battle to begin, rallying the throbbing horde with promises of retaliation. (The rival realm had drawn blood at their last encounter, planting an X-acto knife in the tip of a javelin.) They walked onto the field, waving their arms in defiance at the jeering crowd. This was part of the game: they were hated by the audience, which was stocked with upper middle-class families too proper for such lunacy.

"Go home, freaks!" he heard from a man dressed in a head-to-toe New York Dragons costume. The irony was almost more than he could bear, and it took every ounce of self-restraint not to bludgeon the man on the spot with his two foam axes.

The cacophony of a thousand trumpets blasted from the overhead speakers, and the war began.

"Sink your teeth into them, WelfLanders!" Lukas cried, running forward. He took out the first two other-realmers he encountered with simultaneous left and right blows. He then spun his arms wildly at his sides, imagining himself not as a warrior, but as some menacing medieval machine, slicing a path of death toward the opposing war leader. He spotted him in the distance—a giant with dark leather scales cascading down his torso, eclipsed by a monstrous helmet at the costume's apex—a bull's head with a trio of horns.

Lukas promised to flog himself for not thinking of this arrangement first—the tri-horns were glorious, each of them tipped in bright red blood, viewable even by the people in the cheap seats. He roared so loudly he thought he felt something tear in his throat as he rushed toward his warmongering doppelgänger.

"Dude, chill out," he heard the rival war leader say as he drew near.

Chill out? The words didn't even register with Lukas. His gloved fingers dug deep into the foam of each axe as he cocked them back for a deathblow. And then, he fell. He had been so fixated on the bullheaded leader that he had failed to notice the legion of combatants that had banded to take him down. They crashed upon him like an angry mob at a cancelled death-metal concert. He tried to scream, but his lungs were squeezed flat by the phalanx lying on top of him.

A siren erupted overhead, and the warriors dispersed. Lukas couldn't find the strength to rise. The arena assembly jeered as he was carried from the field on a stretcher.

"Kid, are you severely mentally challenged or just an idiot?" the EMT asked, checking Lukas's abdomen in the medical center backstage. "You've got at least two broken ribs. You sure it's worth it?"

Lukas smiled, working at his bloody front teeth with his tongue.

"The arena won't cover any damage," the EMT reminded him. "Remember that paper you signed earlier?"

"Doesn't matter. My family is rich."

"Whatever . . ." The EMT shook his head. He taped the war leader around his midsection and sent him on his way.

Lukas exited the medical center into a long, fluorescent-lit corridor. It was empty except for the noise of the audience in the distance. Lukas heard the crowd, the cheering, the energetic displays of emotion filled with delight and wonder. Why were they so gung ho to embrace the Dragons and not the WelfLanders? Both wore costumes. Both played by rules of engagement. Both had winners and losers. In theory, there was very little difference. Besides the fact that arena football was for morons.

"I saw you out there."

Lukas blinked. There was a man standing before him. How had he not seen him a second earlier?

"You almost got him, you know. The war leader of the Arnor Realm."

Lukas blinked again. The man wore a suit. An expensive one. He knew it was expensive because it was the kind his father used to wear every day to work, the kind he wore every day after the work dried up, and the kind he wore the day they found him dead in his BMW.

The man walked forward and held out his hand. "Christopher Vallodrin," he said.

Lukas reached out, then suddenly recoiled as the pain in his side flared. "Sorry," he groaned.

The man looked displeased. His hand wavered in the air like a teetering tightrope walker.

Sensing that the tension was real and growing worse, Lukas crossed the void, wincing every inch, until finally making contact with the man, whose sturdy handshake nearly caused him to faint.

"Are you in pain?" the man asked.

Lukas stared into the cerulean eyes—two bottomless lakes centered in the weathered road map of his face—and wondered who on earth this callous reptile could be. "You saw it," he said, bravely testing the waters. "I almost got killed out there."

The man fished in his left pocket and produced three talcum-white pills. "These might help," he said, rattling them in his roomy fist like a gambler about to unleash a perfect roll of the dice.

Lukas took the pills and popped them in his mouth. He was terrible at dry swallowing, so he chewed the pills, an act that stole every drop of moisture from his mouth and left a thick residue on his tongue. "Thanks," he choked.

"There are more of those in my VIP box," Vallodrin said. "If you'd care to join me."

Box seats meant that the guy probably had some food, and Lukas was famished from the fighting. "Sure," he said, following Vallodrin into a passkey-protected elevator. "I wondered where you appeared from," he said as the sleek metal doors shut.

Vallodrin smiled. "There is a series of tunnels and elevators that only I have access to."

"Only you? Man, you must have purchased the premium package."

Vallodrin pushed a button marked with a red star, then slid his passkey through the card reader next to it. "Lukas, there are levels far beyond the 'premium package.'"

Lukas stared at his reflection in the polished elevator door. "I never told you my name," he whispered, feeling a chill travel down his spine.

The doors opened, and a brilliant bath of light spilled into the elevator from the adjoining room.

"Another perk of living above the premium package is being able to find out anything about anyone," Vallodrin said. "For the past month my people have been watching you. I have a proposition I'd like for you to consider."

Lukas followed him out of the elevator but kept a foot at the edge of the door to keep it from closing. *Proposition?* He'd heard stories about older, rich guys liking to get their kicks with younger men. "Listen, dude. I just don't go that way, you know what I mean? I bet you're totally a great guy and everything, and I really am thankful for those pills, which, by the way, absolutely *rock*, but—"

Vallodrin snapped his fingers, and two bodyguards appeared. "Gentlemen," he said, "would you mind showing Lukas the view?"

The bodyguards took Lukas by the arms and dragged him across the plush white carpet toward a series of floor-to-ceiling sliding glass doors on the opposite wall. Lukas thrashed in their tight grip, but the pills had turned his muscles limp.

"Put me down," he pleaded.

The bodyguards, who were apparently hard of hearing, slid the doors open and pushed Lukas through. He was immediately enveloped in the cheers of the crowd, coming from far below the lavishly furnished observation deck they were now perched upon.

"No, no, no!" Lukas yelped, realizing where they were taking him.

"Hope you enjoy the ride," one of the bodyguards said. He grabbed Lukas by the ankles and dangled him over the edge of the railing.

The blood rushed to his head, and Lukas felt like someone had shoved a water hose in his mouth and turned it on full blast. His stretched torso pushed the pain-needle past *unbearable* into the red danger zone of *unbelievable*. He tried not to look down, but found that he lacked the willpower to shut his eyes. The crowd didn't even notice him, and if they did, they certainly didn't acknowledge that he was engaged in some precarious predicament. He imagined some child pointing skyward and the father explaining that there was nothing to worry about, Son, it was just a stunt to entertain the audience.

Vallodrin's nasal purr suddenly filled his ears. "As you can see, I have the best view in the house."

"Please . . ." Lukas gasped. "I'll do anything you want."

Vallodrin laughed. "I can already make you do anything I want. But you've got this all wrong. This was just a test. And so far, you're failing."

"I don't understand."

"Of course you don't," Vallodrin said, as if he were trying to teach calculus to a three-year-old.

Lukas felt his body being lifted back onto the plush precipice of the observation deck. But instead of relief, he felt an even greater sense of fear. The bodyguards left and another man entered the picture, his face obscured by the lights.

"This was your chance," the man said. "I put everything on the line, and you're totally screwing it up."

The voice . . . could it really be?

"*Garrett?* Wha—How did . . . ?"

"You are *Med13valMan*, right?"

Lukas felt like he was watching the conversation take place from some fixed place in space, as if he were somehow a third-party observer, a shadowy spy taking it all in through the safety of binoculars. "*You* . . . you're . . . ?"

"*Marauder1492.*"

Lukas couldn't believe any of this was happening.

"Welcome home, brother."

The rest of the evening was equally surreal. Vallodrin explained the purpose of the Black Vehm, the necessity of their existence. And then he asked if Lukas would join them.

"Why do you need me?" he asked. It was a question he posed to Vallodrin then, and at every meeting since.

The answer always came back the same: "Because you will do what others will not."

Now, standing next to the dead body of a security guard in an elementary school teachers' parking lot, he understood what that meant. The school door opened. He didn't wait to see who came out. He dashed across the parking lot into an alley. He stopped when he reached the front of the school, seeing August with his son and his briefcase climbing into a cab. The goal was still within reach. He grinned, seeing a man pull to a stop at the end of the nearest block in a silver Mercedes-Benz. A convertible. And the top was down.

"Time for some fun in the sun," Lukas said, pulling out Blade Four and running toward his next victim.

FIVE

April Adams opened her purse and retrieved a small red notebook labeled, simply, LISTS. She flipped through the pages, glancing at headings along the way—WORST MOVIES EVER, BEST MEALS EVER, FUNNIEST THINGS CHARLIE EVER SAID, and so on—until she reached the final chapter, which bore the questionable title of WORST DAYS EVER. She regretted ever starting the list, but found that she was compelled to keep it completely current and impeccably ranked. The top three positions had been locked in place for over a year and read to April like the horrible footnotes of a troubling biography:

1. The day my mother, August, and Charlie almost died.

2. The day August signed the divorce papers.

3. The day I got fired from the Library of Congress.

She didn't bother to read further, though her peripheral vision caught that by number thirteen the list became so mundane as to include a bad shrimp cocktail she'd eaten, a fact that depressed her.

She tapped the page with her pen, as if divining the proper ranking of today's catastrophe: August's indictment of her withholding her engagement from Charlie. Why she allowed August to make her feel guilty about anything was a mystery. After all, he wasn't part of her life anymore. He was just Charlie's father, nothing more. At least, that's what her mother, Rose, kept telling her. And April was inclined to believe it.

She clicked the pen, retracting the point, retracting her decision to make an entry. Maybe she was being rash. After all, she was about to go ring shopping. That would make her feel better, right? Surely the day would turn around and somehow make it onto her list of BEST DAYS EVER, a list she had yet to begin. "I'm such a pessimist," she said aloud.

"Something wrong?"

She spun around to meet the adoring eyes of Alex Pierson, who was now her—she grappled with the word for a moment—*fiancé*. The circumstances that had brought them together still amazed her. A year earlier, Alex had sustained a gunshot wound that nearly killed him. Though he survived, the wound left him a paraplegic. His wife at the time—a high-society type who felt embarrassed by his condition—took their three children and left him for good. For months he fought her in court, but the effort ended in defeat. In the midst of the resulting depression, Alex looked to April for support. It wasn't long before they'd fallen for each other.

"I didn't hear you come in," she said, walking over to meet him.

Alex patted the soft rubber tires of his wheelchair. "The Morgan Library made me purchase the quietest ride money could buy. But I'll attach a bicycle bell to it if it will make you feel better." He pulled her onto his lap.

She laughed. "Maybe it would." She relaxed in his arms, falling back against his strong upper body. She raked a hand through his salt-and-pepper hair, ending the journey at his close-shorn beard, which perfectly framed a wide grin. No words escaped her lips for a few minutes, until finally, regrettably, she spoke. "Tell me it's going to get easier."

"It's going to get easier."

"No, Alex, seriously," she said, standing and smoothing out her gray skirt. She tucked her chin-length brown hair behind her ears. "You know I want this more than anything. But I can't help but ask myself why I haven't told Charlie yet."

A hushed whir emitted from the wheelchair as Alex motored across the opulent ruby red carpet of the East Room. The considerable space was girded entirely by glass-protected bookshelves stretching three stories high, bound by a narrow guardrailed walkway. Alex stopped next to the fireplace that dominated the wall opposite the entry.

"You said it was because you wanted to tell him in your own time," he said. "Isn't that true?"

"It *is* true," she said. "But I thought that meant the right time for him. Now I'm realizing that I meant the right time for *me*."

Alex reached inside the fireplace, which had long since ceased being functional, and lifted a briefcase to the arm of his wheelchair. He opened it and removed a small book, delicately placing it on his lap. He then set the briefcase back inside the fireplace, where it was hidden from view. With a wide grin he shuttled the book over to April.

"What is this?" she asked, taking the fragile tome from his hands.

"Something that should prove to you that you're not making a mistake."

She opened the cover and saw that Alex had penned a message inside. "You wrote in it?"

"You seem shocked."

"I am shocked," she said. "I can't believe you would devalue a book like this."

"Devalue?" he asked. "You sound like your ex-husband."

April blanched. He was right. "Alex . . . I'm sorry . . . I . . ."

"You don't need to apologize. Just read it."

She stopped herself from saying any more. "Should I read it out loud?" she asked.

"If you'd like," Alex said, his eyes begging to hear the words.

April cleared her throat. "For April," she said, exchanging a smile with Alex, who was already mouthing the next line. "A small token of my love as our life together begins."

To Kill a Mockingbird. It was her favorite book. She turned to the title page and saw that it was not only a first printing/first edition, but also signed by the author.

"You mentioned it the first day you came to work here," Alex said. "Now it's yours."

"This must have cost a fortune," April said, still not able to fully grasp that the treasured book was hers.

"And you're about to cost me another fortune. Come. It's time to go ring shopping!"

She reached for his outstretched hand. At the exact moment their fingers touched, the lights flickered, and the windowless room fell into darkness. Not one to fall prey to superstition, April still found herself unable to escape the thought that their physical union had created some disturbance in the universe. It was—at the very least—a bad omen.

"What happened?" she asked.

An alarm erupted overhead. "Just a temporary power failure, I would guess," Alex said calmly, squeezing her hand. "Or maybe they're testing the security system. They do this from time to time. You shouldn't worry."

The alarm stopped.

"You see? Everything is fine."

Seconds later they heard a scream outside the door. And then, the distinct crack of gunfire.

"Now should I worry?" April asked, her heartbeat galloping.

"We'd better hurry," Alex said. "If they're coming this way we don't have much time."

April knew there was only one place for them to hide. She ran to the bookcase located next to the door and grabbed a brass handle connected to its wooden frame. She pulled, and the entire bookcase swung out from the wall, revealing a spiral staircase behind—the only means of accessing the additional levels that lined the room. Alex's chair whirred softly as he squeezed into the gap between the staircase and the interior wall. April joined him, pulling the secret compartment closed behind her.

Seconds later the door creaked open. Through a crack between the books, April watched a man enter with measured steps. His lithe figure was lit only by the dimness of the skylights overhead, and April placed her hand over her mouth as she spotted the shimmer of a gun in his hand.

He closed the door behind him with a soft *click.*

"I'm assuming you're still here," he said. "There are few hiding places for a man in a wheelchair."

April felt a tug at her sleeve, and saw that Alex was motioning her to ascend the spiral staircase. She shook her head *no* as he pushed her up a step. She bit her lip and climbed higher.

Alex rolled forward and pushed open the secret compartment. "There are few hiding places in this entire city for someone like me," he said, revealing himself.

April stood frozen, just outside of view, unsure whether to follow Alex or stay back, the rival teams of bravery and stupidity waging war in her mind.

"And where is your adoring little companion?" the intruder asked. "Fiancée, I hear?"

"You said you'd leave her alone," Alex said.

"And I will," the intruder said. "But there's been a complication with August, and I need to ask her a few questions."

A dark cloud gathered in April's mind. Alex and the gunman knew each other. And they were talking about . . . August? Why? She took a deep breath and descended the steps, then exited the safety of the concealed space and stood behind Alex's wheelchair, clutching it like a shield.

"Let me handle this, April," Alex said.

"What's going on?" she asked.

"I think I can answer that for you," the intruder said.

April gazed ahead, her vision fixed on the man's angular skull and the ashen canvas of skin stretched over it.

"Allow me to introduce myself," he said. "My name is Christopher Vallodrin."

April searched the recesses of her brain, digging through her mental shelves, cupboards, and drawers, but came up empty. The name meant nothing.

"Doesn't ring a bell?" he asked. "It shouldn't. I pay a small fortune every year for a pack of PR hounds to sniff out any mention of me and snuff it out. But I know who you are. I know that you used to work at the Library of Congress until you got fired for stealing a rare Gutenberg Bible. I know that you somehow avoided jail time because of some string-puller over at the FBI. I know that you have a son named Charlie, and that he's quite bright, but you worry because he doesn't have many friends at school. I know that you used to be married to August Adams, a book hunter who became too obsessed with his work to take care of his family. I know that you just got engaged, though I'm curious why you would waste your time on a man who can't even take a jog with you in

Central Park. I know many things, April—but I don't know where your ex-husband is taking my book."

"What book?" she asked.

"The Gospels of Henry the Lion," Alex said, entering the conversation. "August has accidentally come into possession of it."

"Accidentally?" April asked. The idea of August unintentionally stumbling upon a highly prized book was unlikely.

"So to speak," Vallodrin said. "Dr. Cleveland Adams used to be an associate of mine. He stole the book from me and sent it to August in order to flee Germany undetected."

"Germany? I thought he lived in London."

Vallodrin smiled. "There are many things about Dr. Adams you don't know. Did August ever explain to you why they aren't on speaking terms?"

"Of course he did."

"Did he tell you it was because of his mother? The way Dr. Adams treated her?"

April remained quiet.

"Untrue," Vallodrin said. "Maybe the next time you see August you should ask him what really happened. Of course, the next time you see him he'll probably be in a casket." He turned to Alex. "Now tell me: Where is August going? To meet his father? Are they trying to find the Stuhlherr?"

Stuhlherr? April had heard that word before . . . but where?

"Our deal is done," Alex said. "I told you exactly where your freak Frohnboten could find August. It's not my fault that he got away."

Another word—*Frohnboten*—so familiar, but April couldn't place it. "Alex, I don't understand," she said, suddenly wondering if she knew her fiancé as well as she thought she did. "Did you set August up? For this . . . this *monster?*"

Alex turned to face her. "I had no choice. Vallodrin said he was going to kill you unless I helped him get August. I knew a public location would give him the best chance to get away alive."

"Public location? You mean Charlie's school?"

"I know it sounds horrible, but there weren't any other options," Alex said, pleading. "Charlie was never going to be in any danger. And look, August got away! Everything's okay."

"Everything's okay? What do you call this?"

"This is called sweetening the deal," Vallodrin said. "I'll make you a new offer: you tell me where August is going, and I'll let you live."

"I have no idea where he is!" Alex said. "How could I?"

"You're right," Vallodrin said. He turned to April. "But *you* could find out. I assume he still takes your phone calls?"

"I won't do it."

"Call him," Vallodrin said, pointing the gun at her head.

April felt the life run out of her. Maybe she could at least warn August. She crossed the room—keeping an eye on the gun—and retrieved her cell phone from her purse.

Alex wheeled over to her. "I don't think you should do this."

"Of course I shouldn't! But there's no other choice." And then she saw the real reason he was talking to her. Tucked beside his leg was a black, palm-sized handgun. She tried to keep the astonishment from registering on her face. She flipped open her phone and dialed August's number.

"You're running out of time," Vallodrin said, glancing at his watch.

April put the phone to her ear. "It's ringing."

Alex gently pushed the wheelchair joystick to the right and turned to face Vallodrin.

"It's going through to voice mail," she said.

"How do I know you dialed his number?"

"Look for yourself," April said, tossing him the phone.

Vallodrin, startled at the sight of the phone flung his way, reached out to catch it, not thinking that his other hand—his gun hand—was inadvertently pointed at the ground.

Alex took immediate advantage. He raised his pistol and pulled the trigger, and Vallodrin dropped to the floor. His gun rattled out of his hand, and April raced to retrieve it.

"Don't touch it!" Alex said. "It will just incriminate you if you pick it up."

"Smart thinking," she said. Instead she picked up her phone, which had smashed against the ground and broken along its plastic hinge. She frowned, holding the phone like a dead pet.

Suddenly, two armed men stormed into the room. April threw the two halves of her phone at them in a futile attempt at defense. Alex followed her action with a more effective offense, firing multiple rounds at the infiltrators, who collapsed on top of one another.

"Now what do we do?" she asked him.

"We get out of here. Because if there are any more of them"—Alex raised his gun and pulled the trigger, producing a hollow *clack*—"we're in trouble."

SIX

Alex and April exited the room and entered the atrium that connected the buildings of the Morgan Library. Sunlight streamed into the spacious glass-walled piazza, which lay entirely empty.

"Where is everyone?" April asked.

"Vallodrin's men must have forced everyone into another room," Alex said, gliding toward an exit. "Come on, the police will be here any minute."

"Shouldn't we stay until they get here? They'll need to know what's going on." *Not that I have any answers*, she thought dismally.

Alex pushed open the door leading to Madison Avenue. There were sirens wailing in the distance, getting closer. "The police will detain us, and we don't have time for that. We've got to find August before the Black Vehm does. Once they find out Vallodrin is dead they'll double their efforts to recover The Gospels of Henry the Lion."

"Wait," April said, replaying what he said in her mind. "Did you say the Black Vehm? I thought they disappeared a century ago."

Alex laughed. "Guess who spread that lie."

She wasn't surprised to hear it. It was a common ploy for covert organizations to provide the public with a story of their demise. And most of the time, it worked brilliantly.

"Vallodrin claimed to be their leader," Alex said. "But I'm sure they'll have no problem replacing him."

"Why do they want that book so badly? Besides the obvious, of course." Like many ancient illuminated works, The Gospels of Henry the Lion was worth millions. But April suspected that any organization calling itself the Black Vehm had more than money in mind.

"I wish I knew," Alex said, engaging his wheelchair into street gear, which April struggled to keep up with as she jogged behind him. "But it sounds like this person called the Stuhlherr has the answers. If we can find him."

They stopped at the street corner as traffic raced by.

"I feel like there's more you're not telling me," April said.

Alex looked up at her and grabbed her hand. "I'll explain everything later. You've just got to trust me for now."

They crossed East Thirty-sixth Street and raced into the shop on the next corner—the Complete Traveler Antiquarian Bookstore, which bore the distinct title of the first travel bookstore in the United States. The wiry, mustached man behind the counter greeted his familiar visitors with a cordial grin, which instantly disappeared when he saw the dismay on their faces.

"Is anyone here besides you?" Alex asked him.

"Well, yes, there's a woman, a rather *rich* woman, trying to find just the perfect book for her husband's new library and—"

"Get her out of here."

The conversation paused for a moment while a squad of police cars whizzed by the front window.

"What on earth is going on?" the wiry man asked, arms twitching.

"Bernie, get any customers out of here and lock the door," Alex said, more strongly this time.

The wiry man looked like a marionette yanked by its strings as he departed for the adjoining room. He returned only seconds later with a stately woman at his arm. She seemed very confused, and he assured her that he would find just the right thing and have it for her by the next morning. She blubbered something about service these days as he ushered her out the door, somehow managing to stuff a few business cards into her hands before closing the door and clasping it shut.

"There," he said, brushing his hands together as though he'd just been working in the garden and now wanted to enjoy the company of his guests. "Now tell me what's going on."

"First, let me use your phone," Alex said, picking up a black, vintage-style telephone on the front counter. He dialed.

"That's strange," he said. "It didn't even ring. It went straight through to August's voice mail."

"Must be dead," April said. "I mean, his *phone* must be dead."

The disquiet was punctuated by two more police cars rushing past the window, followed by a massive armored police truck that shook the floor, causing Bernie to throw his hands over a skyscraper of books threatening to topple.

"There's been some trouble at the Morgan," Alex said.

"Some trouble?" Bernie straightened the pile of books until they seemed sufficiently safe. "April, care to fill in the details for your understated friend?"

"I was hoping you could do that for me," she said.

"And I was hoping you could do that for both of us," Alex said. "Let me explain. We just had an encounter with a member of the Black Vehm."

Bernie sat down on a wooden stool behind the sales register. "How many people are dead from this 'encounter'?"

"*You* know about the Black Vehm?" April asked, surprised. She couldn't imagine someone like Bernie daring to dabble with something as sinister as the Black Vehm.

"The Internet affords enough anonymity for someone as timid as I am."

"You're not timid," April said.

Bernie looked at her with the eyes of someone who'd been told he had the winning lottery ticket, but knew it wasn't true. "I've lived in New York for twenty years, and I've never taken the subway," he said, an unshakeable closing argument.

"You're just shy," April said.

"He's as scared as a matchbook in a gasoline store, and we all know it," Alex said. He maneuvered his wheelchair toward the back of the store where the maps were kept. "Now get over here and help me find something."

"What?" Bernie asked, trailing behind him.

Alex stopped and pointed to the highest shelf. "That."

"*That* doesn't come down," Bernie said, biting his thumbnail.

"I've heard horrible stories of men—grown men—getting run over by angry people in wheelchairs."

Bernie spat out a nail fragment. "It's completely off-limits. I'm sorry. There's absolutely nothing I can—"

"April, would you mind getting the ladder?"

She walked into the next room, returning moments later with a solid-oak three-step ladder, which she propped up on the floor in front of Alex.

"Are you going up there?" Bernie asked.

"Yes," Alex said. "I'm going to miraculously rise from my chair and climb the ladder."

"Ha-ha."

"April, my dear, do you mind?"

April fought back the urge to tell him that she *did* mind. She spent most of her days responding to this same command over and over, climbing up ladders and stairs and fetching Alex whatever book seemed to tickle his interest that day. It wasn't his fault he was wheelchair-bound, and she felt awful for even considering the possibility that he was taking advantage of her.

And she was, after all, more than grateful for the job. Most libraries wouldn't touch her with a ten-foot pole after the stunt she'd pulled at the Library of Congress the year before. But still, she found the work less than rewarding. It was a point that August often mentioned: *You're an expert. Why do you spend your days as Alex's little servant girl? You should be* his *boss!* But she knew that was being unfair. August simply wasn't being reasonable.

"April?"

She smiled and put a hand on Alex's shoulder. There would be time to talk about it later. "Sure."

"No!" Bernie stomped his foot. "I'm serious! I'm going to get in a lot of trouble for this."

April hurried up the steps of the ladder, taking one last glance at a most pitiful Bernie before plucking a thick cardboard tube from the top of the bookcase. "Sorry," she said to him, gracefully making her way back down.

"Whatever," Bernie said. "Just be careful."

"Don't worry," April said, popping off the red plastic end cap and slowly pulling out the fragile map rolled up inside. "You know we won't damage it."

"No," Bernie said, wiping the sweat from his brow. "I mean be careful with what you *find*." He cleared off a nearby desk and covered it with a protective green mat, upon which April unfurled the map.

Alex rolled over to the desk and squared himself behind it, with April and Bernie situated at the opposing corners.

"What is this?" April asked, scanning the yellowed map for clues.

In the upper left-hand corner was a legend bearing the title: NEU-SCHWABENLAND. Beneath the title were three words: DEUTSCHE ANTARKTISHE EXPEDITION and the date 1938–1939. But it was the small emblems in the legend that made the hairs on the back of her neck stand on end: a Nazi flag on a pole, marked GEHISSTE FLAGGEN; a Nazi flag flying alone, marked ABGEWORFENE FLAGGEN; and a tiny, dotted circle, marked SCHIFFSPOSITIONEN.

Alex's hand hovered above the map, as if his fingertips could feel the icy tundra it represented. When he finally spoke, his voice was quiet, reverent. Or maybe frightened. "This was created by the Black Vehm, who hid their organization within the ranks of the Nazis. They claimed to have taken possession of a powerful ancient relic and buried it somewhere in the Antarctic, in a region they called New Swabia—a reference to the ancient lands of Emperor Barbarossa."

"What relic?" Bernie asked.

"The lost relic of the Welf treasure," Alex said. "In the late 1100s, Henry the Lion—arguably the most influential member of the Welf dynasty—became completely obsessed with collecting relics. It was said that a king once offered wheelbarrows full of gold in exchange for his allegiance. Henry the Lion asked instead for wheelbarrows full of relics. The skulls of martyrs, the teeth of saints, splinters of the true cross . . . he gathered everything he could find from around the globe."

"Including this lost relic you mentioned?" April asked.

"Yes," Alex said. "Although *lost* is probably not the right word. *Hidden* would be more accurate. Over time, Henry the Lion's authority dwindled, and in his absence the strength of the Black Vehm grew. He suspected that they might eventually overtake him, so he hid the most significant piece of his collection. But, hoping that one day a member of the Welf family could claim it once more, he created a book that held clues to what it was and where it could be found."

"The Gospels of Henry the Lion," April said.

"Exactly!"

"Aren't you going to tell us what the relic was?" Bernie asked, ticking like a clock wound too tight.

"That, I'm afraid, I don't know."

"Then we've got a problem," Bernie said.

"Sorry?"

"I said, we've got a problem," Bernie said, his tone growing more intense with every word.

"Bernie, what's wrong with you?"

His face contorted slightly as he reached for something under the desk. "I'm sorry," he said, holding up a small, nickel-plated gun.

The front door opened, and the woman whom he had earlier escorted out the door walked back in. This time, however, she didn't bear a befuddled expression. This time, she seemed completely and utterly in control.

Bernie moved to her side. "She got here just before you did. And she made me an offer I couldn't refuse."

"I have a way of being persuasive," the woman said, her voice a refined mixture of vanity and wealth. She took the gun from Bernie's hand and pointed it at April and Alex. "My name is Veronika Vallodrin. Which one of you killed my husband?"

SEVEN

As a child, August remembered hearing his father describe a Yankees game he attended on the hottest day ever recorded in New York.

"It was 105 degrees!" he'd said. "Only one degree less than the melting point of the sun!" He claimed that he cooked a ballpark hot dog on top of the bleachers. "I nearly died!" he had said, with no pretense of exaggeration.

"And who won the game?" August remembered asking.

"Awww!" his father had said, batting the question away like a fly. "It was the worst year for the Yankees ever! But I don't blame them. I blame the heat!"

A hundred and five degrees. August had never forgotten the feeling of dread that triple-digit number had brought to him back then. The same sensation jabbed him now as he jumped out of the cab with Charlie in the middle of Times Square and saw the new headline on every one of the square's massive digital displays: A New Record—107 degrees.

"Dad, a new record!"

"Don't get too excited," August said. But he knew it was no use.

Charlie loved records. All kinds of records. And they sprang from his lips whenever he found the occasion. He'd see a street vendor and mention the most hot dogs eaten in twelve minutes—sixty-six. They'd go to the local gym and he'd recite the most push-ups ever accomplished in one hour—1,940. And the list went on. If there was a record for "most records known by a human," Charlie would have it.

"It doesn't feel that hot," the boy said.

"You're crazy," August said. "What have you got in you, snake blood?"

"Dad! Stop kidding around. Just because a snake is coldblooded—" Charlie stopped talking and pointed his finger at the crowd on the other side of the street. "Hey, isn't that guy getting out of the silver car the same guy we saw at the school?"

August scanned the multitude, instantly spotting the raven-haired punk who'd been waiting for him in the school parking lot. He was staring straight at them. And he was smiling.

"Dad, do you think he's hot in that coat?"

"Probably," August said, directing the two of them toward a nearby trinket shop. "But let's not bother to ask."

Inside the store, August positioned himself behind a shelf of snow globes, which seemed an outlandish keepsake given the day's punishing heat. He squinted through the watery orbs, catching a glimpse of their stalker crossing the street toward them. He turned and walked over to the man behind the cash register. "Is there another way out of here?"

The man shook his head.

"Are you sure?"

The man just shrugged.

August grabbed Charlie by the arm and headed for the door. He stopped, seeing a dark figure blocking the exit.

"Going somewhere?"

August pulled Charlie in close. "We were just about to jump on a tour of the city. Want to join us? Oh, but you probably can't. I heard there's a freak convention going on downtown, and I'm sure you wouldn't want to miss giving the keynote speech."

The punk moved in closer, his right hand stuffed inside his jacket. "All I want is the book."

"The book? I don't have a book. I do, however, have some sandwich cookies in here," August said, lifting his briefcase into view. "They're not Oreos, but they're still pretty good."

The punk snorted. "What's wrong with you?"

"Sorry," August said. "When I get nervous, I say weird things. Like, just a minute ago I was looking at all the trinkets in here and I turned and said to my son, 'Son, wouldn't you love to have a bronze Statue of Liberty?'" Suddenly, August grabbed the very item from the shelf beside him and swung it at the stalker. The base of the statue struck him on the side of the head, and he fell into a rack of I-♥-NY T-shirts. August looked back to catch the reaction of the store owner, but he'd already disappeared, as had the other shoppers who'd been milling around seconds earlier.

"I think you're right, Charlie," August said, stepping over the stalker and motioning for his son to follow him out the door. "He did look awfully hot in that coat."

Once outside, August checked the time. It had been exactly an hour since he had spoken with his father.

"Follow me," he said to Charlie, crossing over Broadway to the center median, which was packed full of people. He had failed to ask his father exactly where they were supposed to meet.

"Dad, why did that guy want your book?" Charlie asked. "Didn't Grandpa give it to you for your birthday?"

"Yes. Well, sort of. To be honest, I'm not sure he was supposed to give it to me."

August's eyes danced from face to face, hoping to land on his father's recognizable visage with his round eyeglasses, brown fedora, and tweed jacket. It was a uniform August could count on no matter the climate, even in 107-degree heat.

"You mean he stole it?"

"No, I just mean . . ." August looked down at Charlie. "I just mean that . . . well, yes, he may have stolen it."

"Grandpa is a crook?"

"We'll never know if we can't find him." August placed his briefcase between his legs and put his hands around Charlie's middle, hoisting him up. Luckily, Charlie was small for his age, but still too big to be sitting on August's shoulders. "Have you gained some weight?"

"Ten pounds since the beginning of the year!" Charlie proudly announced.

The combined heat of Charlie and the sun was already killing August. "Okay, quick, take a look around. Do you remember what Grandpa Adams looks like?" He'd only shown Charlie a picture of him on a couple different occasions.

"I remember."

"I knew you would. Do you see him?" August asked, swiveling around.

"No," Charlie said. "But I do see the guy you hit with the Statue of Liberty! Dad! He sees me! He's coming over here!"

Charlie began kicking his legs in uncontrolled fear, nearly sending August toppling to the pavement.

"Charlie! Stop it!"

"Dad! He's getting really close!"

August yanked his son down from his perch and picked up the briefcase. "C'mon. This way."

With Charlie in tow, he weaved through the crowd to the other side of the median. Luckily, the traffic was nearly at a standstill. They crossed the street and darted into the lobby of a hotel.

"Are we safe?" Charlie asked.

"Definitely not," August said. He put down the briefcase and opened it, removing the book inside. He placed the book in Charlie's arms. "I want you to stay right here with this. Can you do that?"

"Dad, I'm not a baby."

"I know, it's just—"

"I can do it."

August saw the confidence on his son's face and had to admire Charlie's courage. "That guy who's chasing us thinks the book is in here," he said, patting the briefcase. "So I'm going to go back outside and let him come after me. He's going to catch me, and I'm going to give him the briefcase. Then I'm going to come right back here to you. Okay?"

"Okay."

"And if you have any problems?"

"I'll use my telekinetic powers."

August frowned. "Except you don't have telekinetic powers. What will you really do?"

"I'll find a policeman or someone else who can help me."

"Okay, that's better," August said, running to the exit. "I'll be right back."

"Promise?"

At that moment, Charlie didn't look like the young man he was turning into. He looked like the bright-eyed child August had known back when he and April were still together. The memory almost brought tears to his eyes. The old days. The good days.

"I promise," he said, pushing open the door and dissolving into the throng of people rushing by.

EIGHT

Lukas was puzzled. Had August really left the kid behind? On one hand, it made complete sense, leaving the child in the hotel, making sure he was out of harm's way. Harm's way being, of course, *him*. On the other hand, it was idiotic. If he could get his hands on the kid, then August would be forced to trade the book for his son.

And then another idea hit Lukas: What if August didn't even have the book? What if he'd left it with his son? Lukas caught something in his eye—the way August seemed to taunt him, the slight maneuvering of the briefcase to be clearly in sight, a lure to draw Lukas away from the boy. Or maybe he was outthinking his opponent, overthinking the situation. It would be an easy thing to do. Though Lukas had never taken a test to confirm it, he was quite certain he had far beyond a genius level IQ.

He cut through the wall of yellow taxis and chased after August, taking the bait. He waited until August was over half a block in front of him before turning back toward the hotel. He wanted a decent head start, just in case August was faster than he appeared.

Lukas waited until the doorman wasn't looking—he didn't want him to see the gash on the side of his head, fresh from getting smashed by that stupid statuette—and dashed into the hotel. He searched the corridor leading to the lobby, finally spotting his prey in a back corner, seated on a ridiculously overstuffed purple velour chair. And there, placed squarely on his lap, was The Gospels of Henry the Lion.

Their eyes met, and the boy began to rise slowly from the chair.

Lukas placed a single finger to his lips. "Shhhhhh!" he whispered, sliding Blade Eleven—the Moeller Viper I—out from its hidden position in his jacket. He showed it to the kid. The kid seemed impressed, and then horrified.

Sit down, Lukas motioned. But the kid was frozen, a human ice block. Lukas was nearly upon him. The kid looked jittery, the ice melting, his nerves beginning to unwind.

Lukas heard the large revolving door swish open behind him, and a family of six—all decked in their finest New York regalia—came bursting onto the scene. They were laughing and singing and kidding one another—all the normal family activities that made Lukas sick to his stomach. Keeping an eye on the kid, he put a hand up to cover the red blotch on his scalp.

The family passed by, unaware of the signal for help that Lukas's defenseless victim was beaconing with his eyes.

"They don't care about you," Lukas whispered. "The truth is, no one does in this life. And maybe the next one too."

"You're wrong," the boy said, clutching The Gospels of Henry the Lion against his chest. "My dad cares."

"Your dad cared enough to leave you behind," Lukas said, inching closer.

"He'll come back. He promised. And when he does—"

"When he does it will be too late," Lukas said, quickly closing the gap between them. He pressed the tip of the knife into the boy's side to emphasize his point.

"It's never too late," a voice said.

Lukas whipped his head around to see who dared to interrupt his scarefest with the boy.

It was August.

"Took you long enough to get here," Lukas said. "Especially with, you know, the life of your son on the line."

"I met an old friend and stopped to say hello."

Lukas was once again puzzled by August's strange behavior. Vallodrin had warned him that he was a tad off-kilter, even by book-collector standards. He looked around to make sure August wasn't still holding the statue weapon he'd wielded earlier. "So, who was your friend? Batman? Because you're going to need him."

"Close," said a voice from behind him.

And that was the last thing Lukas heard before something slammed into the other side of his head, in mirror-image harmony with the wound he already bore.

NINE

August watched Charlie jump onto the back of his knife-employing assailant and wrap his arms around his grandfather's neck. "You got him, Grandpa Adams!" he said.

Dr. Cleveland Adams bowed. "Lord Imaginary Hart, at your service!" he said, tucking his cracked cane under his arm.

Charlie looked puzzled. "Lord Imaginary Hart?"

August ran to Charlie and threw his arms around him. "*Lord Imaginary Hart* was a children's book your grandfather wrote. It was about a magical ten-point stag that always saved the day at the last minute, just when the whole world seemed to be falling apart. But the stag was never seen by anyone but the main character."

". . . Whose name was August," Cleveland said, completing the tale. He put one hand on August's shoulder and the other on Charlie's. "I'm sorry for the circumstances, but it's good to see you. *Both* of you."

"I've missed you, Grandpa," Charlie said.

"Missed me? But you've never even met me."

"That doesn't mean I couldn't miss you."

"Is that right?" Cleveland questioned, stroking his well-groomed goatee.

"Totally. I mean, sometimes I feel like I miss the characters I read about in books, even though I've never met any of them. But I've heard the stories about them, so it *seems* like I really know them."

Cleveland smiled. "He sounds just like you," he said to August. "Bright, energetic, filled with wonder at the world around him."

"But he'll soon learn how that wonder can get him in a lot of trouble," August said, taking The Gospels of Henry the Lion out of Charlie's arms. "What should we do about our friend in the black trench coat?"

"Leave him here," Cleveland said. He leaned over the still figure of the Frohnboten and opened his jacket to reveal the bounty of weapons hidden inside. "When hotel security finds him, they'll look like heroes dragging him off to the police."

"Sounds good. No need for us to get involved directly. Especially while we have The Gospels of Henry the Lion," August said. "We need to get this to a museum, pronto."

"You'll do no such thing!" Cleveland said, striding over to him and plucking the thick volume from August's grip.

"We can't keep it," August said. He glanced around nervously. "If you don't turn it in now, you're going to be put away for a very long time. And if the Germans get hold of you—"

"The Germans are the ones who started this whole mess!" Cleveland said, hustling to the hotel exit. "I'll tell you more about everything on the way to see the Stuhlherr."

"The Stuhl-*what*?" Charlie asked.

"The Stuhlherr was a judge who presided over the Court of the Holy Vehm," August explained to his son as they followed Cleveland out the door. "But I don't know why your grandfather keeps talking about it, because none of them exist anymore."

"You're half-right, and a hundred percent wrong," Cleveland said, edging his way to the street and sticking out his hand to flag a cab. "The Holy Vehm disappeared. But a splinter group, the Black Vehm, is still very much alive."

"That's not possible."

"Who do you think sent that vicious little Frohnboten?"

"What's a Frohnboten?" Charlie asked.

August began to explain. "It's an unfriendly—"

Cleveland cut him short. "A Frohnboten is an assassin for the Black Vehm—ruthless killer! Charlie, you need to know *exactly* how dangerous this situation is."

A taxi stopped, and Cleveland threw open the door, letting the boy in first. He stopped August. "You never should have brought him with you."

"I didn't have a choice."

"Then his life is in your hands, not mine."

"There you go again," August said, sliding into the cab. "Washing your hands of all responsibility. I'll have you remember that none of this would be happening if you hadn't stolen that book!"

The cab driver glanced at August in the mirror apprehensively.

"It's just an expression," August said to him, hoping the whole conversation was lost in translation.

Cleveland entered the vehicle and slammed the door shut. "Here's the burgled item!" he exclaimed, holding up the book for inspection.

The cab driver just grinned. "Where to?"

"Let's go to the Morgan Library," August said. "April will know what to do."

"We can't get her involved," Cleveland said. "This matter can only be resolved by talking to the Stuhlherr."

"Who is this Stuhlherr you keep talking about?"

"Honestly, I'm not sure. I've only corresponded with him through e-mail."

"Then *he* could actually be a *she*?"

Cleveland frowned. "I never thought about that."

"That's because you're a chauvinist. I should know. April always said that I was one too."

"A female Stuhlherr . . ." Cleveland said, mulling over the idea.

"Where to?" the cab driver asked again, this time not as happily.

"The public library," Cleveland said. "And make it snappy. No telling when Lukas is going to wake up."

"Who's Lukas?" Charlie asked.

"That's the name of that psychopath who almost cut you to pieces," Cleveland said.

"He's just kidding about that," August said to the cab driver.

"No, he's not, Dad!"

"Charlie . . ."

"But, Dad—"

"Enough," August said. He turned to his father. "Did you know that kid you knocked out?"

"No," Cleveland said. "There was a patch on the inside of his jacket that said PROPERTY OF LUKAS DARAUL. I figure that must be his name. I'm surprised you didn't take note of it yourself."

August was surprised too. He was an information junkie. He never missed a detail, especially the small ones. Was he losing his touch? "This whole April-getting-engaged-to-Alex-Pierson thing has me on edge, I guess."

Charlie gasped. "What? Did you say that Mom is engaged? Does that mean she's getting married?"

The question sent a river of panic through August's blood. Charlie wasn't supposed to know. At least, not yet. And especially not like this.

"That's wonderful!" Cleveland said. "Alex Pierson is a first-class bookman."

"Alex Pierson is a first-class—" August bit his tongue. "How do you know him?"

"I've sold many books to him over the years," Cleveland said.

"You have? It's just . . . it's kind of strange that he never mentioned it."

"Maybe he didn't want you to know."

Charlie broke into the conversation. "So is Mom marrying Alex or not?"

There was a pregnant pause.

"Yes," August finally said. "Not right away, but soon. *Too* soon if you ask me." He tugged at his shirt collar. "Is it hot in here?"

"Hottest day ever!" the cab driver said.

"One hundred and seven degrees!" Charlie chimed in.

August hoped the conversation would continue in this direction, away from the unavoidable truth of April and Alex's future. But when Charlie tugged at his arm, he knew the discussion wasn't over—it had simply stalled in midair.

"Dad," Charlie said.

August breathed deeply. "Yes?"

"Are you going to be okay?"

"I think so," he said. "What about you?"

"I think so too," he said, his bottom lip trembling just a little. "But why didn't Mom tell me? Why didn't *you* tell me?"

"Because he was trying to protect you," Cleveland said. "But as you're going to learn, Charlie, he *can't* protect you."

"Stop scaring him," August said.

"Scaring him would be telling him that everything was going to be fine when it isn't. Scaring him would be lying to him, hoping that things were somehow going to magically work out. But the truth is, the whole world is a mess, and it's just getting messier. So don't scare him. Empower him. Tell him the truth."

The cab pulled over on Fifth Avenue in front of the stately gray marble archways that gated the New York Public Library. August paid the driver, and he, Charlie, and Cleveland all tumbled out the door.

"So what *is* the truth?" August asked.

"Well, I don't mean to frighten you," Cleveland said, "but the future of the world is in our hands!"

August watched his father sprint up the steps of the library, his broken cane tucked neatly under one arm, The Gospels of Henry the Lion under the other. This was the man he had revered as the finest mind on rare books in the world today. Everything he had learned about books he had learned from him, watching during his childhood as his father would pore over volume after volume looking for clues from the past, which he would turn, like a modern-day alchemist, into a significant profit.

But that's all it had ever been: a good business plan, nothing more. His father had never shown attachment to any book. In fact, he had preached almost daily the practice of noninvolvement, a detached objectivity that allowed decision making based solely on financial profitability. It was a gospel that August had devoured and made his own.

But as he saw his father reach the top step and turn back to him with a smile as wide as a child's on Christmas morning, he knew that this was a different man—not a man gripped with the worldly worth of the book he held, but a man energized and revitalized by the adventure the book brought. The sight was both alarming and inspiring.

"Dad," Charlie asked, "did Grandpa really mean that about the future of the world?"

August leaned down to his son, searching for the right phrase, the proper way to portray the situation in terms the boy could fully under-stand. "Charlie," he said. "I think the heat may have fried your grandpa's brain."

Charlie seemed unfazed. "So he's probably going to need our help."

"Probably," August said.

"I think *definitely*," Charlie said, pointing to a frightening figure looming in the distance.

It was Lukas.

TEN

April looked at her watch. Five o'clock. "We missed our appointment," she whispered to Alex.

"What?"

"With the jeweler. He was expecting us at five."

Alex looked at her like she was crazy. "I think he'll understand, given that we're being held at gunpoint. It seems like a reasonable excuse."

April wondered whether they would ever have the opportunity to reschedule. To die now seemed like such a shame, right on the brink of a whole new life. And not just for her—for Charlie too. She still hadn't had a chance to tell him the news about her engagement to Alex. Maybe he knew by now. Maybe August had already taken the liberty of letting the cat out of the bag. It would be just like August to do something like that. Of course, it was just like *her* not to tell Charlie in the first place. She was a world-class card-carrying conflict avoider.

"Don't worry," Alex said, smiling as if he knew every thought in her head. "We'll reschedule as soon as this whole escapade is over."

April hoped he was right.

"Young lovebirds," Veronika Vallodrin mocked. "How sweet. You better start praying you can find each other in the afterlife."

"Wait," Bernie said, putting his hands up. "You don't need to kill both of them. Alex is the one who shot your husband."

"Why do you care?" Veronika asked.

"I just . . ." Bernie struggled for the words. "I just think it would be a waste to kill April."

Veronika considered the sinewy little fellow twittering before her. "Very well," she said, reading into the situation. "I suppose we can keep her around."

"Thank you," Bernie said, winking at April.

She turned away, disgusted. Bernie was nice enough, but the thought of him pawing her made her skin crawl.

"Why would you do this to me?" Alex asked.

Bernie's lips began to tremble as he approached his old friend. "I'll tell you why," he said. "Because you've done nothing but take advantage of me. When you got hurt last year, who filled in for you? Who made sure everything was taken care of? Me. And did you do anything to thank me? No. Don't think I don't know what you said about me at the Morgan . . ."

"What are you talking about?"

"There was a position open, and you told them not to take me. Why would you do that? After everything I did for you?"

"I never asked you to do anything for me, Bernie."

"You see? There you go again! I could rip my heart out of my chest and hand it to you, and you wouldn't even care! *You wouldn't even care!*" he erupted, foam spraying from the sides of his mouth.

The room stood still.

"Well, *that*," Veronika said, stepping forward, "was absolutely revolting." And without another word, she drilled a bullet-shaped hole in Bernie's chest.

He staggered backward into a pile of books, which capsized under the weight of his crashing torso. He wheezed wetly and then, with one final tremor, became deathly still.

April clasped a hand over her mouth to keep from crying. The repulsion she had felt for Bernie only seconds ago was suddenly replaced with pity, thinking of all the time he must have spent lusting after Alex's life one block down the street. At least he had had one glorious moment to release the steam from his festering boiler tank.

"I'm sorry for being such a witch," Veronika said, poking a pointed toe in Bernie's side to ensure his lifelessness. "But my husband's death has put me in a foul mood."

"You had no right to do that," Alex said.

"I have every right to do whatever I please," Veronika said. "So tell me, should I kill you, or do you know more than you were telling our poor friend Bernie?"

"How do you know . . . ?"

Alex's voice trailed off as he watched Veronika walk over to a pile of books in the corner and pick up the top one in the stack. She opened the cover, revealing the book's innards, a carved-out set of pages with a listening device stationed carefully inside.

"You heard everything," April said.

"The only difference is, I'm not as gullible as Bernie," Veronika said. She walked over to the desk and stabbed a finger onto the map placed there. "What is all this about?"

"I wish I knew," Alex said.

Veronika drummed her nails on the desk, making a noise like a tiny plastic horse in full gallop. "I'd take your kneecap off with a bullet," she said to Alex, "but that really wouldn't do either of us much good." She walked over to April. "But she's a different story . . ."

"Don't you dare."

"Dr. Pierson, I'm not playing around. What do you know?" She placed the muzzle of the gun on top of April's knee.

Alex's face turned dark. "I don't know anything."

Veronika looked April in the eyes. "You know, maybe he *wants* me to shoot you in the leg. I suppose it makes sense . . . being handicapped would give you one more thing in common."

"Stop," Alex said.

"I'm giving you three seconds," Veronika said, tightening her grip on the gun.

"He said he doesn't know anything!" April cried.

"Three . . ."

"Please!"

"Two . . ."

April felt her heart stop beating in her chest. She tried desperately to keep the blackness from blotting out her vision, but it was just too much.

Why don't you believe him? she heard herself say as her head fell back and the world spun madly away.

ELEVEN

Rumbling. A soft rumbling from underneath her head. April forced open her eyes to blackness. Where was she? She waited a moment for her vision to adjust, but still, all she could see was blackness. No. Wait. It was black leather. The bottom of a car seat. She was lying on the floor of a car. How long had she been here? Her head was killing her. Had she blacked out? Had Veronika shot her in the knee?

"Finally awake?"

"Did you shoot me?" April asked.

"Check for yourself," Veronika said, without a hint of compassion.

April slowly sat up, finding herself in the aisle of a lengthy limousine. She and Veronika appeared to be the only passengers. She inspected her left knee, which seemed to be fully intact. She stretched out her leg, checking for abnormalities. Everything looked completely fine. Which meant . . . *what?*

"Missing something?" Veronika asked. "Or maybe someone?"

Alex! "Where is he?" April asked, suddenly struck with concern.

"In the car behind us," Veronika said. "Go on. Take a look."

April moved to the rear of the elongated vehicle and stared out the tiny tinted window. Behind them followed a large, black SUV. She could only vaguely make out two figures sitting in the front. "How do I know Alex is in there?"

"How do you know he's not?" Veronika opened a compartment at the front of the limo and poured herself a drink of something golden and venomous looking. She took a shallow sip, closing her eyes as if the experience was almost too much to bear. "Besides, shouldn't you be more concerned with the fact that he lied to you?"

"He didn't lie."

"My dear," Veronika said, slithering down the seat to meet April, "he almost let me *cripple* you. And all he had to do was tell me what he knew."

"But he said he didn't know anything," April said.

"Which is exactly why I said he lied to you."

April wasn't sure whether to believe her. It seemed perfectly in character that Veronika would simply play mind games with her. "What did he tell you?"

Veronika acted surprised. "You mean you really don't know?"

"Of course not," April said, pushing herself into the back corner of the limo. "Because he's protecting me."

"I don't think protecting you was part of his plan," Veronika teased, draining the remainder of her glass through her cherry-painted lips.

"What do you mean?"

"I know it might be painful to hear this," Veronika said, "but I counted all the way down . . . three, two, one . . . and he didn't even flinch. Didn't say a word. I could have blasted your kneecap off, and he wouldn't have told me anything." She let the words sink in before adding, "You didn't matter to him even a little."

"You're lying," April said.

"Am I?"

They sat in silence, listening to the sound of the street passing by.

"Where are we going?"

Veronika adjusted her hair, pulling it back in a tight ponytail. "One of our operatives spotted August taking The Gospels of Henry the Lion into the New York Public Library. After his capture, we're all meeting at a warehouse to . . . um . . . figure things out."

"Sounds like a party," April said.

"I can assure you it won't be," Veronika said. "But before we get there, I need to ask you a few questions about the book in question. I'm assuming you know quite a bit about it, being that you're a rather famous bibliophile."

April liked hearing that she was famous, until she remembered the reason why. Her connection to the theft of the Gutenberg Bible from the Library of Congress in Washington DC had made national headlines. Maybe not the front page, but not too deep in the paper to keep her from being noticed on the street every once in a while. It was awful.

When Alex had taken her in at the Morgan Library, she was in terrible shape, racked with guilt and shame. But Alex protected her from the savages of the media, and even helped her reclaim some small shred of dignity. In the midst of her personal storm, he had acted as a shining beacon of hope. That was the man he truly was, not the one being cleverly portrayed by her captor now.

"To be honest," she said, "the only things I know, I heard from my ex-husband."

"Care to explain?" Veronika asked, as if she were simply a reporter on the prowl for a scoop.

"Mysterious things, mostly. He told me that the book vanished after the Second World War, only to suddenly reappear fifty years later on the auction block at Sotheby's."

"True," Veronika said, as if checking April's words against some hidden database. "Did he know who had it for all of those years?"

"If you've done your homework, you already know that no one knows the answer to that."

"*Someone* knows," Veronika said, her eyes turning to slender slits.

"Well, that someone certainly isn't me," April said, deflecting Veronika's penetrating glare.

"What else did he tell you?"

"Not much," April said. "But I do remember a story he told me about Henry the Lion. Apparently, in 1172 Henry the Lion made a pilgrimage to Jerusalem. During his journey he stopped in Byzantium, modern-day Istanbul, to meet with Emperor Manuel the First. Henry the Lion was met with a grand reception and was lavished with many rare religious relics. When it finally came time for him to leave, he was given a very special parting gift."

"What was it?"

"A lion! A real, live lion. Fitting, wouldn't you say? Henry the Lion brought the beast back with him to his home in Brunswick. I've heard that the cathedral he built there shortly after his return is marked with the lion's scratches."

"Fascinating," Veronika said. "But not exactly the kind of information I was hoping for." She made her way back to the front of the limo and poured herself another drink. "Did he happen to mention anything about the relics that Emperor Manuel gave to Henry the Lion?"

"No."

"Or anything about the Black Vehm?"

April paused to ponder the question. "Alex told me your husband might have been their leader."

"He did, did he?" Veronika said, which seemed like her way of confirming the information without actually saying so.

"Are you part of the Black Vehm too?" April asked.

Veronika grinned. "My dear girl, if you knew anything about the Black Vehm, then you would know that I can't answer that."

"I'm just curious," April said. "I haven't read about any medieval orders that included women."

Veronika swirled the drink in her hand. "Then perhaps you need to read more."

April decided to push the issue further. "I can't imagine the Black Vehm would ever put any real power in the hands of a woman. Which means that you're just as much a pawn in this game as I am."

"This is no game," Veronika said.

April was about to respond, when she turned her head just in time to see the SUV crash directly into the back of the limo. The impact was forceful enough to throw her from her seat. "What are they doing?" she asked, picking herself up from the floor of the vehicle.

"I don't know, but I'm going to find out," Veronika said, incensed that the blow had made her spill her drink. "What on earth—"

A second crash, this one stronger. April lost her grip and went tumbling toward the front of the limo, directly into her captor.

"Get off me!" Veronika shrieked.

"Aren't you going to stop them?" April asked, seeing through the back window that they were being pushed forward faster and faster by the SUV.

The strength Veronika had shown earlier was quickly melting. She pulled a phone out from the wall of the limo and dialed. "The collision must have killed it," she said, slamming it back into place.

April clawed her way up to the Plexiglas divider between the front and back of the vehicle and peered ahead. She banged on the divider with her hand, trying to awaken the driver, who was unconscious, or dead, his head bobbing like it was connected to his body by a spring. The SUV had pushed them off the road, and a street vendor jumped out of the way as the limo struck his cart, sending a bath of hot dogs spilling out.

The SUV revved its engine and slammed again into the back of the limo, pushing them onto a loading dock at the edge of the East River. The hapless vehicle flew across the thick boards of the dock, heading directly toward its edge and the watery grave beyond.

April panicked, crawling down the seat toward the doors. She jerked at one of the handles, but it didn't respond.

"Don't waste your time!" Veronika said. "The doors can only be opened by the driver."

"I don't think he's going to be able to help us," April said, grabbing onto the wall for support. "If we're going to get the doors open, we need to get through that divider! Where's your gun?"

The limo bounced like a speedboat over a choppy sea. April felt her stomach sicken, not from the cataclysmic motion, but from the awareness of impending doom.

Veronika pulled out her gun and pointed it at April. "Stay away!"

"Shoot the divider, not me!" April said. "It's the only way we're going to get out of here!"

"I said stay away! There's no way I'm letting you out of this car alive."

"But what if they've been using you? What if they're trying to get rid of both of us?"

"No," Veronika said. "You're wrong."

"Look out the window! Look out the window and tell me I'm wrong!"

The limo lurched violently, sending the two arguing women hurtling into the long side window. The gun fell out of Veronika's hand, and April scrambled for it.

"Give me that!" Veronika wailed, her voice high and shrill, like an animal in the heat of attack.

April's hand closed around the gun just as Veronika's fingernails dug into her neck. Like tiny daggers, they tore at her skin. April cried out in pain and lost her grip. Veronika crawled over her to retrieve the weapon, smashing April's face against the floor.

After struggling toward opposite ends of the vehicle, the women turned to face each other. April put her hands up, seeing that Veronika had the gun trained on her. She'd squandered the one opportunity she'd had, and now she was going to die.

Veronika's hand tensed to squeeze the trigger.

Suddenly, the SUV roared behind them. The cabin filled with the harsh sound of ripping metal as the rear of the vehicle received a devastating jolt. The gun fired at the same instant, the bullet rebounding off the bulletproof rear window. April closed her eyes, hearing the bounding projectile as it whizzed by her ear. She opened her eyes and found the bullet's final resting place—the middle of Veronika's forehead. A slim trail of crimson trickled down her face as she collapsed into a lifeless heap.

Despite the horror of witnessing Veronika's timely demise, April's immediate instinct was to find a way out of the ill-fated limo. She grabbed Veronika's gun and—after a slight hesitation as to the brittleness of the barrier before her—fired a round directly at the divider. She heard the bullet lodge in the seat beside her, a Plexiglas showing only the slightest indication that a bullet had ricocheted against it. Tears flowing down her cheeks, April desperately slammed the gun against the divider over and over until her hand felt broken. The Plexiglas didn't even show a single scratch.

As the limo launched off the end of the dock, pointed like a plummeting missile at the dark waters of the river, April realized that this was the end, the final call, her last few remaining seconds of life. She curled up on the seat, watching with fright-induced awe as the waters bubbled up around the limousine, which cruised slowly, almost leisurely, toward a final destination on the river's murky floor.

April had always heard that drowning was a peaceful death, but as the water began to find its way into the cabin of the vehicle, she wondered how anyone could know such a fact.

Soon I'll know whether they were right or not, she thought morbidly as the limousine was enveloped in sweeping, unfathomable darkness.

TWELVE

"Run!" August yelled as he grabbed Charlie and charged up the steps of the New York Public Library. The top of the stairs seemed miles away, and Lukas was gaining on them fast. If they could make it inside the front doors, they would be safe. The security checkpoint wouldn't be a problem for them, but Lukas and his personal armory would be stopped cold.

"Dad!" Charlie said. "I can't keep up!"

"Yes, you can!" August said, dragging him forward.

Lukas was getting closer—only a few stairs stood between them.

The people congregating on the steps didn't seem to notice the commotion. Or they didn't seem to care. No one had died yet. No one had screamed *bomb* or *terrorist*. For all they knew, it was just some freaks acting stupid.

The door was almost within reach. August had lost track of Lukas in a swarm of tourists. He could be anywhere, waiting to pounce on them.

August twisted around, just to make sure Lukas hadn't somehow gotten behind him. But there was only Charlie, looking deathly afraid.

The two of them sprinted the few remaining feet, and August threw open the door to the library. As they crossed the threshold, August breathed a sigh of relief. "That was close," he said, looking back.

But Charlie wasn't relieved. His other arm was still out the door, held tightly in the clutches of Lukas Daraul.

"Dad!"

Lukas drew a knife from his trench coat.

"Don't let go of me," August said to Charlie, pulling on him with all his strength. "No matter what, just don't let go!"

"Dad!"

"Hang on to me, Charlie!" And with that, August gave a final tug, pulling so hard that he feared Charlie's arm might come free of its socket. Luckily, the boy came tumbling forward all in one piece, landing safely in his father's arms.

A burly security guard lumbered to their side. "What's going on over here?"

August saw that Lukas had already vanished. "My son just got his arm caught in the door," he said, holding tightly to Charlie, who was shaking violently.

"Son," the guard said, "is everything okay?"

"Yeah," Charlie answered, putting on a brave face. "I just got a little scared. No big deal."

"You're sure?" the guard asked, giving August a suspicious glance.

"Totally."

"All right," the guard said, tapping Charlie on the shoulder. "Just try to keep it down while you're here. This is a library, after all."

"We'll keep that in mind," August said, directing Charlie away from the scene by his shoulders.

August kept a wary eye on the entrance as they jogged up a long, curved staircase. There was no sign of Lukas. August wondered if he was looking for another way inside or simply waiting for them to exit. Either way, their troubles weren't over.

"Where's Grandpa?" Charlie asked.

"I'm not sure," August said. "I was hoping he'd wait for us. But I suppose that's not really his style."

They wound their way through the building until they reached the library's famed main reading room. At nearly three hundred feet long, with fifty-foot ceilings that literally mimicked the sky with a series of Tiepolo-inspired cloud-painted inlays, the room acted as a church for the bibliophiles of New York. Grand chandeliers hung from the roof. Immense wooden tables adorned the floor. And legions of books surrounded the room, like tiny sentries ready to do battle with the ignorance of the world.

August and Charlie made their way down the lengthy middle aisle, a familiar trip for Charlie, though he still gazed around the immense space in gape-jawed wonder.

After their journey across the room, August stopped to ask a librarian if she'd seen a man fitting his father's description. She remembered him easily. He was the only person in the library—and perhaps in the entire city—wearing a woolen sports coat.

The librarian directed them to the room behind her. "Ask for Dr. Jonathan Rothschild," she said.

August was perplexed. Dr. Rothschild was an old family friend, and had on many occasions helped to shed light on the lurid histories of ancient books. But August hadn't seen him in years.

"I thought Dr. Rothschild didn't work here anymore."

"He gets that a lot," the librarian said with a grin, as if the statement were the beginning of some inside joke. "But he was only on sabbatical."

"That's one long sabbatical."

"What's a sabbatical?" Charlie asked.

"It's just a fancy word for vacation."

"What's *vacation*?"

"It's—" August stopped. "Ha-ha. Yes. I get it. Your parents are both workaholics who never take a break. Very subtle."

"Maybe you should take a sabbatical sometime," Charlie suggested.

"Maybe so," August said. "But not right now. Right now, we've got to figure out what your crazy grandfather is up to."

They exited the main reading room, Room 315, and entered a smaller room, Room 328—the reading room for rare books and manuscripts. They stopped at the desk and asked for Dr. Rothschild. A few moments later he arrived, his usual droopy frown adorning his face, curving in the same manner as the thick gray mustache that crested his upper lip.

"Your father said you'd be here shortly," he said, glancing around nervously. "Come. Follow me."

THIRTEEN

August followed his peevish host, making sure to keep Charlie close by. The boy had fallen into trouble on many occasions in the rare book stable. He simply couldn't keep his hands off the colorful, ancient tomes. August understood his son's urgings, but he understood even more the importance of keeping the exceptional value of the library's collection fully intact.

Dr. Rothschild shuffled over to a librarian and asked her to kindly remove all the other patrons from the room. The librarian jumped to the task, shooing the surprised habitués away. Dr. Rothschild remained comatose until the room was empty, then promptly toted August and Charlie to a ponderous oak table in the back where Cleveland was situated.

"Whatever took you so long?" he asked, as if he'd been sitting with a stopwatch, counting off the seconds.

"We had another run-in with our friend Lukas," August explained.

"Is everything okay?"

"For now," August said. "But he'll probably be waiting for us when we leave."

"Well . . . first things first," Cleveland said, turning back to The Gospels of Henry the Lion, which lay open on the table like an exhumed corpse.

Dr. Rothschild cleared his throat. "Your father was just explaining to me that the Black Vehm is desperate to get their hands on this book."

"You know about the Black Vehm?" August asked. He'd always imagined Dr. Rothschild as a rather studious type, a bookworm gnawing his way through literature, with little appreciation for the flavor.

"Know about it?" Cleveland said, nearly chuckling. "Dr. Rothschild was *in* the Black Vehm!"

August's hand involuntarily clutched Charlie's arm. "Dad, you knew about this? What if this is all a trap?"

Now it was Dr. Rothschild's turn to be amused. "Son, your father has obviously not told you the rest of the story," he said. "He was once in the Black Vehm too."

August grabbed a chair and sat down. "Why didn't you tell me?" he asked his father.

"You never asked," Cleveland said.

"*I never asked?*" August said angrily. "I shouldn't have to ask if you ever belonged to an organization that's trying to kill us, should I? Shouldn't it just be a *given* that information like that might be good for me to know?"

"It was a long time ago," Dr. Rothschild said. "For both of us. The Black Vehm was much different then. It was just an intellectual community, not the monster it's turned into."

"I would love to have seen this intellectual community," August said. "What did you discuss? How to take control of the world economy? Which president to overthrow? Something tells me your 'intellectual community' probably wasn't as charming as you make it sound."

"Maybe not," Cleveland said, "but we certainly weren't going around killing people."

"When was this?" August asked.

"Back when you were a child, when we lived in England," Cleveland said. "Back when your mother was still alive."

August hesitated at the mention of his mother. Then he said, "Tell me everything."

"Very well," Cleveland said, as if he were about to confess to a horrible crime he'd committed long ago. "You should know that I never intended to join the Black Vehm. They were—as the name would clearly suggest—a dark and nefarious bunch. But our paths became tangled, and in time, I was given no other option."

"There's *always* another option," August said.

"I used to think that too," Cleveland said, his voice thick with regret. "It was a long time ago. I had just opened the bookstore on Sackville Street, right in the heart of London's West End. It was a grand opening. A member of the royal family even attended, though I never saw him, nor was I introduced. Maybe it was just a story invented by my business partner, Bartholomew Randall. In any case, the story worked. During our first week we sold enough rare books to fill Big Ben. It became fashionable to say that you had visited our store, and even more fashionable to say you had purchased some rarified digest from our lot. But the attention wasn't all good. It attracted many ne'er-do-wells, the worst of which was a man named Wesley Chaw."

"He sounds evil," Charlie said.

Cleveland nodded in agreement. "He was! He came into the store one day and demanded to see Bartholomew. When I asked why, he explained that Bartholomew had acquired a book for him, and he wanted to make good on the transaction. Sensing that this was a potentially powerful new client, I immediately fetched Bartholomew from his office and introduced him to Wesley. If only I'd known . . ."

"Don't feel so guilty," Dr. Rothschild chimed in. "He fooled many of us."

"I wasn't fooled," Cleveland said. "But Bartholomew certainly was. He fell immediately into Wesley's trap."

"How?"

"Wesley frowned when I introduced him to Bartholomew. He explained that the Bartholomew he was looking for was much older, much more seasoned in the book-hunting trade. Bartholomew asked what he was trying to find and suggested that perhaps it was still something he could help with. Wesley explained that he had contacted this other Bartholomew—who I can now safely say did not exist—to find a book called The Gospels of Henry the Lion. The other Bartholomew claimed to have the book, and was more than willing to sell it, for a very hefty fee. Unable to contain my curiosity, I asked what the fee was. I nearly dropped to the floor when he replied eight million pounds."

"Eight million pounds of what?" Charlie asked.

"A pound is like a dollar," August explained.

"Dad. I'm kidding." Charlie turned to his grandfather. "But what was eight million pounds worth back then?"

"I don't remember exactly, but it was certainly much more than any book sale I had ever heard of. Wesley left the store shortly after, but not before placing a business card in Bartholomew's hand. From that moment on, Bartholomew searched for The Gospels of Henry the Lion. The chore proved to be entirely more difficult than he thought it would be. The book had disappeared over four decades earlier in the hands of the

Nazis. But the dream of eight million quid was more than enough to fuel his quest, and eventually he found it."

"He really found The Gospels of Henry the Lion?" August asked.

"This was still nearly a decade before the auction at Sotheby's, during the period that remains a veritable black hole of information concerning the book. Though I never saw it with my own eyes, I believe that—to this day—Bartholomew was telling the truth. Perhaps it's the loss of his life that convinced me of that fact."

Charlie gasped. "The Black Vehm killed him?"

Cleveland continued. "It was about six weeks after the meeting with Wesley that Bartholomew disappeared. His absence wasn't surprising at first—he would travel the world on a whim if he got wind of a rare book. But I became concerned after discovering his calendar lying open on his desk. December 6 was circled—that day's date. *MEETING WITH WESLEY AT BOOKSTORE—3 P.M.*, it read. I remember looking at my watch. It was four o'clock. Maybe they had changed the meeting place, I thought. But a voice inside me knew the truth—something terrible had happened. His body was discovered two days later, washed up along the shores of the Thames. His throat had been slit, and there were letters scrawled into his chest—*SSGG*."

"I've seen that before," August said, combing through his memory for a connection. "But I don't know what it means."

"I didn't back then," Cleveland said. "And neither did the police investigating Bartholomew's death. They thought it was a gang sign. After no leads showed up, they eventually let the case die. But I kept hunting, and eventually I found something that led me straight into the belly of the Black Vehm."

"It's surprising to me now, but I don't think I've heard this part before," Dr. Rothschild said. "I'm curious to hear what led you to the Vehm."

"It's not quite as exciting as *your* introduction to them!"

Charlie looked at Dr. Rothschild eagerly.

"A tale for another time," Dr. Rothschild said.

Cleveland returned to his story. "My discovery of the Vehm—and their connection to Bartholomew's death—came about quite by accident. A German businessman sold me a book that had been in his family for nearly six hundred years. It really wasn't much of a book, but it was in excellent shape, and I knew it would fetch a decent price on the open market. I was looking through the book one night, carefully inspecting its pages, when an envelope fell out. It was fragile and yellow with age. Inside was a single folded piece of paper—a handwritten note in German. I understood just enough of its antiquated language to read the letter."

"What did it say?" August asked.

"It was a warning, sent to a friend. For some unexplained reason the Black Vehm had marked this person to die. The letter mentioned the evidence—the signature of the Black Vehm was upon his door. *SSGG*."

"Just like the markings on Bartholomew's chest."

"Exactly."

"But you still haven't told us what it means," August said. "Do you know?"

"I'm afraid I do. The four letters stand for four words—*Strick, Stein, Gras, Grun*—meaning *Rope, Stone, Grass, Green*. It refers to the ritual induction each member of the Black Vehm goes through. The Stuhlherr—the Vehmic head judge—places a noose made of linden fibers around the inductee's throat. This is the Rope, the *Strick*. The Stuhlherr then draws a few drops of blood from the inductee's neck with a two-handed sword. This is to remind the inductee that his life is now in their hands, and if he is ever found to be a traitor, there will be a deadly penalty. Thus the *Stein, Gras, Grun*—the headstone and grassy grave. Finally, the inductee kisses the Stuhlherr's sword between the hilt and the blade—a sign of the cross—and swears a solemn oath, which is burned in my memory like a brand:

"I promise, on the holy marriage, that I will from henceforth aid, keep, and conceal the Holy Vehm from wife and child, father and mother, sister and brother, fire and wind, from all that the sun shines on and the rain covers, from all that is between sky and ground, especially from the man who knows the law, and will bring before this free tribunal, under which I sit, all that belongs to the secret jurisdiction of the emperor, whether I know it to be true myself, or have heard it from trustworthy people, whatever requires correction or punishment, whatever is Fehmfree, that it may be judged or, with the consent of the accuser, be put off in grace; and will not cease so to do, for love or for fear, for gold or for silver, or for precious stones; and will strengthen this tribunal and jurisdiction with all my five senses and power; and that I do not take on me this office for any other cause than for the sake of right and justice; moreover, that I will ever further and honor this free tribunal more than any other free tribunal; and what I thus promise will I steadfastly and firmly keep, so help me God and His Holy Gospel.

"That same poisonous passage has been spoken by every person who has joined the Holy Vehm. It cost me dearly to find them. But I needed to know the truth about Bartholomew's death, and the reason they were so desperate to get their hands on The Gospels of Henry the Lion."

August was about to ask his father whether he had answered those two mysteries when the power to the building failed. The lights died, the air-conditioning expired, and the entire building fell into a strange silence. At first August wondered if Lukas was responsible. But only a moment later a librarian entered and explained that she'd been listening to the radio—on headphones, of course—and had heard that the massive overuse of air-conditioning throughout the city had caused a blackout.

"How extensive is it?" Dr. Rothschild asked.

"All of Manhattan, just like 2003," she said. A worrisome expression creased her face, barely visible in the dim, golden glow emanating from the skylights overhead.

"Make an announcement," Dr. Rothschild said. "Send everyone in the building home."

"But we don't close until—"

"Things will only get worse after nightfall. Make the announcement. Now."

The librarian dashed away. They heard her call out to the people in the next room, explaining the situation. Her broadcast was followed by the sound of dozens of chairs rumbling, then hundreds of feet making their way to the exit.

"Lukas will be able to sneak in," August said.

"Or we'll be able to sneak out," Cleveland said, rising from his seat and picking up The Gospels of Henry the Lion.

"Sneak out? But don't we need to talk to Dr. Rothschild more about the book? Isn't he the one we were looking for?"

"If you think I'm the Stuhlherr, you're wrong," Dr. Rothschild said, answering the question of his own accord. "But I know where he can be found."

"Where?" August asked.

Suddenly Charlie called out quietly from the other side of the room. "Dad!"

"What are you doing over there?" August asked, wondering when his son had stolen away. "And why are you whispering?"

"Come here!"

August hurried over to Charlie, who was hunched by the door that led out to the main reading room.

"Look up there," he said, directing August's attention to the narrow balcony that surrounded the vast adjoining space.

August saw six men in black suits walking along the balcony. They were clearly surveying the departing crowd.

"Do you think they're looking for us?" Charlie asked.

"No," August said. "I think they're looking for The Gospels of Henry the Lion."

He and Charlie jogged back over to Cleveland and Dr. Rothschild. "We need to go. The Black Vehm has arrived."

"You mean Lukas?" Cleveland asked.

"I didn't see Lukas, but I think we can assume he's here too," August said. He turned to Dr. Rothschild. "You said you knew where we can find the Stuhlherr?"

"I do," Dr. Rothschild croaked in reply. He seemed reluctant to reveal the answer.

"Is there a problem?"

"I'm afraid you won't like the answer."

Just outside the door, they heard a deep voice talking to one of the librarians.

"We have to get out of here," August said anxiously. "Dr. Rothschild, you have to tell me where we can find the Stuhlherr!"

Dr. Rothschild took a notebook out of his pocket and ripped a page out, folded it, and handed it to August. "I prepared this earlier. Don't read it until you're out of my sight."

August took the paper warily. "Why?"

Dr. Rothschild grabbed August by the arm, leading him to a door along the back wall. "Because I don't want to be within five hundred feet of you when you figure out who the Stuhlherr is!" He opened the door and August went out, followed closely by Charlie and Cleveland.

August, too anxious to heed Dr. Rothschild's advice, opened the note. It read:

Slaughter the librarian's horrid myth.

"What does this mean?" he asked.

"I told you not to read it yet!" Dr. Rothschild said, angrily waving him onward. "Now get out of here!"

"Good-bye, old friend," Cleveland said.

"Don't worry about me," Dr. Rothschild said. "I've been ready to die for a long time." And with that, he shut the door.

Not a second later, they heard the sudden burst of gunshots, followed by the sound of a body hitting the floor.

FOURTEEN

Ice.

It was everywhere. It covered the land. Ninety-eight percent of it, to be exact. There was enough ice, in fact, that if it all melted at once, the world sea level would rise by two hundred feet, enough to destroy the coastlines of every continent. In America, Washington DC, Baltimore, Philadelphia, and New York would all disappear, as would the entire state of Florida. And that was just the East Coast. Other places in the world—London, Copenhagen, Oslo, and Bangkok, to mention a few—were in equal jeopardy of being plunged under water. It wasn't a reality yet, but given the current global conditions, it could happen.

But it wouldn't happen tonight.

Ivonne Segur checked the outside temperature. Negative thirty degrees Fahrenheit. Considering what some of the other Antarctic bases were experiencing, it was a warm night. But not warm enough to keep from needing several layers of protective undergarments, not to mention her ECWs—extra cold weather clothing—which included a substantial weatherproof parka.

Ivy stared at herself in the mirror. She looked like a snowman. A bright orange snowman. All the parkas were colored for high visibility, easily seen from a distance, even in the constant haze of gray that enveloped their surroundings. But not at night. Nothing would be visible at night.

"Ivy, what are you doing?"

She turned, startled. "Nicolas, you scared me."

The Frenchman entered the room, holding a wine glass in his hand. He always seemed to be holding a wine glass. "The others are wondering where you are," he said. "I've been wondering, too."

"I bet you have," she said. Nicolas had spent the last few weeks trying to convince her to give up her boyfriend, who was thousands of miles away. So far he had been unsuccessful.

"I can help you get out of that costume," he said, impressing the last word heavily with his accent. He walked over and picked up the thick gloves on the table next to her. "What are you doing getting into your ECWs, anyway?"

"I'm going out."

"Out? What on earth do you mean?"

They both knew that going out at night was more than stupid—it was dangerous. She swiped the gloves from his hand. "O-U-T. *Out.* Or are you still having trouble with English?"

He looked at her curiously. "Are you playing with me?" He reached out and grasped the front zipper of her parka. "Because if you are . . ." The zipper came down an inch.

Ivy grinned. "When are you going to learn?"

Nicolas laughed. "Never, I suppose." The zipper slipped down another few inches.

"I told you—I have a boyfriend."

"And I told you—I don't care," he said, pushing the zipper down the rest of the way.

"But won't the others be wondering where we are?"

"Don't worry about them," Nicolas said. "They're all half-drunk."

"*You're* half-drunk."

Nicolas set his wine glass on the table and navigated his hands inside of Ivy's parka, placing his palms firmly on either side of her waist.

"You seem surprised that I'm letting you do this," Ivy said.

"I *am* surprised," Nicolas replied, quivering with excitement as he kissed her just below the ear. "You never let me get this far before."

Ivy wrapped her arms around his neck. "Maybe I was just waiting for the perfect moment." And then she plunged all six inches of the blade she'd been concealing into the soft space beneath his shoulder blade. She let his body slump gently to the floor. She frowned at his inanimate form, wondering if different circumstances would have allowed them to be together. No time to wonder now. There was still a job to do.

She checked her watch. There was still an hour before anyone would come back to the sleeping quarters. Nicolas was probably telling the truth when he said the others were half-drunk. The crew of Neumayer spent most nights drinking wine, playing board games, drinking more wine, and occasionally—when things got boring—analyzing field data.

Ivy swabbed Nicolas's blood off the floor with a blanket, then wrapped it around his body and pushed the entire package beneath one of the bunks. She zipped up her parka, grabbed her gloves and other essentials, and exited the room, turning down the hallway toward the loading dock.

"Ivy?"

She kept walking.

"Ivy, is that you?"

She turned. "Dr. Marsh, are you already done going over the satellite readings?"

"Not quite," he said. "Have you seen Nicolas?"

"I'm on my way to meet him in the rear access port. Apparently there's a problem with one of the lifts. He wanted me to take a look."

"I can send Malcolm to look at it if you want."

"That's not necessary," Ivy said. "I think Nicolas and I will be able to fix it."

"All right," Dr. Marsh said. He paused. "Is everything okay? You've seemed a little on edge lately."

"I guess I've had a lot on my mind," she said, nervously watching Dr. Marsh reach for the door handle of the room where she'd killed Nicolas.

"We all do," Dr. Marsh said, opening the door.

"Talk to you later," Ivy said, turning back down the hallway. Her heartbeat boomed like a cannon inside her parka. She strolled quickly away, hoping she hadn't left any visible clues of Nicolas's termination.

"Ivy!"

She froze. "Yes?" She reached inside the parka for her gun and slowly twisted around. Her finger trembled on the trigger.

"Is this yours?" He held an object in his hand.

In the dim light of the hallway, Ivy couldn't make out what it was. She clicked off the safety on the gun. "What is it?" She ran through the possibilities in her mind. Had she forgotten to retrieve the knife? She suddenly couldn't remember.

Dr. Marsh moved forward until he was directly under a hall light. He was holding Nicolas's wine glass. "It might be considered rude to waste a perfectly good merlot, Ivy. We aren't expecting another shipment for a month."

"I'll try to remember that," Ivy said. Ordinarily she wouldn't have taken the scolding with such grace, but the circumstances required restraint.

The walk down the hallway seemed endless. She finally reached the door to the air lock and allowed the security system to scan her retinas. The air lock opened, and she stepped inside. She put on her gloves, goggles, and other protective layers to ensure that none of her skin was exposed to the outside air when the loading dock opened. Thirty below zero wasn't the worst she'd endured, but it was bad enough to cause severe damage in a short amount of time.

The air lock whooshed open, and the floor of the loading dock began lowering to the frozen landscape outside. Ivy wondered if the racket she was raising was audible to the rest of the Neumayer crew. It probably didn't matter. There wouldn't be enough time for them to react anyway.

The bright lights that hung from the ceiling illuminated the object of Ivy's escape—a red Piston Bully snow tractor. She clomped down the ramp to the vehicle, opened the side door, and climbed inside. She sat in the seat and turned the key, which never left the ignition, listening as the engine grumbled like a bear woken from hibernation.

Ivy put the tractor in reverse and backed away from the loading dock ramp, which gradually rose until it was once again flush with the bottom of the ice station. She flipped on the tractor's front lights, viewing the building in all its strange, futuristic glory, with its wide, tubular body set upon a series of tall, curved legs. It looked like a giant white bug, something from a science-fiction movie, which made sense given that the station had originally been designed to be a space station for the moon. Not that its current location was much less remote.

Ivy peeled off her goggles and gloves. She sighed, watching the condensation of her eupnea collect in the air like a puff of smoke from a pipe. Shivering, she turned up the heat in the tractor. She then reached into an interior pocket of her parka, retrieving a device that resembled a walkie-talkie, but instead had a long series of buttons along its front. She pressed the first one, waiting to see a tiny red warning light awaken on the underside of the station.

There it was. A red dot in the distance.

Ivy imagined in her mind what the people inside Neumayer would soon be experiencing. A sudden shortness of breath. A diminishing sense of reality. Nausea, followed by an even worse bout of *unbearable* nausea. Muscular cramps. Nosebleeds. A burning sensation in the lungs. And then, finally, death.

She checked her watch. It would take about ten minutes for the station to be completely filled with the airborne necrotoxin. There was nothing to do but wait. Why hadn't she remembered to bring a book?

She looked at the time again. Nine and a half minutes left. How was that possible? The seeming slowdown of time reminded her of a mission she'd had in Hong Kong—one of the worst waits of her life. Posing as a prostitute, she'd connected with a British diplomat and poisoned him with a glass of wine. For the first few minutes, as she watched him struggling for air, she contemplated picking up the phone and calling for an ambulance. Finally, her better judgment took hold, and she locked him in the bathroom.

The wait for him to die was excruciating. She still remembered the sounds of him gasping and scraping at the door. It was awful. Over an hour later, the noise from the bathroom subsided. She wiped the tears from her eyes and crept away, praying she'd never have another encounter like that in her life. But here she was, only a few months later, in remarkably similar circumstances. She could lie to herself, but the truth was that she was as stuck in her position as the people lying dead on the floor of the ice station.

Ten minutes passed. None of the station's side doors were open, meaning that no one had escaped. She pressed the second button on the device in her hand, activating a massive ventilation system that was built into Neumayer. The abatement of the fatal air inside the station should only take a few minutes. Her earlier adrenaline rush had worn off, and sitting in the warm, purring tractor was only making Ivy drowsier. It was imperative to stay awake. She tapped her foot and drummed her hands and tried to hum a song she'd heard on the radio the day before. Her eyes drooped, but the reminder of the importance of her mission kept her awake.

She pressed the third button on the device, a sensor that would detect whether the air was breathable inside the station. The answer would be shown the same way as earlier, by the small beacon hidden under the station.

It blinked yellow. Conditions were still unacceptable.

Ivy groaned, again wishing she'd brought a book. "Come on," she begged. "Just give me the green light."

And then suddenly it was there. The green light. Apparently all she had to do was ask.

She drove the Piston Bully forward, flipping a switch on the dash to lower the station ramp. Lights blazed from the yawning entryway, making the ramp look like the path to heaven itself. But Ivy knew that the sight awaiting her inside was far from heaven. It was, in fact, quite the opposite.

She yanked on the door latch and jumped out of the tractor, her feet crunching on the snow below. She scurried up the ramp, slipping along the way. She slowed down. There was no need to hurry. No one was waiting for her.

Ivy approached the air lock, and the computer scanned her eyes, permitting her to enter. A twinge of fear rippled through her as she stepped into the hallway. What if the sensor had been faulty? What if the green light had lit by accident, and Neumayer was still a death trap? *Too late now*, she thought glumly.

"Hello?" she said, listening to her voice bounce along the tubular metal wall of the hallway. There was no reply. She imagined the shock if someone had called back. The thought made her quiver. She felt as if she'd just stepped aboard a haunted ship.

At the end of the hallway she entered the main living space, which was normally bustling with activity. Tonight, unfortunately, it was not. Bodies were everywhere, slumped over the couches and the chairs, splayed out on the floor—it was as if the entire station had suddenly come under the sleeping spell of a wicked witch. Only they weren't asleep, they were—

Hhhhhhhhhhh.

Ivy nearly leapt to the ceiling. She turned to see where the sound was coming from, hoping to see a pipe loose from a fitting in the wall, or a small weather balloon losing its air. That's what the sound was like. Air escaping. Or maybe like—

Hhhhhhhhhhhhhhhhhhhh.

Ivy spun around, realizing the source was different this time. "No," she said aloud. "This can't be right."

The sound was coming from the crewmembers. They were still alive— but just barely. She got closer to one of the bodies. She leaned down, half expecting him to jump at her like a zombie in a horror film. But instead, he just lay there, frozen, the faintest drifting of his chest up and down visible through his thick blue sweater. It was sad, really. A shame. Ivy had grown to tolerate most of the crew. But now—despite her growing fondness—they were going to have to die.

She reached in her jacket for her gun. It was missing. What? Had she dropped it outside? She was tempted to run back to the snow tractor and see if she'd left it there, but she began to worry that the necrotoxin might wear off, and if she left she'd return to find an angry crew coming slowly back alive.

That was simply unacceptable. She needed a quick solution.

She entered the adjoining kitchen and rummaged through the drawers for a knife. *Knives*, actually. She would probably blunt quite a few of them in the next hour. The thought of what she needed to do made her sick to her stomach. It was supposed to be so easy—she would gas the joint, and everyone would die. Quick. Painless. At least for *her*. But now . . .

Hhhhhhhhhhhhhhhhhhhhhhhhhhhhh.

The wheezing continued to grow in the other room. She wondered what had gone wrong, whether the mixture of the gas hadn't been potent enough, or . . . well, did it really matter now?

She set six knives out on the counter in front of her, blades all pointed to the right, arranged from smallest to largest. She picked up the one in the middle and contemplated the method to employ. A stab to the heart? A slit across the throat? She tried to keep the matter scientific in her mind, devoid of any human element, but she found it difficult. She'd heard them talk about their families, their plans for the future. And now all of that had been cut short.

Hhhhhhhhhhhhhhhhhhhhhhhhhhhhhhhhhhhhhhhhhhh.

"Let's get this over with," she said, stirring up the nerve to forge ahead. She had no other option. The Black Vehm had spoken, and she had no choice but to help carry out their master plan.

FIFTEEN

The limousine sank down through the turbid river muck like a giant black obelisk, a leviathan drifting into the deep beyond, a fish of biblical proportions with its own Jonah—the panic-stricken April Adams—fixed snugly in its belly. The *glug glug glug* of entering water continued to fill her ear, a constant reminder of her inevitable doom. She stood upright on the divider between the driver's seat and the passenger compartment and stomped with all her might, hoping that her foot would do what a bullet could not and break through the barrier.

Veronika's dead body lay slumped like a mannequin beside her, the glazed orbs in her puttied face looking as vacuous as a runway model's. April tried to tune out the fact that she was trapped inside an increasingly shrinking space with a corpse.

How do I get out of here? she asked herself, hoping that some tinder of wisdom would catch fire in her brain. She looked up, and to her amazement, saw a possible solution—a fold-down armrest in the rear seat—an escape route into the trunk, and therefore, to the outside. The only problem was getting there.

There was nothing to grab onto, nothing to use as a ladder to scale the interior space, which was easily twice her height. But the water was filling in quickly, and fear brought new confidence that there must be a solution.

The seats were top-grade leather and nearly seamless, providing little for April to pry her fingers into for a grip. The floor was equally slippery and impenetrable—a solid mass of black, rippled rubber. The only surface that remained was the supportless, spongy material of the ceiling. And then she spotted the series of six small rectangular lights running down its spine.

April began scaling the lights like an amateur rock climber. She wished August could see her in action. It would certainly prove that she was tougher than he gave her credit for.

Now as high as she could get in the vehicle, she reached up and grabbed hold of the armrest in the backseat. The armrest folded down, revealing a leather divider behind. She stuck her arm through the crease in the middle of the divider and reached into the trunk. She put her other arm through as well and began pulling herself up through the space. It was a tight squeeze—tighter than she had imagined. Her frame barely fit through. She wriggled upward and got halfway into the trunk when her skirt caught.

She couldn't turn back, so she planted her hands on either side of the opening and pushed down with all her might. She struggled and twisted and contorted her body to get free. The water continued to pour in. She pushed again, harder, and felt her skirt rip its entire length as she finally entered the trunk. *Unbelievable!* she thought. *I just bought this!*

She curled up in the lightless space, listening as the water seeped in from the trunk lid above and the crawl-through below. Her nerves frayed, and her mind churned in terror. She tried to remember the lessons she'd learned in panic school to fight off claustrophobia and nyctophobia—slowing her breathing, calming her thoughts—but she found a third uncontrollable phobia had overtaken the other two—the fear of death.

The trunk was half full of water. April focused on finding the handle to open the trunk lid. She frantically felt around the latch, groping for the release cord. It was missing.

The trunk was over three-quarters full of water, and April pressed her face against the lid in order to suck in as much oxygen as she could. In her mind she envisioned the lifeless bodies of Veronika and the driver floating only a few yards below her. She prayed their fate would not be her own as she searched the area once again, feeling for the release cord. Suddenly she found it. She yanked on it, too hard, and the cord broke loose. "No!" she screamed.

Knowing the cord was attached to a release mechanism, she guessed at its whereabouts and found a tiny metal loop three inches to the right of the trunk latch. She put her finger in the loop and pulled, but the device didn't give way.

The water was only inches from wholly covering her. A vision entered her mind—it was Charlie, encouraging her onward. *You can do it, Mom!* he said. *You've just got to try a little harder.* She knew it was her own words she heard in her head, but it was the reminder of her precious son that made the difference. She jerked the latch one more time, knowing it was her last attempt.

It came loose.

She pushed the trunk open, and through the distorted lens of the river water April saw radiance from above. She swam toward the glow, unsure if the gasp of air left in her lungs was adequate for the journey. Her arms churned in the water. She was exhausted beyond measure, but she forced herself onward, upward. The light was getting closer. But her lungs were giving out.

April closed her eyes, willing herself to stay alive.

An eternity passed.

Blackness enveloped her.

And then . . .

She broke through the surface of the water.

She choked, releasing the water that had collected in her lungs, and fought to breathe normally. Remembering that Alex could be in trouble, she swam to the side of the river and climbed up a ladder of decayed boards. She peered over the edge of the dock and spotted the SUV that had pushed the limo off course. It was swallowed in flames. She pulled herself up and ran to the vehicle, where she saw a man lying on his back only a few yards away.

April fell beside him and grabbed his face between her hands. "Alex! Can you hear me?" she asked, praying for a response.

He blinked at her and smiled. "I can't believe you're alive," he said.

"You either," April said, wiping the blood off his face with the corner of her blouse. "What happened?"

"They had me tied up in the backseat of the SUV," he said, gaining his composure. "They lied to me. They said Veronika killed you. When I found out she was in the limo in front of us, I knew what I had to do . . ."

April listened intently, trying to make sense of the melee that had just occurred.

"People always underestimate a 'cripple,'" Alex said. "And lucky for me, that motto held true today. The knot around my hands wasn't tied properly. I slipped out and grabbed the gun from the guy next to me. I shot him, then shot the men in the front seats too. I pulled myself forward and pushed down the dead leg of the driver. The SUV crashed into the limo, and in a mad rage I drove it right into the river." Alex closed his eyes and shook his head woefully. "I had no idea you were inside."

April pulled him close to her. "There was no way you could know." She felt his chest heaving beneath her. He was crying uncontrollably. April wasn't sure what to think of the outburst—she could count the number of times August had cried in front of her on one hand, maybe even one finger. But Alex had just been through a terrible ordeal. Surely he was due a tear or two. She didn't think less of him for it.

Alex cleared his throat and collected himself, putting his normal mask of strength back on. "You have to get out of here," he said. "The cops could show up any minute. If you're going to find August, you have to leave now."

"But what about you?" April asked.

"I really don't have any choice," Alex said, slapping his legs. "Besides, someone has to explain this scene to the cops."

April hesitated. It seemed wrong to leave, especially when she was dashing in the direction of her ex-husband. "No," she said. "I can't leave you here."

"I'm fine," Alex said. He pulled her close and kissed her cheek. "You've got to try and save August."

"And Charlie. He might still have Charlie with him."

"Then that's reason enough to go," Alex said.

April stood. She could hear sirens in the distance.

"Wait!" Alex said. He reached into his pocket and pulled out the Nazi map from the bookstore. "August might know what to do with this."

"How did you get it?"

"The driver of the SUV had it in his pocket. I'm lucky I didn't put a bullet through it. They kept talking about some link between the map and The Gospels of Henry the Lion. Maybe you and August can figure it out."

April took the map. She didn't have a pocket or a purse, so she just stuck it into the top of her sopping wet, ripped skirt.

"I always said you have nice legs," Alex said with a grin.

"Stop it," she said, turning red. It wasn't just her skirt—her whole appearance was embarrassing. Her hair was stringy, her makeup was a mess, and her blouse was sticking to her like it was painted on. If it weren't a matter of life and death, she would take the time to change her clothes. But there wasn't a chance. She held together the two ragged sides of her skirt as she scurried away. Suddenly she stopped.

"What is it?" Alex asked.

"It just dawned on me that I have no idea where I'm going."

"Where do you think August would try to find you?"

April answered immediately. "The Morgan Library. I'm never any-where else."

"Then go there, and he'll end up there too," Alex said. "But please be careful."

"I will," April said. It was a paper-thin promise. She sensed that as bad as things had been, they were about to get worse.

SIXTEEN

August held his hand over Charlie's mouth. The boy was scared out of his mind, and rightfully so. He had just heard an old family friend shot to death. August crept down the stairwell, following Cleveland through the erubescent bath of the emergency lights. He towed Charlie along in a head-grip, squashing the chance of a squeal escaping from his lips.

The door behind them rattled, and August felt his heart skip a beat. Maybe the Black Vehm had seen them escape. Maybe they were flushing them to the outside, where Lukas would be waiting, blade ready to dice them.

They hit the bottom of the stairwell and took a hard left into a short hallway. There was an emergency exit waiting for them ahead. Their pace picked up dramatically, especially after hearing the door behind them splinter and shatter.

"Hurry it up!" August said, letting go of Charlie's mouth and pushing Cleveland forward.

"Not all of us are spring chickens," Cleveland said.

"What's a spring chicken?"

"Not now, Charlie!"

"But if they kill us, then I'll die without knowing what a—"

August clamped his hand over his son's mouth again, then kicked the exit door open. "I said *not now*."

Charlie said a muffled *sorry*.

Outside, Lukas stood only a few yards ahead of them. He was facing away, watching another exit, and hadn't spotted them yet. August watched and waited, unsure whether to retreat or attack. Behind him, he heard the sound of feet clomping down the stairs. Only seconds remained until the other members of the Black Vehm would be upon them. They were trapped.

But just as August was about to make a mad rush toward Lukas, he had a better idea. The mob of people outside provided an opportunity to escape. August had never seen anything like it. People were leaving their cars on the street. Streaming out of every exit of every building. With the power off across the entirety of Manhattan, no one wanted to be left on the great island in the dark. Every person had one thing on his or her mind—getting home, and getting home *now*, before the night came and things spun out of control. In the midst of the chaos, Lukas must have seen someone in the trail of people who took him away from his post. And it couldn't have happened a moment later.

August sprang from the exit with Charlie and Cleveland close behind. They shot off to the right, in the opposite direction of Lukas, and apparently in full opposition to the growing exodus. They were salmon traveling upriver. August placed Cleveland before him like a shield and hauled Charlie behind him like a wagon, feeling at once like a medieval warrior advancing toward an impenetrable citadel. The plan—however crazy—did have its merits. August glanced back in time to see the Vehmic mercenaries spill out of the library and take the more luxurious route, flowing downstream with the swell of fleeing New Yorkers.

"Where are we going?" Charlie asked.

"I'm not sure yet," August said. The three of them crossed the street and stopped at a coffee shop halfway down the next block. There was a tugboat-sized man in a green apron posted at the door.

"Can we come in?" August asked, pulling Charlie close, hoping the man would take pity on them.

"Man, I don't know . . . things are getting crazy . . ." he said, shaking his head.

Charlie put on a winning grin, the one he usually reserved for asking incredibly big favors.

"You got cash?" the man in the apron asked.

"Yes," August said. He shot an eye over his shoulder and saw the mercenaries scanning the crowd. It wouldn't be long before they figured out where they'd gone. "So . . . please?"

"All right," the man said, already regretting the decision. "But I'm not letting the old man in."

"I beg your pardon?" Cleveland said.

"Just kidding," the man said, opening the door for the three guests. "Just don't cause any trouble."

"I can assure you we won't," Cleveland said. "But if you happen to see someone in a long black trench coat and a rather dour expression, you may want to keep him at bay."

"Okay," the man responded. "I'll try and do that."

"Good man!" Cleveland said, clapping him on the shoulder.

August, Charlie, and Cleveland all shuttled themselves inside the store, which lay largely empty. The girl at the register informed them that they were out of decaf, and couldn't make any espresso drinks, but if they wanted a cup of their dark roast, they could have it for free.

"We'll take three," August said, glancing back at the door nervously. He grabbed the cups and the three of them sat down.

"Coffee?" Charlie scrunched his nose.

"Gotta start sometime. Just dump in a bucketful of sugar and you'll be fine."

Charlie grabbed a handful of white packets from the concession cart and returned. "Shouldn't we get out of here?" he asked, doctoring his hot brew.

"We need to lie low for a few minutes. Hopefully Lukas and his crew will move on and give us a chance to get away." August looked at his father. "Something wrong?"

"I just feel bad about this mess I've gotten us into."

"You should feel bad."

"Dad, that's not very nice to say."

"I know it sounds mean, but since I was younger than you, I've had to deal with your grandfather's mistakes."

"August, stop. He doesn't need to hear about our troubles."

"Weren't you the one in favor of openness and truth? Well, here it is!"

"You're not being fair. After your mother passed away, I was trying to raise you *and* keep a full-time job. It was an impossible task."

"One that took you out of the country almost every week," August said.

"Sounds familiar," Charlie said quietly.

August shook his index finger. "No, my situation—*our* situation—is different. You live with your mom and Grandma Rose . . . people who really care about you. I had whoever your grandfather could pay to watch me, which included some people that I swear were escaped convicts."

"Cool."

"No, Charlie, not cool. Not cool at all."

Cleveland cleared his throat. "May I make a suggestion?" he said. "As interesting as this conversation is, perhaps it would do us good to focus our attention on the problem at hand." He placed The Gospels of Henry the Lion on the table.

"You're right," August said. "Tell us how you got involved in this mess. But make it quick. No telling when Lukas might show up again."

"Agreed," Cleveland said. "Earlier I explained my connection to the Black Vehm. After moving away from London, I didn't hear anything about them for almost twenty-five years. I figured the brotherhood had either disappeared or forgotten about me and my connection to Bartholomew's death and The Gospels of Henry the Lion."

"But you were wrong," August said.

"Yes . . . I was wrong," Cleveland said. "The Black Vehm was just waiting for the right time to reemerge. I was living in Berlin. I had a small bookshop, concentrating most of my selling and buying through online sources."

"Online? You?" August was amazed.

"I hired a beautiful, bright young woman who was quite adept at Web-based retail."

"Woman? Were you two . . . involved?"

Cleveland laughed. "No. It wasn't like that. I was like a father to her. That's why it was so sad when . . ." He trailed off.

"What happened?" August asked, already suspecting the answer.

"I had been receiving threatening letters. They read *contact us or else*—that kind of rubbish. Honestly, I thought it was someone I'd unintentionally wronged in a book deal. So I ignored the letters. Until finally one day Ivonne disappeared."

"Ivonne? That was her name?"

"Yes."

"Did they kill her?" August asked, whispering the last two words.

"I'm afraid so," Cleveland responded, visibly pained at recalling the memory. "The Black Vehm left clues that they were responsible. I contacted them after the loss of Ivonne, for fear that they might come after someone even closer to me." He looked at August.

"I appreciate the fact that you didn't want them to kill me. It's touching, really. But you never should have gotten involved with them to begin with," August said. "What did they want?"

"They wanted me to go to the Herzog August Bibliothek in Wolfenbuttel and do some research—some *private* research—on The Gospels of Henry the Lion."

"And you went."

"Did I have a choice? In exchange for my services, they promised to pay me handsomely and leave my friends and family alone."

"Obviously they decided to break that promise."

"Yes, but only because I broke my promise first," Cleveland said. "Once I started digging into the history of The Gospels of Henry the Lion, I discovered information that I knew I couldn't hand over to them."

SEVENTEEN

August knew they should leave the coffee shop soon, but first he needed to understand what secrets his father had uncovered. "What did you find?"

"Something that had eluded the Black Vehm for centuries." Cleveland patted the book that covered the majority of the undersized coffee shop table, as if recalling the many hours he had spent exploring its pages. "The text is taken from the four biblical Gospels—Matthew, Mark, Luke, and John. But the pictures inside tell a different story." He opened the cover and delicately turned the vellum pages, stopping at an enormously colorful miniature.

"What story does this picture tell?" Charlie asked, pointing to the luminous illustration before him.

"This is called the dedication miniature," Cleveland began, setting up the context of the scene. "It's split into two sections, top and bottom. On the top half sits the Virgin Mary, holding the Christ child in her lap."

August studied the picture. The Virgin Mary was seated on a golden throne. She wore a ruby red robe, and her head was covered with a sapphire blue stole. Her arms were stretched wide, as if she were worshipping or accepting worship. The Christ child was stationed in an orb in her lap, and though he bore the dimensions of a youngster, he wore the visage of someone much older and wiser. An ornate gold and burgundy aureole surrounded the two figures—an almond-shaped mandorla that was typical of the scene.

"To the right of the Virgin is John the Baptist, holding a palm branch. And opposite him is the apostle Bartholomew, clutching a cross." Cleveland shrugged. "It's all very normal. But *here* is what sets this book apart."

He pointed to the leftmost of the four characters stationed on the bottom of the page. "This is Henry the Lion. He had the bravado to set himself within this scene, which shows quite clearly his enormous ego. In his left hand he holds up the book we are now looking at, while the patron saint of Brunswick Cathedral—Saint Blaise—leads him forward with his right hand."

"Saint Blaze, like a fire?" Charlie asked.

"No. B-L-A-I-S-E," Cleveland answered. "Saint Blaise had a very strong . . . um . . . fan base in medieval times. He was one of the Fourteen Holy Helpers, whose names slip my memory . . . August, you always had a knack for information like this. Can you help me here?"

August's eyes flicked back and forth, as though searching through a vast storehouse of knowledge. "Is an alphabetical list okay?"

"Oh, don't be such a show-off."

"The Fourteen Holy Helpers," August said, putting out his thumb to begin the countdown. "Saint Achatius, Saint Barbara, Saint Blaise, Saint Catherine, Saint Christopher, Saint Cyriacus, Saint Denis, Saint Erasmus, Saint Eustachius, Saint George, Saint Giles, Saint Margaret, Saint Pantaleon, and . . ."

Cleveland and Charlie waited anxiously.

"Saint Vitus!" August exclaimed. "Wow. For a second I started to freak out there."

"Enough, enough," Cleveland said. He turned to Charlie. "The Fourteen Holy Helpers all had different areas of expertise, I guess you could say. Saint Blaise's name was to be invoked against illnesses of the throat."

"Why?"

"As the story goes, he once performed a miracle, saving a woman's son from choking to death on a fish bone."

Charlie's gaze returned to the book on the table. "Is the man standing next to St. Blaise another one of the Fourteen Holy Helpers?"

"Ah! Smart boy! Yes, the man next to him is Saint Giles, whose name was to be invoked against plague. In the picture he is holding the hand of Henry the Lion's wife, Matilda."

"So what's the big deal?" Charlie asked. "Why does it matter that Henry and Matilda had themselves painted with people they liked?"

"Think of it this way," August said. "Say you created a picture in Photoshop that showed you hanging out with the president, Oprah, Bono, and Michael Jordan."

"Who's Michael Jordan?"

"Let's also pretend you didn't ask that, Charlie."

"But who is he?"

"The best basketball player ever."

"Really?"

"Really. So there you are, in this picture, with all of these extremely famous people. And then, let's say, you bring the picture to school and show all your friends."

"They'd know it's a fake."

"Sure they would. But let's say that you tell all your friends that you *belong* with these famous people, that you're just as cool and amazing and fabulous as they are."

Charlie thought about this for a second. "Then my friends would say I'm a pompous buffoon."

August blinked. "Pompous buffoon? Where did you get that?"

"Mom."

"Mom?"

"Yes. She uses it sometimes to talk a—" Charlie clamped his mouth shut.

"About . . . ?"

Cleveland jumped in. "Obviously, about *you*. Now can we please move on?"

"Well, phraseology aside, you're completely correct," August said. "Your friends probably would say you thought too much of yourself. Now, remembering that, think about who Henry the Lion put himself in the company of—the Saints, the Virgin Mary, even Christ himself."

"So Henry the Lion was a pompous buffoon?"

"You really need to lose that," August said. "But in essence, yes. People thought Henry the Lion was extremely arrogant. And his egotism showed in other ways too, including the people he chose to create his gospel book. He hired the monk Herimann, who was from the Helmarshausen Abbey, known for its artistic prowess in multiple fields, including metalwork, wall coverings, and stained-glass windows. And that's precisely why, in the end, The Gospels of Henry the Lion is worth so much. It's more than just a book; it's a prized work of art." He turned to his father. "But I'm guessing that's not why the Black Vehm hired you to study it."

"I wish it were," Cleveland said. "During the first few months, they led me to believe that their aims were purely academic. But I had my own suspicions, and it didn't take long for them to be confirmed."

"What do you mean?"

"They began by giving me a simple assignment. For instance, they wanted me to figure out the proper name and title of any person illustrated in the book. This made complete sense—like the Dedication Miniature, most of the illustrations combined people from different eras and places. Creating a thorough, chronological list of these characters made sense, and it wasn't difficult. But once that chore was accomplished, they added a second layer to my work—listing any relics associated with any of these characters. At first I thought nothing of it. But as I began to search through the history of those relics, I began to grow more distrustful of the Black Vehm's inquiry."

"I know relics are old, but what are they exactly?" Charlie asked.

"Most often a relic is part of a saint or martyr—a fragment of a tooth, a broken bone, a severed arm, or even an entire head."

"A real-life *head*?"

"Strange, but true. For example, the Knights Templar claimed to have the head of John the Baptist."

"A lot of people claim to have that head," August said. "The monks of Saint-Jean-d'Angély, for example."

"Oh, rubbish!" Cleveland said. "You're ruining the story for Charlie. Now, where was I?"

"You were telling me about relics," Charlie said.

"Ah, yes! I think the idea of relics came about because of a verse from the Old Testament, in Second Kings. The passage says that some people were burying a man, but because of some advancing raiders, they were forced to hide the body. They rolled it into the tomb of the prophet Elisha, and when it touched his bones, the dead body suddenly sprang to life!"

"Wow!"

"People began wondering what other miracles could be performed

with the bones of saints and martyrs. So they collected them. Enshrined them. Covered them with gold and precious stones. And some royalty—like Henry the Lion—set themselves to the task of gathering every relic they could find. But not all relics were made of bone. Some were made of wood and steel. Some were weapons."

"Like swords?"

"Yes. Going back to John the Baptist, the sword that cut off his head was considered a highly valued relic, and it reached legendary status after being mentioned in the Arthurian tale 'Perlesvaus, the High History of the Holy Grail.'"

"Is John the Baptist's sword what the Black Vehm wanted you to find?"

"A perceptive question, Charlie. But no, it wasn't the sword they wanted me to find. It was something else."

"What?"

"Let's see if you can find it for yourself," Cleveland said, gently turning the pages of The Gospels of Henry the Lion. He stopped upon finding an exceptionally gruesome image. "This miniature is called *The Scourging and Crucifixion of Christ*."

An ornate border framed the picture. Each corner held a circle containing a famous biblical figure. In the upper left-hand corner was David, majestic and crowned. In the upper right-hand corner was Jeremiah, gray-bearded and wise. In the lower left-hand corner was Abel, holding the sacrificial lamb. And in the lower right-hand corner was Melchizedek, holding a chalice high in his hands.

Inside the frame were two settings, one on top of the other. The top half of the illustration showed Christ fixed to a marble pillar, his back bloody and raw, being thrashed by two branch-wielding men. The bottom half portrayed Christ on the cross, with the Virgin Mary and Saint John standing watch. On either side of the cross were two unidentified figures. One of them—presumably a woman, from her appearance—held out a wooden goblet to catch the blood coursing from the wound at Jesus' side. The other figure—completely cloaked with the face rubbed out—held a rod and a banner that read: MALEDICTUS OMNIS QUI PENDET IN LIGNO.

"What does that mean?" Charlie asked, pointing to the banner.

"It's Latin, a reference to the last line of Galatians, chapter three, verse thirteen. It translates *Cursed is every one that hangeth on a tree*. It's to remind the reader that Christ bore the shame of the entire world."

"That explains the banner," Charlie said, scratching the side of his face with his finger, thinking through the matter. "But what about the rod?"

"Are you sure it's a rod?" Cleveland asked.

August leaned in for a better look. "Of course he's sure. I mean, just look at how it starts up here and ends up down . . . Wait a second . . ."

"Yes?"

Charlie figured it out first. "It's not a rod! It's a *spear*!"

August rubbed his eyes to make sure he was seeing the image correctly. But there was no mistaking it. Down at the end of the "rod" was a large, triangular metal tip—the point of a spear. And it was even stabbing into the side of a camouflaged lion. "How did I never notice this before?"

"Because you've never viewed with your own eyes the *real* Gospels of Henry the Lion. You've only seen copies, facsimiles of the original."

"Is this the spear the Black Vehm was looking for?" Charlie asked.

Cleveland beamed at his grandson. "It is, Charlie. This spear is actually a very important relic, one of the most sought after and talked about in history. It's been called by many names—the Spear of Christ, the Holy Lance—as well as my personal favorite, the Spear of Destiny. It was said to have belonged to a Roman soldier named Longinus, as evidenced by the spear's Latin name—*Lancea Longini*. There are hundreds of legends surrounding it. And now—for some terrible reason—the Black Vehm wants to get their hands on it."

"But why?" August asked. "Do the Black Vehm really think the spear is magical? Do they really think it has the mystical powers the legends describe? The power to conquer the world? It just doesn't make sense!"

"I wish you could have been there to tell that to Hitler," Cleveland said. "Perhaps you could have talked some sense into him."

"What are you talking about?"

Cleveland carefully closed the cover of The Gospels of Henry the Lion.

"Hitler believed in the spear," he said, "and he went to unthinkable lengths to try and obtain it. And there's a long list of people before him, including Napoleon, the Holy Roman Emperor Barbarossa, and many others throughout history. Each one of them believed in the power of the spear, and they laid everything on the line just to *see* it. Don't underestimate people's belief, and what it can drive them to do."

August leaned back in his chair. "Is that what this is about? Is that why we have men with guns and knives trying to kill us? Because if that's the case, then I say let's give them the book. Let's give them exactly what they want so they can find their precious lance." He stood up from the table, waving his arms. "I'm sorry, but I'm not willing to bet my life—or anyone else's—on saving some myth."

"It's not a myth," Cleveland said.

"I'm sorry?"

"It's not a myth. The spear is real. But that's only the beginning. I think the Black Vehm has something much greater in mind."

"What?"

Cleveland picked up The Gospels of Henry the Lion and tucked it under his arm, then nodded his head toward the front door, where a brawl had broken out between the coffeehouse bouncer and men wearing black suits and dark expressions. "Maybe they came to explain."

August frowned. "Or maybe they came to take care of this once and for all."

EIGHTEEN

It was midnight in the Antarctic. Ivy peered through the front window of the snow tractor with her electronically aided binoculars. The night vision showed only a series of scant outlines, but she knew it was the advancing troops of the Black Vehm. No one else would dare traverse the icy landscape at this time of night.

She grabbed her two-way radio. "This is Ivonne Segur of the Neumayer Base Station. Jeremiah, do you have a copy?"

Jeremiah was the code name for the operation, coined from the prophet who wrote the so-called "broken book." It was a play on words—the Black Vehm was breaking the cryptogram found in The Gospels of Henry the Lion.

"This is Jeremiah," came the static-drenched reply.

"Do you have an ETA?"

"Not long. Twenty minutes. There's not much out here to slow down our advance."

"Nothing but ice," Ivy said.

She watched through the binoculars as they got closer. Five hundred of them—that's what she'd been told. More than enough to accomplish their goals. And this was just the beginning. Another deployment was scheduled to arrive in less than a month.

Ivy retrieved her copy of Norman Mailer's *The Castle in the Forest* from her backpack. This time she'd been smart enough to bring something to read. The book reminded her of her early days, and the way she had first come to know of the serpentine organization known as the Black Vehm.

She had just graduated from Yale. An article she'd written about Nazism had caught the eye of a prominent German publisher. The company contacted her and asked if she was interested in joining a project devoted to researching Hitler's biographical data. She accepted the job, more out of excitement to work overseas than for the job description itself. In truth, the whole thing made her a bit nervous. She wondered why they thought she was a good fit for the job—her article in the Yale paper bore a severely negative slant. She even remembered using the phrase "fascism's drug-addled teenage son" in reference to Nazism. Why they thought she would want to devote years of her life to extending the legacy of Hitler was beyond her.

Packing took no time—she owned practically nothing—and before she knew it, she was living in an apartment in downtown Berlin. David Bowie had once called the city the greatest cultural extravaganza that one could imagine, and she instantly understood why. It was a city of split personalities—quite literally, after its East-West unification. Rich beside the poor. Modern next to the ancient. The city was culturally interleaved in a way that Ivy had not anticipated.

Her first day on the job was terrible. For some reason everyone was under the impression that she spoke German, which she did not, having taken French at Yale. This didn't, however, keep anyone from barking orders to her in German, a detail that added a unique frustration to each task. Midway through the day, she found someone even lower on the totem pole, and after striking a bargain—doing the dolt's laundry once a week—she made him her personal translator. That night she cried until she fell asleep, fully planning to quit her job and move back to the States.

Her second day on the job changed those plans.

She was sent to the *Staatsbibliothek zu Berlin*—the State Library of Berlin—to meet with a curator claiming to possess Hitler's personal journal. It was a fool's errand. If the journal really existed, someone more important would have been sent for the job. She went anyway, dragging her "translator" with her, having promised to press and starch every shirt in his closet.

Upon arriving at the *Staatsbibliothek*, she was met at the door by a man who introduced himself as Dr. Rothschild.

"I assume you're here to see the Gutenberg," he said.

"You speak English?"

"Everyone here does."

"Everyone here *can*," Ivy clarified. "But not everyone *does*."

"I suppose you don't eat currywurst either."

"Sorry?"

"Never mind. Are you here for the Gutenberg or not?"

"I'm afraid there's been a mistake. I'm here to see a journal." Ivy didn't say more. She didn't want to be laughed away quite yet.

"A journal? And what journal is that?"

Ivy looked around. No one else was within earshot. "Hitler's," she whispered, barely breathing the name.

"I'm sorry?"

"*Hit-ler's*," she said again, splitting the word into two bite-sized portions.

Dr. Rothschild stared at her as if deciding her eternal fate. Finally he spoke. "I was told someone of a little more *stature* was going to be sent."

"Are you telling me you actually have it?"

"I said no such thing."

Ivy stepped in closer. "If you have it, show it to me right now, because if I go back and tell everyone you have it, but you're waiting for someone with 'more stature,' we're both going to look like fools." She stopped and bit her trembling lip.

Dr. Rothschild pulled off his glasses and cleaned them with a handkerchief. "You're certain you don't want to see the Gutenberg?"

"Thanks, but no."

"Your loss," he said, walking away.

Ivy turned to her translator—a worthless investment for the day—and told him she was ready to leave.

"Well?" Dr. Rothschild asked. "Are you coming or not?"

"Yes!" Ivy said, surprised at her change of fortune. She sent her translator away and scurried down the hall. "Sorry. I thought—"

"Be quiet until we get to my office," Dr. Rothschild said.

Ivy followed, wondering what she was getting herself into.

They entered Dr. Rothschild's office, which was small and simple and barren of any personal touches. If he spent time there, it didn't show.

He produced the journal with little fanfare. "Here it is," he said, handing it to her.

Ivy took it cautiously. "I don't understand. If this is real, then it belongs in a museum, or behind glass in a library, not in my hands."

"Your hands are *exactly* where it belongs, Ivonne," said a voice behind her.

Ivy spun around.

He shut the door. "My name is Christopher Vallodrin."

Ivy shook his outstretched hand, which felt cold, like the hand of a corpse. "Who are you?"

"Please, take a seat," he said, motioning with a flourish to the chair beside him. "This will take some explaining."

"*What* will take some explaining?"

"Our recruitment methods."

Ivy was lost. "Recruitment? I already have a job."

Vallodrin pointed at the chair.

"Fine," she said, taking a seat. "But make it quick. I'm due back to my boss in an hour."

Vallodrin laughed. "You won't have to worry about that."

"No, you certainly won't," Dr. Rothschild added.

Ivy felt like she was stuck in some nightmarish version of a hidden camera show. "What's going on here?"

"Ivonne . . . or may I call you Ivy?" Vallodrin asked, sitting across from her.

"You may call me Ms. Segur," she said.

"Then, Ms. Segur, I regret to inform you that you've been part of a rather cruel charade. The publishing company you work for doesn't exist."

"What?"

"It's fake."

"The employees? My boss?"

"Completely fabricated."

"Then what am I doing here?"

"As I said earlier, you've been recruited. The only difference between this recruitment and all others is that you've been unaware of the interviewing process."

Ivy looked across the room at Dr. Rothschild, who was positioned as far away from Vallodrin as possible. "Were you 'recruited' too?" she asked him.

"Dr. Rothschild has been with us for quite some time," Vallodrin said, answering the question for him. "And has been an active participant in evaluating your personal file."

"Personal file?"

Vallodrin's eyelids dropped a millimeter, his gaze fixed on Ivy like a viper ready to strike. "We know just about everything there is to know about you, Ms. Segur. You were a history major at Yale, but you secretly wished you had pursued a life as an artist. You had a boyfriend at school, but he lost interest after meeting your best friend, Lara. You hate the color pink. You enjoy a glass of red wine—Shiraz, if I'm not mistaken—and a good book. You only drive foreign-model cars. You have a small chip on the corner of your left front tooth. You don't speak German, but you've ordered a language study course that you think might help. Should I go on? I have more intimate details . . ."

"Please stop."

"Most people react like you . . . angry, scared. But don't think for a second that your privacy has been invaded. Privacy is an illusion, and a clever one at that. It makes you feel safe and secure. But it's not real. Every detail of your life has already been gathered, stored, and filed for later use."

"Why would anyone want to know about my life?"

"Because of your history, Ms. Segur. Though you don't know it, you belong to a very long line of Vehmists."

"I'm sorry?"

"Vehmists. People who belong to the Holy Vehm."

Fear swept into Ivy's heart. She felt like she'd just been told she was a vampire. "I'm not sure what the Holy Vehm is," she said, "but it sounds a little like a cult, and I'm really not cult material."

"The Vehm isn't a cult," Vallodrin said. "It's *royalty*. But instead of being bestowed with jewels and gold, you receive power. Enough power to have anything you want."

Ivy rose from her chair. "This is just too much. I'm going to leave now, and my life is going to return to normal."

Vallodrin stood, towering over her. "I'm sorry, Ms. Segur, but your life will never be normal again. But you never wanted *normal* anyway, did you? Not when you're meant for so much more."

Ivy ran out the door without saying another word. Surely it was all a clever game, a prank by some coworkers, a strange initiation by her employers. But when she returned to the office and found it empty, when everyone she knew was nowhere to be seen, when her apartment key didn't work, when her credit cards and identification were deemed invalid, she knew something was horribly wrong.

Luckily, she hadn't opened a local bank account yet, so every dime she owned was in her pocket. It wasn't much, but was more than enough to afford a cheap hotel for the night. She slept only a few scant minutes at a time, plagued by dark visions of the Vehm.

The visions didn't stop when the sun finally rose. The next day she could feel the eyes of the Vehm watching her everywhere she went. She finally decided to return to the *Staatsbibliothek zu Berlin*, hoping to locate Dr. Rothschild or Vallodrin. But they were not there. A quick chat with the receptionist revealed that they had never been employed there, that they didn't seem to exist at all.

She returned to her decrepit hotel room, defeated. They had taken everything from her, and they had done it with ease. But what had Vallodrin said? This was an *interview*. If that was true, then this was the final test. She didn't care about joining their beastly brotherhood, but she certainly wanted her life back. If that meant deciphering the clues they'd left behind, then so be it. But what had they left behind?

And then she remembered.

Hitler's journal.

NINETEEN

Ivy sat in the Piston Bully, listening to the wind whistle outside the door. She shivered, not from the cold, but from the memory of opening Hitler's journal for the first time. In her mind she was back in the hotel in Berlin, digging in her bag for the leather digest that Vallodrin had left in her care. The book was so fragile it cracked in her hands like a pile of dry leaves as she carefully turned the pages, unsure of what she should be looking for. It was handwritten in sharp, pointed lettering. Ivy guessed that even if she could read German the journal would be illegible, the words were so small and tightly spaced. She continued to search through the pages, already beginning to doubt that this was the proper course of action. What did she expect to find?

And then she saw it—a word, fully comprehensible—standing in solitary defiance against a background of cacography. *Vehm.* She looked again, just to make sure. *Vehm.* She studied each letter, hoping to see a loop she had missed, something that would steer the word in another direction. But there was no mistaking it.

She needed to find out more. *But who could help her?* She ran to the front desk of the hotel.

The kind-faced woman behind the counter looked up from her cross-word book. "Help you, luv?" she asked.

"Sorry to bother you," Ivy said. "I have something I need translated. Do you know German?"

"*Ich spreche ein kleines Deutsch,*" the woman said, smiling. "Now, what have you got for me?"

"Really? You'll do it?"

"Won't be many more people coming through tonight. What else is there to do?"

Ivy handed her the journal, open to the section that talked about the Vehm.

The woman put on her reading glasses and pushed her bushy gray hair out of her face. She grimaced as she read. "Whose journal was this?" she asked.

"It was . . . it was my grandfather's."

"Was your grandfather Hitler?" the woman asked.

Ivy froze.

"I'm joking, love. But he obviously had an attraction to the Nazis. And this group of people called the Vehm."

"What does it say about the Vehm?" Ivy asked, anxious for answers.

"Well, the author—your grandfather—speaks very highly of them. Apparently the Vehm has some connection to a legendary king named Charlemagne. They were the ambassadors of his court and carried out the enforcement of his laws. They were a powerful bunch. A secretive bunch. And your grandfather was seeking to reestablish their authority."

"Does it say anything else?" Ivy asked. She thought harder. "Does it list any locations where they may have met?"

"Let me look, luv," the woman said. She read for a moment, then paused. "Your grandfather had terrible penmanship, by the way."

"Runs in the family," Ivy said.

"Let's hope that's all that runs in the family," the woman said. "Because if you don't mind me sayin' it, your grandfather had some ghastly ideas."

"Like . . . ?"

The woman put her hand on Ivy's. "Let's not dwell on such things. But I do think I saw a location written down in reference to the Vehm. Would you like to know that?"

"Yes. Please."

The woman took off her glasses. "Wewelsburg. It's a castle. A triangular one. Very strange. I've not been there, but I've heard plenty about it. My brother went a few years ago. He talked about it for months."

"How far away is it?"

"About four hours by train. You'll need to speak with someone at the station, but just remember *Paderborn Hauptbahnhof.* That should be the nearest drop-off for Wewelsburg."

Ivy smiled and took back the journal. "Thank you so much."

"No problem, luv," the woman said. "And stay away from that grandfather of yours."

"Don't worry. He's dead."

"Ah, well then . . . forgive me for sayin' it, but thank God."

Ivy returned to her room and immediately fell into her bed. She rose groggily the next morning to the sound of someone rapping on her door.

"Who is it?" she asked, checking the locks.

"It's me, luv."

Ivy breathed a sigh of relief and opened the door. "Hi," she said, wiping the sleep from her eyes. "Was there something you forgot to tell me?"

"I couldn't stop thinking about you all night long," the woman explained. "I was just worried sick."

Ivy glanced up and down the hallway. "Maybe you should come in."

"I just wanted to give you this," she said, holding out a folded blanket.

"Is it cold where I'm going?"

"Just take it."

Ivy took the blanket from the woman. "But I—"

The woman shushed her and waved her hand. "I was never here," she said.

Ivy watched the woman retreat, then closed the door and carried the blanket to the bed. She unfolded it, and her mouth fell open. "Son of a gun," she said, seeing the silvery weapon hidden inside.

She dressed and exited the room, leaving the gun behind. She'd only taken a few steps down the hallway when the paranoia hit her. She rushed back to the room and retrieved the weapon. "What have I gotten myself into?" she asked herself, shoving the cold steel under her clothes.

She left for the station and took the first train out. As promised, the trip was relatively short, and she soon found herself standing before Wewelsburg's walls. She expected the structure to be sinister and dark, but the brightly hued brick of the castle glowed in the day's warm sunlight. The castle rose from the green canvas of the surrounding trees like something out of an Arthurian legend.

She joined a tour of the castle and took in the sights of Wewelsburg. She learned that the castle was built in the early 1600s by the prince of Paderborn, and that the SS took over the building during the 1930s under the direction of Hitler's second-in-command, Heinrich Himmler. Himmler used Wewelsburg to conduct his *germanische*

Zweckforschung—Germanic Purpose Research—and planned for the structure to be the center of the German world, as well as, eventually, the center of the *entire* world.

The tour ended. Ivy wasn't sure what to do next. Had she gotten it all wrong? She was halfway out the exit when a tour guide grabbed her arm.

"Excuse me, miss," the woman said. "If you would like a private tour of Himmler's Crypt, I could arrange that for you."

"That's okay," Ivy said. "I've seen enough for one day."

"It's free of charge. I *highly* recommend it."

Ivy suddenly realized she wasn't being asked. "I suppose I have time."

"If you could just follow me . . ."

"Is anyone else coming with us?"

"Maybe you didn't hear me," the guide said. "This is a private tour."

Ivy followed her to the North Tower, then down to the tower's lower level.

"You're on your own from here," the guide said. She scurried away like a roach caught in daylight.

Ivy called after her, to no avail. She considered making a quick exit but found that she was drawn by an uncontrollable urge to enter the large, circular room known as Himmler's Crypt. She walked cautiously into the space, listening as the bottoms of her feet clapped the stone floor, reverberating in an endless echo.

Ivy remembered that the crypt was to be the marvelous epicenter of Himmler's domain. Around the perimeter of the room were twelve ominously lit stone stations, built to represent the Twelve Knights of the Round Table. Himmler viewed himself as the King Arthur of his day, a fact that made Ivy's blood run cold. At least he was stopped before his sinister plan was carried out.

She looked up above her head. In the center of the domed ceiling was a round yellow stone, pressed with an image. She strained her neck upward, trying to decipher the rough-hewn icon.

"It's hard to see in this light. But I can assure you that it's a swastika."

Ivy swiveled on her heel and met the blood-drained face of Christopher Vallodrin.

He continued. "Above this room is the *Obergruppenführersaal*, the Supreme Leaders Hall. Its floor is adorned with another brilliant figure, the *Sonnenrad*, or Black Sun."

"A black sun for a blackhearted people," Ivy said.

"You're one of those people."

"I'm definitely not."

"That's why you're here, isn't it?" Vallodrin said. "To confirm your history?"

Ivy's body tensed. She hated the pages of her life being so easily thumbed through by this monster. "In Berlin, you said you knew my family. Was that a lie?"

"No."

"Then tell me who my parents are." She reached behind her back and pulled out the gun. Her hands shook as she pointed it at Vallodrin.

He didn't even flinch. "I know the names of your father and your mother," he stated calmly. "And your siblings as well."

Siblings? Ivy tried to keep her emotions in check. She'd gone through life believing she was alone. To know that she had siblings was almost more than she could bear. Family. Blood family. She pulled back the hammer on the gun. "Tell me who they are."

"I will tell you this, and only this, for now. Your mother and father are alive. They live in the United States, in the Northwest. You have an older sister and a younger brother. One of them lives in the West, the other in the East. They are all doing well. Quite well, in fact."

Ivy tried to calm her erratic breathing. "That's not enough," she said. "What are their names?"

Vallodrin strolled forward, stopping at the edge of the circular sunken pit situated in the middle of the crypt. He inspected the orna-mented depression with the inquisitiveness of a visitor. Just taking a look. Never mind the woman holding a gun on him. He spoke to Ivy without looking at her. "Each name has been written on a card and placed in a safe-deposit box. Four cards, four deposit boxes, scattered around the world."

"I'm not much for games," Ivy said. "And besides, if you were the one who wrote each name, then I really don't need the cards."

"That's the interesting part," Vallodrin said, stretching the words playfully. "I didn't write the cards. I don't know the names." He held out his palms innocently. There was nothing he could do about it. He was simply the messenger.

"You're lying."

Vallodrin shook his head. "I've seen their faces. And I know the details of their lives. But I don't know their names. That I have kept from myself, as a protection from situations like the one we're in now."

Ivy's finger relaxed on the trigger. "What do you want from me?"

"If you want the names, then you must embrace the Holy Vehm as your temporary family, until you are provided with the names of your *real* one."

"I'll never join you."

"It's your choice," Vallodrin said with a shrug.

"I'll hunt you down one by one until I get the names of my family," Ivy said. Then she pulled the trigger. Over and over she pulled it.

Vallodrin laughed. "You can't even kill me, and I'm just one man. There are thousands in the Vehm. But we need you. Your gifts and tal-ents are necessary to our future plans."

She stared at the venomless gun in her hands, which was just another prop in Vallodrin's grand charade. "Never."

The puppet master walked to the door. "Four tasks for four names. That's all the Vehm asks. It's worth it, isn't it?"

Ivy watched him depart, then listened as his footsteps grew fainter. "How will I find you?" she called out, instantly regretting the question.

"Don't worry," came the distant reply. "We'll be waiting . . ."

IVY CLOSED THE BOOK. SHE'D READ TWO CHAPTERS BUT COULDN'T remember a word, caught in the memory of her past. Since the meeting in Himmler's Crypt, she'd collected two of the names—her brother's and her sister's. They were doing far worse than Vallodrin had reported. Both were down on their luck, desperate for money, and riddled with problems, drug-related and otherwise. The situation with her brother had gotten to the point where she could no longer communicate with him. And the last time she'd seen her sister was dropping her off at another rehab center. In addition to that, they had absolutely no information about her parents—they had grown up just as alone as she had.

She'd performed another grisly job for the Vehm in exchange for information about her mother. This time, the safe-deposit box she earned contained coordinates to a cemetery plot. Her mother had died the year before, stricken with lung cancer. Ivy was so distraught over the ordeal that she killed three of Vallodrin's men and was about to kill him too when he pleaded with her to complete the fourth and final task. Her father was still alive, he said. One more job, and his name would be hers. She wrestled with the decision for weeks before giving in. But she'd gone too far to turn back now.

The radio squealed in the seat next to her. She grabbed it. "I'm here."

"We need you to open the station," said the voice.

"I'll be right there," she said. "Have all the details been taken care of? We need to make sure this looks like an American job."

"You're American, aren't you?"

"Yes."

"Then it was an American job."

For a brief moment, Ivy wondered if she'd been set up. The laughter crackling from the radio let her know it was a wisecrack, albeit a badly timed one. "Joke like that again and I'll rip your throat out," she growled into the radio.

"Sorry, Ms. Segur," came the reply. He knew she wasn't kidding.

"Meet me at the front of the station in five minutes." She clipped the radio to her belt and jumped out the door. She breathed deeply, the cold air crystallizing in her throat like a million tiny shards of glass. It felt good. A reminder that she was still alive. *Just one more job*, she told herself, preparing for the difficult night ahead. It was time to complete Task Number Four and be done with the Black Vehm forever.

TWENTY

April caught a glimpse of her frowsy self in a store window as she passed by. She shook her head, wondering what her mother would think. Barefoot. Dripping wet. Clothes ripped. Hair matted. Makeup an absolute mess. She looked like an escapee from an underwater insane asylum.

Not that anyone cared.

The streets were clogged with distressed individuals. They had homes to get to, children to care for, loved ones to find—all before the city plunged into the blackness of twilight. April wasn't much of a sight compared with the spectacle around her.

Glass exploded behind her. She turned and saw people dashing in and out of a fractured window, their arms full of flat-screen televisions and other high-tech appliances. There was no alarm, no signal that the store had been invaded. The employees had apparently vacated the space, or were hiding in the back, or had simply given up any hope of stopping the looters. There were no police on hand, and no one bothered to save the day. There were no heroes this day. Only victims.

April suddenly felt hyperaware of the map tucked into her skirt. She knew it was irrational, but there was a persistent, gnawing uneasiness in her stomach. Unlike the pillagers of the electronics store, her conscience didn't have a switch she could shut off.

At the next intersection she made a sharp right, happening to catch the eyes of two men in black suits. There were plenty of men in black suits—it wasn't that in particular that bothered her—but there was some-thing in the way their eyes pierced hers when they met. They recognized her. And her awareness of their recognition confirmed her hunch: she was being chased.

She quickened her pace. She didn't want to turn back and look, but after a block she had to find out if they'd gotten closer. Maybe she was just being paranoid. It would be easy to fall prey to such a mind disease in the midst of all the madness. But there they were—two men with angled jaws and shorn heads—getting closer with every step she took.

The street and sidewalk became more congested. People were pack-ing in from everywhere. April struggled forward, feeling the slowdown with every moment. She was treading through water, then mud, then quick-dry cement. Her pace dipped to nearly nothing, and she could feel the men advancing on her from behind. She needed to find another route. Something unexpected.

She pushed her way through the mob of people toward a storefront. BARRY'S PAWN AND JEWELRY, the hand-painted sign read. Had the electric-ity been working, a metal gate would have protected the store. But the blackout left it fully exposed.

As the people bumped and shoved her from behind, April plastered herself to the glass, cupping her hands around her eyes to look inside. The store was deserted. She turned and saw that her pursuers were upon her.

"Give us the map," the first one said.

"I don't know what you're talking about," April said as the second man blocked her from behind.

The three of them stood close together, lapped heavily by the waves of people pushing by. April used the proximity to her advantage, reaching into the jacket of the first man and fumbling for his gun.

"What do you think you're doing?" he yelled, his voice lost in the din around them. He tried to grab the gun away from her, and the firearm expelled its heat directly into the window of Barry's Pawn and Jewelry. The glass shattered in a shower of sparkling debris. But rather than people shrinking back from the scene, they poured into the shop, as if Barry had suddenly decided to have an "everything must go!" sale.

April slipped into the store with the iniquitous horde, her assailants momentarily cut off. She ran behind the register and into a dimly lit back room lined with metal shelves, all filled with additional goods. Seconds later the room was invaded by the strip-mining marauders, who devoured the remaining treasure.

April escaped through a sliding steel door into a long, dark hallway. At the end she spied a fracture of light, a clear sign that this was the way to the outside. She sprinted down the passage, hearing footsteps behind her. Whether the sound belonged to the two dark-suited men or just the lawless thugs robbing the place, she didn't know.

She reached the door at the end of the hallway. It was completely covered in rust. She tried to twist the handle, but it didn't budge. A man suddenly pushed her aside and worked furiously at the exit. Others piled against April, shoving her against the door like a human vise. Her lungs collapsed under the pressure. Hands groped her and elbows smashed into her. In the midst of the horror, she caught the faces of the two black-suited men bringing up the rear. They were smiling.

Suddenly the door gave way, the entire pack literally flooding out onto the dirty pavement of the alleyway. People scattered everywhere, the remnants of Barry's Pawn and Jewelry spewing from their pockets like candy from a piñata. April pulled herself up. She ran in the opposite direction from the gang until she discovered why they had chosen the contraroute: the police had arrived, and stood like a wall in front of her. She stopped and turned to run the other way, but the two dark-suited men blocked her flight. They brushed the rubble from their expensive clothes and walked toward her. Where was she going to go? Into the arms of the police?

Both parties closed in, and neither had her best interests in mind. She was about to give up and let the two opposing forces duke it out when she discovered a possible means of escape. She climbed on top of a large trash bin and jumped up, stretching out her arms. The tips of her fingers grazed the fire ladder hanging down, but she failed to get a grip. A man stealing a ten-point mounted deer head distracted the police, but the black suits were getting close. April leapt again, and this time—fueled by fear and a stomach-ulcerating surge of adrenaline—she wrapped a hand around the bottom rung. She pulled herself up and quickly scaled the ladder.

The black suits were right behind her. April scrambled up the rungs like a four-legged spider, reaching the roof in record time. Once there, her plan faded. She hadn't gotten any further in her mind, and the roof didn't provide any easy solutions. There were no helicopters waiting to whisk her away. No soldiers ready to defend her. She was alone with nowhere to go.

The growing clamor of heavy shoes against steel bars announced the approach of the black suits. She needed a getaway. *Or did she?* Another plan began to form, one she wouldn't have considered in less dire circumstances.

She picked up a short metal pipe. It was weighty, but she knew she could swing it with enough force to cause severe damage. Before there was a chance to reconsider the violent action, the skull of the first black suit came into view. April swung her makeshift weapon with deadly imprecision, nearly missing his face altogether. But she nicked him, and given that the nick was dealt with the tip of a metal pipe, it was enough to cause the black suit to fall backward onto his friend below.

April dropped the pipe and gazed over the edge of the roof, seeing the two suits sprawled at awkward angles on the concrete below. They weren't moving. The police surrounded the bodies. April pulled her head back. Had they seen her? She wasn't sure. She didn't hear anyone coming up the ladder, but she knew it wasn't a good idea to wait around.

Had she killed the two men? April felt dreadfully ill. She retched, bargaining with her emotions that her hand was forced, that she had no choice. It was the truth, but it didn't make her feel any better. She looked down and saw the blood on the pipe, which caused her to heave once more.

Fully emptied of both her nourishment and her guilt, April searched the roof for an escape. She found a square plate in the northwest corner and removed it, revealing a utility shaft that extended down the entire interior of the building. She lowered herself into the hole and made a swift descent, ending up in a bantam electrical closet on the ground floor. She slowly opened the door marked FOR USE IN CASE OF FIRE and found herself once again on the street among the swollen mass of people still struggling toward their homes. She slipped into the human river and ventured downstream in the direction of the Morgan Library.

The map! April suddenly worried that she'd lost it in the ruckus. She checked the top of her skirt.

It was still there.

Afraid that it might come loose and get trampled under the plodding, unyielding feet that stomped along the street, she slipped it out from its hiding place and held it tightly in her hand as she hurried down the street.

TWENTY-ONE

Though books were her specialty, April held a particular fondness for maps, especially strange ones—the ones devoted to buried treasure, both real and imagined. Maybe her affection had something to do with the map that had introduced her to August.

It was years ago, back when she was working for MIT Libraries in their special collections division. A memo arrived at her desk. The institution was sending her to a party that evening.

Party? Why was she being sent to a party? The idea almost repulsed her. Plus she had nothing to wear. She pleaded with her boss not to make her go.

"Don't think of it as a party," he said. "Think of it as research. Besides, you need to get out. I never see you without your nose shoved in a book. Don't get me wrong, I love your dedication to the job. But you've got to live a little, April."

"But—"

He raised a hand. "I won't hear it! Go, or you're fired."

"You're kidding."

"Do I look like I'm kidding?"

She raced out and bought a new ensemble for the event. If forced to go, she figured she might as well represent MIT with some style. She begrudged the decision with each step she took in her freshly purchased stilettos.

The first heel broke as she ascended the long flight of stairs leading to the ballroom. The second broke when she threw the shoes into the trash in the ladies room. She sat in one of the stalls crying, until she overheard a couple of women talking in front of the mirror. They were gossiping about some hot book hustler who was about to arrive at the chic soiree. His name was August Adams, and apparently all the women were after him.

"Oh, please . . ." April said, then suddenly realized she'd said the words out loud. The women laughed, then left April to stew in her embarrassment. She waited to make sure they were gone, then reapplied her makeup and quickly exited. She'd read articles about August and wanted to see the tome trafficker in the flesh. He represented everything she hated, especially in relation to books: he was the first rare bookseller to clear over a million dollars on eBay alone.

She entered the ballroom, dazzled by the opulent display. There were ice carvings as tall as trees, waiters in tuxes dashing to and fro with plates of decadent desserts and fine wine, a live band playing swanky jazz numbers, and at the heart of it all—a book. Not just any book, of course. It was an extremely rare book—The Nuremberg Chronicle, also known as The Book of Chronicles from the Beginning of the World. Anyone who was anyone in the book world was there to view it, and her boss wanted her to mill around, to keep her eye open for any potential donors to MIT's own rare books collection.

April decided to take a look at The Nuremberg Chronicle for herself.

She crossed the dark, polished floor, hoping no one would notice her shoeless feet in the muted light. Approaching the thick glass display box, she was amazed to find herself alone to study it. She admired the book, which lay open to a colorful, almost otherworldly-looking map.

"Do you know much about this?" asked a man behind her.

"Some," she said, remembering that this could be a possible donor. She aimed to impress. "I believe this map is based on the Cusanus map of 1491."

"Cusanus? As in Nicholas of Cusa? But didn't he die in 1464?"

April couldn't help but grin. Such an amateurish question. "Yes, but you see . . . well, the answer probably wouldn't interest you."

"Oh, but I'm sure it would," the man said. "After all, aren't we talking about the same Nicholas of Cusa who was a 'Renaissance man' before there was a Renaissance? The genius who inspired Kepler, Leibniz, and Cantor too? Not to mention his ideas about metaphysics and religion. The man was practically the definition of *interesting*, so I'd be more than happy to hear any ideas you have about him."

April turned in wonder to view this strange man. She fought back a gasp. "You're August Adams, aren't you?"

He smiled. "And you are . . . ?"

April opened her mouth and found that she couldn't remember her name. Or anything else, for that matter. What was wrong with her? "April!" she blurted, on the verge of a brain aneurism.

"April. I like that."

"You do?"

"Of course I do," August said. He leaned in close to her, then peered over her shoulder at the book. "What do you think?"

April felt a little dizzy having him so close to her. It had been awhile since she'd had a boyfriend, or even a date. She'd been locked away at the institution for far too long. "What do I think of *what*?"

"The book, of course," August said.

"Yes! The book! I think it's great."

"Great? It's more than great. In fact, it's about a million-and-a-half more than great, if you know what I mean."

"Dollars?" April exclaimed.

"Shhhh!" August said, putting a finger to her lips. "It's not polite to talk about such things in public."

"Oh. I'm sorry."

"I'm joking," August said. "Tomorrow morning on the front of the *New York Times* there's going to be a picture of me, The Nuremberg Chronicle, and the check I received for selling it."

April felt the spell begin to lift. "Just when I thought I had you all wrong . . ."

"What does that mean?" August asked.

"This is all about the money for you, isn't it?"

"No. It's not."

"Then what is it?"

"It's the adventure. The money just makes the adventure possible."

A pair of white-gloved arms crept over August's shoulders. He turned to meet a shapely blonde who was apparently ecstatic to see him.

"The money makes a lot of things possible, doesn't it?" April said. But she was talking to herself at this point, watching as August was dragged away into a swirling pool of admirers.

April stayed long enough to get a few business cards. It was the only evidence she needed to prove the night was a success. She nibbled on cheese and sampled a plate of luxurious sweets, then stole out the door in deep need of her quiet apartment. She was hailing a cab, tiptoeing back and forth to keep her bare feet from freezing on the pavement, when she felt a hand on her arm.

"Leaving already?"

It was August.

"Yes. Some of us have to work tomorrow."

"I have work too."

April shot him a frown. "You'll sleep until noon, then get up and go have a midafternoon drink with one of your fans."

"My fans?"

"You know . . . one of those girls."

"You think after talking to me for five minutes you have me all figured out?"

"Maybe," April said, finally catching the attention of a cab. She opened the door and climbed inside, more than ready to end the discussion, and the night. She started to close the door when August slid in next to her.

"You're wrong, you know."

April groaned. "I don't care. I just want to go home."

"No, you don't. Not yet, anyway. First, you have to come with me somewhere."

April looked at him suspiciously.

"It's not like that," August said. "I've got a secret, and I want to share it with you."

"Why?" she asked.

"Because unlike the people in there, you'll appreciate it."

"Appreciate what?"

August gave the cab driver an address.

"Where are we going?" April asked.

"Like I said, it's a secret."

April considered her options. She could jump out of the cab and return to her humdrum life. Or she could stay with this dashing devil and see if his secret was as good as he promised. Against her better judgment, she stayed.

"If you try anything, I swear I'll mace you," she warned.

"Do you really carry mace?"

"Always."

"Good. Because the area of town we're headed to isn't the greatest."

"I can't go. I don't have any shoes."

August stared at her feet. "Shoes are all the rage right now. You really should own some."

"It's a long story."

"I bet. But listen, if shoelessness is the only thing holding you back, I'll buy you some shoes."

April chuckled. "Where are you going to find me shoes at this time of night?"

"This is New York!" August said. "The city that never sleeps! We could shop for shoes all night if we wanted."

April shook her head. "I don't know."

August gave the driver another address.

"Where are we going?" April asked.

August smiled. "I just thought of a little store I think you'll like."

"How do you . . . ?"

"With 'fans' like mine, you learn quickly about the best places in town for shoes."

An hour later, after a successful shoe detour, they pulled up in front of an unmarked warehouse.

"Don't go anywhere," August told the driver, handing him a wad of bills. He climbed out and motioned for April to follow him to the warehouse door. He unlocked the door with a key he produced from a hidden compartment in his belt. "You can't be too careful," he said, glancing around nervously.

Too careful about what? April wondered. Maybe she was going to need her mace after all.

They entered the warehouse, and August threw on the lights. The cavernous space lay entirely empty except for a black BMW situated squarely in its middle. August approached the rear of the vehicle and removed his shoe, shaking another key out of it. "Like I said, you can't be too careful."

April approached cautiously as he unlocked the trunk and pulled out a sizeable silver briefcase. "Need another key?" she asked.

"No," August said, unfastening the latches. "I figured at this point it was probably overkill." He pried up the lid.

April was shocked at the sight before her. It was The Nuremberg Chronicle. "But . . . I thought . . ."

"The book at the party was a fake," he said, turning the briefcase for April to get a better look. "This is the *real* Nuremberg Chronicle. I couldn't display it in an unsecured public area."

"I can't believe it."

"Believe it," he said, setting the briefcase on the ground and reaching back into the trunk of the BMW. He pulled out two sets of gloves, handing one pair to April. "Here, put these on so you can take a closer look!"

"Really?"

"Of course!"

April slipped her hands into the gloves. "Do you do this with all the girls?" she asked, carefully removing the book from its nesting place.

August grinned. "I can assure you I don't do *this* with any of them."

They spent the entire night looking at the book together, comparing notes on its history, its creators, and the myths and legends that surrounded both. At some point—April didn't remember when—August sent the cab driver away.

"I kept him around in case you wanted to leave," he told her.

"Don't worry," she said. "I'm not going anywhere."

At daybreak August returned the book to its hiding place, then fired up the BMW and drove April to work.

"Are you going to be okay?" he asked her, concerned over her sleepless state.

"I'm going to be fine," she said. "And I'm going to be even better if you follow through with that donation you talked about."

"Now who's the one talking about money!" August said with a wink. "Tell you what. I'll give you the check tonight, right after we have dinner together."

"We're having dinner together?"

"It's the least I can do after keeping you up all night."

UP ALL NIGHT. APRIL FELT CERTAIN THAT THE UPCOMING NIGHT would be equally sleepless. She tucked the map away and punched in the code at the back door of the Morgan Library. She didn't have a clue if the Black Vehm was waiting for her inside, but it was the only place she had a chance of connecting with August.

She crept inside and quietly shut the door behind her. She tiptoed down the hallway, then stopped to listen as she reached a staircase. At first she heard nothing but the dull buzz of an emergency exit light. But then there were voices, hushed and low, accompanied by the soft shuffle of feet. April strained to hear the two distinct voices, their words all but indecipherable. They were getting closer. Too close.

April turned to make a swift escape, but someone was waiting for her. The man held a gun, its laser sight trained on her, pricking her chest with a solitary dot of red.

"I've got her," the gunman yelled to his comrades up the stairs.

April heard them coming from behind. Every fiber of her being told her to run, but she was frozen in place. She was trapped, and this time she knew she wouldn't be as lucky as she'd been on the roof. This time, they would kill her.

TWENTY-TWO

August knew they needed to act quickly. The coffee shop security guard wouldn't be much of a match for the Black Vehm, especially Lukas, who wouldn't hesitate to slice the guard's green apron to shreds.

"Give me the book," August said.

"Why?" Cleveland asked, holding The Gospels of Henry the Lion protectively under his arm.

"It's the only thing the Black Vehm wants. If I have it, they'll follow me. Then you can get Charlie to safety."

Cleveland shook his head. "This is all my fault. I'm the one who should have to deal with them."

"You won't make it half a block."

"I may be an old man, but I'm faster than you think."

"Not fast enough. Give me the book."

"Fine," Cleveland said, shoving the book into his arms. "Just make sure they don't get their hands on it. Or on you, for that matter."

August, Cleveland, and Charlie darted behind the front counter and entered a storage room. An employee sat there watching a movie on his laptop, unaware that disaster was about to strike. August yanked the earbuds from his head. "Call the police."

"Why?"

A mad clatter broke out in the other room. The employee jumped up from his chair.

"Forget the police," August said, escorting the entire party down a hallway toward the back door. "Just get out of here!"

Cleveland, Charlie, and the employee all exited the coffee shop into the alleyway.

"The coast is clear," August said. "Better move fast."

"Where do we go?" Cleveland asked.

"Charlie knows. Just follow him and stay out of sight. I'll find you later." He kissed his son on the head, then handed him his cell phone.

"I thought these weren't working."

"Not right now. But if the blackout ends, call the police. Okay?"

"Okay," Charlie said, shoving the phone deep into his pocket.

Cleveland put his arm around the boy, and they disappeared.

August turned and sprinted for the front door. Lying a few feet in front of it was the coffeehouse security guard, his throat slit wide open. Lukas and two of his Vehmic compatriots stood over him like hawks.

"Get him," Lukas snarled.

August darted through the tables, knocking over the mugs that had been left behind, the ceramic bowls smashing on the floor like hollow hailstones. Still clutching The Gospels of Henry the Lion, he grabbed a chair with his other arm and threw it through the front window, which shattered on impact. August hurdled the spiky expanse and took off down the sidewalk at a breakneck pace. The two Vehmites and Lukas were close behind.

The streets were still full of people. August weaved left and right through the crowd like an NFL player, the opposing team managing to stay within a few yards of him. August knew if he was going to escape their reach, he needed a new plan.

And that's when he saw the bike.

The midnight-black Buell 1125R looked fast. And from what August had heard from his thrill-seeking buddies, it was rip-roaring fast. When Charlie was born, he'd promised April not to ride a motorcycle again. Ever.

She'll get over it, August thought, running to the sport bike.

He waved his wallet in the air like a badge and screamed something about police business. The motorcyclist didn't move. August felt a tap on his shoulder and swiveled to find a second cyclist on a matching bike. They both took off their helmets. Brothers. Twins.

"Those guys sent me," August said, pointing to Lukas and his friends, who had just arrived on the scene. "They had a message: real men drive Harleys."

"They said that?" the first brother said. He was obviously drunk and looking for a fight.

The second brother got off his bike. "They're going down!"

A fight erupted in the street between the brothers and the Black Vehm. August picked up one of the bikes and tore away from the scene, watching in his rearview mirror as Lukas grabbed the other and followed him. He gunned the engine and shot through an endless line of cars straight toward his destination—the Lincoln Tunnel. He glanced back. Lukas was getting dangerously close.

August hit the throttle, and the bike screamed forward. He squinted his eyes to fight off the wind and prayed nobody would decide to open a car door unexpectedly. He heard the second bike rev loudly behind him. The gap between them was rapidly shrinking. They charged through an intersection, nearly colliding with a garbage truck stuck in the center. Motorists yelled as they sped by, but August didn't hear them, intent on reaching the dark channel in the distance.

Before the blackout, August knew, the Lincoln Tunnel would have been clotted with cars. But now it lay before him like a wide-open battle-field. A security guard chased after him in vain as he blasted through one of the closed gates and jetted into the center tunnel. The passageway was a dark abyss, and August felt that instead of burrowing under the Hudson River he was shooting away into the blackness of space. He found the headlight switch, but decided to keep it off. He didn't want to give away his position quite yet. Not when it was his only advantage.

TWENTY-THREE

Lukas hit the accelerator and plunged the cycle into the lightless tunnel. Though he couldn't see him, he knew August couldn't be too far ahead. He reached inside his jacket and pulled out the weapon that felt most effective for the moment—an Emerson CQC-T—a perfectly balanced, razor-sharp steel tomahawk. It would make quick work of carving up his prey.

He drove faster, holding the tomahawk down, angled by his side, ready for action. In his mind, he envisioned a clean swipe through August's neck, which, if he were lucky, would fully sever his frowning face from his body. Lukas almost laughed at the thought; it was so gruesomely perfect.

In the distance, he saw a taillight flicker alive. He knew August was too deep in the tunnel to go any further without illumination. His disappearing act had ended, and there was nothing left for him to do but die. Lukas kept his own lights off, knowing that the element of surprise would give him a clear advantage. Soon The Gospels of Henry the Lion would be in his hands, and he would be the savior of the Black Vehm.

He dipped his blade down until it skimmed the flesh of the pavement, causing a cascade of sparks that blazed a trail toward his target. He gained ground quickly, almost too fast. Had August stopped in his tracks? It made the whole scenario seem almost sad—the poor defenseless bookworm sitting scared in the dark, awaiting his fate like a man trapped in the craw of a guillotine.

The taillight was only a few yards away when Lukas noticed something curious about its angle. It wasn't square with the road, but rather slightly tipped off axis. He swore and hit the brakes, but not before August stepped out of the shadows and swung a two-by-four directly at his face. The tomahawk rattled out of his hand as he fell from the bike and landed with a sick thud against the pavement.

The last thing he remembered before the darkness took him was the sound of a bike thundering away into the distance.

TWENTY-FOUR

August was shaking, his nerves rattled by the encounter with Lukas. He'd barely escaped being sliced in two by his fire-breathing blade. The orange-and-white-striped board he'd struck him with was part of a discarded traffic barrier. His hands still stung from the impact, but he knew he got the better end of the deal.

A minute later he blasted out the end of the tunnel, cutting a path through the gates and merging back into the thick stew of Manhattan traffic. The other two members of the Black Vehm were nowhere to be seen, and August hoped that they hadn't gone back to the coffee shop in search of Cleveland and Charlie.

He took the note Dr. Rothschild had given him out of his pocket and read it once more:

Slaughter the librarian's horrid myth.

He'd wondered at first if the phrase were a quote from a famous book, something Dr. Rothschild would have figured him to know. But nothing came to mind. The answer must lie elsewhere. He remembered that Dr. Rothschild was a puzzle lover; he took time every morning to complete the crossword in the *New York Times* and was a notorious letter jumbler and anagram solver.

August knew Dr. Rothschild wouldn't have given him the puzzle without some clue. But what was it? He thought through the solution. It was supposed to reveal information about the Stuhlherr, so perhaps STUHLHERR was the key to figuring out the rest. He subtracted the word from the phrase, thinking through the remaining characters:

What else had Dr. Rothschild said? Something about not wanting to be there when August figured out who the Stuhlherr was. Most of the people August knew closely worked at libraries, so he wondered if LIBRARY was another clue. He subtracted the word, just to test the theory:

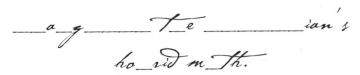

Stuhlherr . . . something something . . . library. So far so good. He braked hard, almost running into the back of a cab. The man inside stuck out his head and yelled something unintelligible. August waved back kindly, as if misunderstanding the angry display. Driving while talking on the phone was bad, but driving while trying to solve a madman's riddle was infinitely worse.

Now it was time to eliminate any smaller connecting words. He tried many combinations—IN, AND, THE, AT—and on and on. The combinations were endless. How was he ever going to figure it out? There weren't many letters left, but he needed a clue to solve the phrase. He was so close. He could feel it. What was he missing?

Down the street, the Morgan Library came into view. And suddenly the answer to Dr. Rothschild's puzzle struck him. It was so simple. *MORGAN*. That's the clue he needed. The rest of the phrase fell immediately into place:

Stuhlherr is hid at the Morgan Library

But there was another message implied, a more profound and important one—the identity of the Stuhlherr.

Alex Pierson.

No wonder Dr. Rothschild feared his discovering it! August ran the possibilities through his head a million times, but he kept coming back to Alex. In some terrible way, it confirmed every suspicion that he'd ever felt about his old friend. But it was a confirmation he never wanted to be true, especially now that April was engaged to him. How would he explain it to her? And how would he convince her to believe him? She would probably think he dreamed it up as a reason she shouldn't marry Alex. And August had to admit that it wasn't a far-fetched idea.

His track record wasn't the best. He'd been caught blackmailing a potential suitor with digitally altered photographs. He was spotted spying on her during a business trip in London. His jealousy made no sense. He had no right to interfere with April's life, especially when he was the one who screwed everything up in the first place. And now he was going to do it again. She'd never forgive him, even if she understood that he was telling the truth.

But was it the truth? Doubt crept into his head. What if he told her that Alex was the Stuhlherr, and he was wrong? She'd have him committed. And she'd keep Charlie a safe distance away. But would she really do that? Who wouldn't? And could he blame her?

He pulled up to the curb near the Morgan Library. It was time to make a decision. Telling April what he believed about Alex meant putting their relationship, such as it was, at risk. Not telling her meant putting her life in possible danger. It was a terrible choice, but August knew what he had to do. He had to tell her, even if it meant sacrificing everything they had. And everything they *could* have.

He parked the bike next to a tree and removed The Gospels of Henry the Lion from behind the seat, then jogged to the side entrance of the Morgan and pulled on the door. It was locked. He contemplated breaking the glass, but knew it would cause too much of a racket if the Black Vehm was waiting for him inside.

The massive brick-walled library loomed before him like a medieval castle. *There's got to be another way into this place*, he thought. An image popped into his head, a scene from the top of the Empire State Building. He'd been there with April, and she'd felt dizzy. August had thought at first that the sensation was simply due to the high altitude, but then a second reason came to him. He looked out from the viewing deck and found his attention grabbed by the whirling of a thousand giant air-conditioning fans—the colossal churning rotors that topped every building in Manhattan. That had been the cause of April's vertigo. At the time, the information created an excuse for her to close her eyes and cling to him for support, but now it could be a lifesaver.

He ran to the edge of the building and found a drainpipe extending down from the roof. He took off his belt and wrapped it around his chest, securing The Gospels of Henry the Lion to his front. Grappling the fittings that held the drainpipe firmly against the brick, August began a labored ascent. He wished he were ten years younger. Reaching the roof, he hurried to the air-conditioning vent and stared down into the chasm. Normally, a set of substantial spinning blades would block his entrance, but the blackout had taken care of that problem.

He dropped into the hole. There was little to hold on to, and the support bars inside the shaft bent easily under his weight. He descended a few feet at a time, trying desperately not to lose his grip. Despite his carefulness, his foot slipped, and he slid down the throat of the metal leviathan toward an uncertain end.

His body slammed against the sides as he fell, his clothes and skin catching on loose nails and half-turned screws. August felt as if he were trapped in some evil child's torture device—a tornado slide fitted with tiny daggers.

He hit bottom with a resounding clang. He shuddered at the impact, an excruciating headache instantly gripping his temples. Slowly he raised himself up, feeling at the many sore spots across his body, all wet with fresh blood. He winced, finding an especially tender tear along the side of his head. Despite his sorry state, he'd made it inside. Now the problem was getting back out.

He found a narrow air duct leading to the right, and climbed inside. He crawled forward like a sewer rat, The Gospels of Henry the Lion still attached to his chest. He wondered if anyone, including the Black Vehm, had heard his clattering fall. It was a large building—there was still a good chance he had gone undetected. Soon enough he would know.

The air duct led to a dead end. August was about to turn back when he felt a cool draft of wind beneath him. His eyes adjusted to the dark, and he saw that he was situated directly over a slotted grate. He found two latches on either side of the grate and unfastened them. Holding on to the fixture, he let it unfold on its hinges into the space below. He stuck his head out upside-down through the opening and saw that he was located in a large storage room.

He dangled out of the air duct and grabbed onto a water pipe that extended to the back wall. Hand over hand, he led himself to the end of the pipe, then climbed down a set of shelves to the floor. He carefully crossed the dimly lit room, through columns of cleaning solutions and mop buckets, and made his way to the door. He put his ear against the wood and heard nothing. Slowly, he turned the door handle and slipped out into the hallway. He glanced around at the unfamiliar setting. He knew the Morgan Library extremely well, but he'd never seen this area before.

Where was he?

TWENTY-FIVE

August heard voices.

He crept to the end of the hallway and peered around the corner. Only a few yards away he spied two men standing before a steel door. One of them flipped open a panel in the wall, revealing a digital lock. August listened as one of the men recited a seven-digit code to the other, who punched in the numbers.

"Did you hear something?"

August pulled his head back.

"Shhhh! Did you hear that?"

"Yeah. It's my stomach. Let's get out of here."

August listened as the two men left in the opposite direction. He waited until their footsteps disappeared before stealing his way to the door. He opened the wall panel and punched in the code. A green light flashed, and he heard a soft click as the door unlocked. Jackpot.

He slipped in the door and gasped at the sight before him. It was—for lack of a better description—a cave. Not a large one, but a cave nonetheless. Fiery torches lit the greasy walls. Thick oak benches lined the rock floor. And the most curious sight was the object at the end of the cave—a ten-foot golden statue of the Virgin Mary.

This must be the Stuhlherr's court, thought August. Whoever had constructed the arena had obviously modeled it specifically on an ancient plan. There was nothing haphazard about it—everything clearly served a precise purpose in the room's grand design.

August heard voices from the hallway. He swore and scanned the room for a hiding place. There weren't many options. He ran toward the statue, noting a fissure running along its front. He set down the book, then placed his hands inside the statue and split it open. Inside, gleaming in the flickering torchlight, was a wicked assembly of triangular spikes. August shook his head. Not a good place to hide.

Across the room, the lock turned in the door. August shut the statue and slipped behind it. The narrow expanse barely concealed his frame. Then he remembered: *The book! It was still sitting on the floor!*

The door opened and two men entered, intent on shutting up the woman they were dragging in with them. It was April.

August's dark instincts begged him to race out and bludgeon the two men to death with his fists. But he knew he wouldn't make it halfway across the room before they shot him dead. If he had any chance to save April, he was going to have to wait for the right opportunity to strike.

"I'll tell you where the map is," April said. "But you have to let me go."

Map? What did the Black Vehm need with a map? Wasn't it the book they were after?

"We have to wait for the Stuhlherr before making that decision," the first voice said.

August peeked out from his hiding spot and saw that the voice belonged to a stocky muscle-bound man stuffed into a suit. His face appeared to be a mass of ripples, like the wrinkled face of a bulldog.

His partner was a study in contrasts—rail thin and over a foot taller. His suit hung off him like he was made of clothes hangers. His gaunt face was fixed in a frown. "We need to take care of this now, before the Stuhlherr gets here," he said to the bulldog. "Besides, she could be lying. She could have the map with her now."

August pulled his head back, hoping he hadn't been spotted as the thin man glanced in his direction.

"Check her," the man said.

August heard April cry out in protest. The bulldog was obviously not taking a very gentle approach in his investigation.

"Get your hands off me!" April said.

"Hey . . . she's got something here," the bulldog said.

August heard the sound of parchment being unfolded. April's deal had fallen apart. Now that they had the map, there was no reason for them to keep her alive. August was planning his next move when it was made for him.

"What's that over there?" the thin man said.

"Looks like a book," his partner replied.

August heard heavy footsteps coming his way. He held his arms in close, tensing for the attack. And then he saw a second option.

The bulldog got closer. "Hey," he said, "isn't that the book the Stuhlherr told us about?"

"It can't be," the thin man said.

August put his back to the wall and pushed against the statue with every ounce of strength he possessed. He strained until he thought his head might explode, then found another boost of energy when he saw the golden head sway in the room's orange glow.

"I'm serious!" the bulldog said, still advancing. "Look, it's got the two little angels and the cross in the middle, just like he showed us!"

The base of the statue groaned and cracked; then the entire structure broke free and fell forward like a toppled timber. The bulldog screamed and put his arms up in protest, but it was too late. The golden Virgin bent down and kissed his forehead, crushing his cranium in the process. He flailed limply as he and the statue crashed to the ground, the cave trembling in response.

His shield gone, August was now fully exposed. He watched helplessly as the thin man drew his pistol and pulled the trigger. A bullet exploded from the muzzle, instantly ricocheting off the wall just inches from his head. He knew he wouldn't be so lucky with the next shot. But it never came. April sprang to his defense, hitting the thin man in the jaw and wrestling with him for control of the gun.

August jumped over the gap exposed by the fallen statue and ran toward the brutal scene. April took a nasty blow to the head just as August reached them. The man stumbled to his feet and wiped the blood from his mouth. He pointed the gun squarely at August's heart. "Don't move," he warned.

April lay unconscious on the floor.

August put his arms up. "Whatever you want, we can give you. Just don't do anything stupid."

"Stupid was letting this girl get the best of me," the man said, licking his cut lip. "But don't think I'll be that stupid again."

August closed his eyes and prayed that the road would be short from this life into the next.

TWENTY-SIX

Charlie looked up at the angel high above his head. She held her hand out to him, a gesture of kindness, or perhaps of warning—he couldn't decide which. Her wings were stretched outward, but he knew she wasn't going anywhere. This was her permanent home, a place he loved to visit whenever he had a chance, especially with his father.

"C'mon, Grandpa," he called out. "We're getting close."

"I hope so," Cleveland replied, sitting down at the edge of the fountain. "I'm about to faint from exhaustion."

"We can wait here a minute," Charlie said, taking a seat next to him. "You ever been here before?"

"To Bethesda Terrace? I don't make a trip to New York without coming to Central Park to see Angel Fountain."

Charlie smiled. "When I was little, I thought the angel was real."

"Sometimes I still do," Cleveland replied. He glanced around nervously.

"What is it?"

"Just making sure we're not being followed."

Charlie stood and scanned the crowd. There were plenty of people milling about, but no one too suspicious looking. At least no one wearing a black suit like the guys he'd seen back at the coffee shop. "I think we're okay for now."

"Good."

The two of them sat peacefully for a moment, which felt odd to Charlie, given the events of the day.

"Where is this place your father knew you'd be?"

"Are you ready to see it?" Charlie asked.

"I think so," Cleveland said, splashing the waters of the fountain with his fingers before getting up.

Charlie ran and entered one of the archways that led beneath Terrace Bridge. Cleveland caught up to him, and they walked together through the tunnel, coming to a set of stairs. Charlie jumped up them two at a time, stopping at the summit and raising his arms like a prizefighter.

"I win!" he said.

Cleveland huffed as he made his way to the boy. "I lose!" he said, raising his arms in mock defeat.

"Don't worry. We're close now." Charlie followed the wall along the walkway to a square pillar. "This is it!"

Cleveland joined him and grinned. "Now I understand."

Carved into the side of the pillar was a scene any bibliophile would notice—an open book. Set behind it was a lamp, and though its flame was inanimate, the gray pages of the book glowed with the final fires of the setting sun.

"Isn't it cool?" Charlie said. "I like to imagine what words were on the pages before they got rubbed off."

"Rubbed off?"

"Yeah. Maybe there used to be a magic spell written into the stone. But someone washed it away with acid!"

Cleveland ruffled the hair on his grandson's head. "You're so much like your father."

"Really? People tell me I'm a lot like my mom."

"Who says that?"

Charlie's cheeks went red. "Mostly my mom."

"I have no doubt there's some truth to that. But you are your father's son. No doubt about it."

"I'm pretty sure I got his brain skills."

"Please explain," Cleveland said.

"My dad makes me memorize stuff all the time."

"Like this meeting spot?"

"Yeah. But a lot more too."

"Anything interesting?"

"I guess so. All the stone carvings around here were designed by a guy named Jacob Wrey Mould. It's easy to remember if you imagine green mold covering everything."

"Charming."

"Some of the carvings represent morning, and some night. My dad made a deal with me that if we ever got separated from each other in the morning, we would meet at the carving of the rooster. But if we got separated from each other later in the day—"

"You would meet at the book and the lamp," Cleveland filled in. "A representation of night."

"Right!"

"Sounds like your 'brain skills' are in perfect working order."

"That's exactly what Dad says!"

The conversation paused. All the talk about his father made Charlie wish he would show up. Ten wordless minutes passed, and the sky became a thick curtain of deep purples and ruby reds, an endless cascade of colors that stretched across the sky to become the darkest indigo.

"Why weren't you and Dad speaking?" Charlie asked, curling in closer to Cleveland.

"Didn't he ever tell you?"

"No."

"Then I suppose he refrained for a reason. You should ask your father after all this foolishness has settled down."

"But what if . . ." Charlie didn't want to finish the sentence. "What if he doesn't ever come?"

Cleveland mumbled something under his breath. "Oh, all right," he finally said. "But if your father ever tells you this story, you have to act like you've never heard it before. Agreed?"

"Agreed," Charlie said, showing a scout's promise.

"I should start by saying that your father is a very good man. And he started as a very good boy. But he still made some very bad choices."

"Is this going to be a sad story?" Charlie asked.

"Somewhat. Do you still want to hear it?"

Charlie stirred his courage. "Yes."

Cleveland continued. "The trouble all began after Violet died. She was your grandmother. I wish you could have met her. She was wonderful, smart as a whip, and oh, so beautiful. I was lucky to have had her for as many years as I did. August was only twelve years old when she passed away. It was a very hard time for him. For both of us. Things between us became difficult. I suppose most of it was my fault. Every time I looked at his face I saw her. I never meant to pull away from him, but looking back, I have to admit that all the time I spent on the road was an effort to escape the pain I was feeling. That was the mistake I made. Your father's came later."

Charlie sat in rapt attention. He hadn't heard many stories about his father's early years.

"Six years passed," Cleveland explained. "I was spending more and more time on the road, and August was spending more and more time getting into trouble. I finally took notice when he and some of his ruffian friends broke into their school and spray-painted graffiti across the walls of the gym. I was in Russia at the time and had to make an overnight trip back to get August out of jail."

"My dad was in jail?"

"I'm not surprised he never told you. It wasn't his finest moment."

"Did someone try to stick him with a shiv?"

Cleveland couldn't help but chuckle. "He had a rough time, but there was no shiv involved."

"What happened after you got him out of jail? Did you ground him?"

"I tried," Cleveland said. "But he was eighteen. Almost a man. And at least enough of a man not to have to listen to me. Against my wishes, he moved in with a friend, a dropout, who I discovered was peddling goods on the black market. Not drugs, but artwork. But don't think because it was art that it was any less dangerous, or any less illegal. I never could find out if August was directly involved, but the more I discovered, the more I pleaded with him to come back home."

"Did he?" Charlie asked.

"I wish I could say yes. My last conversation with him was on the phone. It was dreary and cold, raining like the dickens. I was in Scotland, I believe. I called to tell him that I was coming back home the next day and asked if he would have lunch with me, just to talk. He refused. Just lunch, I told him. Nothing more. But he still said no. I told him that I loved him, and he hung up. And that was it."

"Why?"

"Because then he did the unthinkable. He stole my book."

"What book?"

"The Book of Chronicles from the Beginning of the World. It's also known as The Nuremberg Chronicle, and even more properly as the *Liber Chronicarum*. Have you heard of it?"

"Yes. My mom told me about it. I think it had something to do with how she met Dad."

"That's true," Cleveland said, smiling sadly. "But here's the unfortunate truth of the matter. The book was originally mine. I found it many years before August was born. It was my prize possession, the artifact that put me on the map in the world of rare books. It was special to me for another reason too. It was how I met Violet."

"I've never heard any stories about her."

"That's too bad, because she was an incredible woman. Of course, she didn't start that way. Her father was a wealthy man and gave her everything she wanted. When I first met her she was incredibly spoiled."

"I know kids like that at school."

"Probably not the most popular, are they?"

"If they have an Xbox, they are."

"I think I understand what you mean," Cleveland said. He continued his story. "On Violet's eighteenth birthday her father asked her to choose anything she wanted as a gift. I suppose he thought she would choose an extravagant diamond necklace or a mile-long string of pearls. But she chose something else."

"An Xbox?"

"No. She asked for The Book of Chronicles from the Beginning of the World."

"The same book my mom talked about!"

"The very same. Why it was so important to her, she never revealed. But nonetheless, he was compelled to find it. He called on some of his friends for help, but no one was even familiar with the title, much less its whereabouts. Eventually, he took a more drastic route to find it. He hired me."

"And that's how you met Violet?"

"Not quite yet. Her father was the one who hired me. To this day I'm not sure why. He must have received a strong recommendation from a colleague or ex-employer of mine. I was eager to take the job, having had only a few modest successes in the field of book hunting. It was my biggest assignment so far, and a tall order at that. He told me I had *no budget*, which I thought meant I'd have to finance the quest myself. But I quickly realized that he actually meant an unlimited budget. There were no restrictions. If I needed to fly to Hong Kong, I could do it on a moment's notice. If I needed to hire a boat captain or an air captain or an entire regiment of zeppelin captains to take me where I needed to go, I could do it without hesitation."

"That sounds cool!"

"It was. But the job also came with a lot of hard work. I spent the first three months becoming acquainted with the major players in the book world. They were a strange lot, stranger than any of the book characters they talked about. But they were also helpful, and led me step-by-step closer to the goal."

"You found the book?"

"Not yet. I hit a snag. Violet was becoming impatient. She began to question my methods and my inexperience. She even said that she could do a better job herself. So from that point on, she went everywhere with me."

"Did you already like her then?"

"Not at all! Her constant complaining caused me to pray for my own deafness. *The soup is cold. The spoon is dirty. The room is too hot. The room is too cold*. And on and on. Finally, in a fit of rage, I lost my temper and let her know how I felt. I heard words come out of my mouth that I didn't even know I knew. It must have been an effective speech, because when I finished, she cried for the rest of the night. I felt horrible, of course, but something told me not to console her."

"You just watched her cry?"

"I know it sounds cruel, but you have to believe me when I say it was for the best. From then on, things got better and better. We were honest with each other about our feelings. She explained to me how she didn't like who she had become and wanted to change. And then, almost magically, she did. We both did. Adventure after adventure came our way as we pursued the elusive Nuremberg Chronicle. Finally, one very sad day, we found it. Our journey ended."

"Then what happened?"

"We did what any normal couple in love would do. We got married."

"And what happened to the book?"

"We put the book in a glass case by our front door. It wasn't the safest of locations for such a priceless item, but we knew we couldn't hide it away in some bank vault. Every time we walked by it we were reminded of how our relationship started . . . and why it would never end."

Charlie felt a few tears begin to collect at the edges of his eyes. He brushed them aside. "Why would my dad steal the Book of Chronicles away from you, then? Didn't he know how much it meant to you?"

Cleveland put his arm around him. "He knew *exactly* how much it meant to me. That's why he did it. He knew that taking it from me was like putting a dagger through my heart. He knew that I'd leave him alone, that I'd stop asking him to change his ways and come home. But he was wrong."

"You forgave him?"

"Of course I did," Cleveland said. "Not right away, but a person can only stay angry for so long. After a while I realized my feelings were for Violet, not the book. The book was important to me, but in the end, it was just a book."

"A pretty important book," Charlie said.

"Yes," Cleveland said, "it was. But that's the past. We have new problems before us now."

"Including my dad, who's still missing," Charlie said. "How long do you think we should wait?" The shadows were beginning to crawl out from the corners, and Charlie was beginning to hear his mother's protective words in his head. *Never be in the park after dark.* It was like a scary nursery rhyme.

"We've waited long enough," Cleveland said, a sorrowful tone inflecting his voice. "It's time to leave."

Charlie put his hand on the book carved out of stone, as if to say good-bye to it. "Where are we going?"

Cleveland smiled. "It's always good to have a backup plan," he said, leading Charlie down the path toward Central Park's eastern edge.

"You have a backup plan?"

"Always."

TWENTY-SEVEN

Garrett Daraul ran toward the colossal C141 Starlifter parked on the runway. The plane had been purchased from the military and fitted with equipment more suitable to the needs of the Black Vehm. The customization was the first and simplest job he'd performed for the organization. Since then the assignments had become increasingly more complex and deadly.

He longed for the days when he first joined, when the Vehm's direction was clearly defined, not muddled with internal politicking. Now there were factions to recognize, egos to soothe, and sways in the balance of power that needed to be navigated with the utmost care. Now it was tricky. He longed for the days when *kill or be killed* was all you had to know.

Garrett jogged up the metal steps of the Starlifter and rapped on the door. It opened immediately. He climbed inside and offered the good news to his superior.

"They're on their way."

"It's about time," came the slurred reply.

"Are you drinking the Remy Martin the Stuhlherr was saving for later?" Garrett asked quietly, trying not to stir up trouble.

"It's okay to celebrate a little early," his superior said, bolstering the statement with a slow sip. "The war has already been handed to us."

"I'll make sure not to be in your company when you explain that to the Stuhlherr," Garrett said, exiting the plane.

He meant what he said. The Stuhlherr was merciless and had no trouble extinguishing another life if it impaired his progress. Garrett once witnessed the Stuhlherr cut off the forefingers of ten men who had failed to finish a job on time.

He jogged over to a limousine stationed near the Starlifter and tapped on the driver's window. The tinted glass slid down a few inches, barely enough to make out the features of the man inside.

"Do you have the pickup point?" the driver asked.

"I do," Garrett said. He made sure no one was watching, then handed over a folded piece of paper.

The driver unfolded it. "This is different from the location we discussed earlier."

"Plans change," Garrett said, unfazed. "You should know that by now."

The driver said nothing. He rolled up his window and sped away.

Garrett made a mental note to replace him as soon as the opportunity arose. But first, there were more pressing situations to attend to. He retrieved a slim cell phone from his pocket and dialed a long string of digits. The call went through to voice mail. He hung up and dialed again.

"Hello?"

"Ivy. Always pick up."

"Sorry. I was busy burying a dead body in the ice."

"Sounds amusing," Garrett said, not sure if she was serious or not. He checked his watch. "How are things going?"

"We're on schedule," she said. "We'll be ready when you get here."

"I'm not looking forward to the flight."

"You should. Things will be much worse once you get here." She paused. "It'll be good to see you. It seems like a long time."

"Too long," Garrett said. He tried to remember the last time he'd seen her. Was it after the job in Berlin? Or London? They were all starting to run together in his mind—an endless string of dirty cities and dirtier errands they were forced to forget. "They don't have any fancy hotel rooms down there we can use, do they?"

"Afraid not. Just you and me and the ice."

Garrett checked his watch again. It had become a habitual action. Things were always falling off track, and his main responsibility was to see that they got back on. "I better go," he said, feeling the pressure of the impending flight.

"Okay."

"Be careful."

"I will."

"And don't trust anyone."

"Not even you?"

Garrett laughed, then hung up. He straightened his jacket and tie and headed back to the plane. "Not even me," he said, knowing that the price was high to find favor with the Black Vehm.

TWENTY-EIGHT

Ivy had been to the South African National Antarctic Expedition base only once before. It was located in Queen Maud Land at the *Vesleskarvet*, a word that meant "flat-topped mountain" in Norwegian. The name perfectly described the area, as the ice station lay at the edge of Ahlmann Ridge, a set of cliffs that rose over eight hundred feet above the Antarctic ice shelf. During daylight hours the setting was stark and stunning, like something out of a children's fantasy book. But in the darkness Ivy could only see the tiny glowing lights of the base, hanging like paper lanterns in the cold air of the hinterland.

She landed the helicopter a safe distance away from the base, but not far enough to go undetected. Not that it mattered. The members of the SANAE had nowhere to go, and certainly no means of defending themselves.

Ivy turned to the commander of the operation, who sat next to her in the chopper.

"Who were you talking to on your sat-phone earlier?" he asked her.

She wanted to tell him it was her boyfriend, but she knew it would sound juvenile. Even more juvenile was her not knowing if Garrett would agree with the label. Their relationship had been on-again, off-again since they'd first worked together.

"It was the unit in New York," she finally said, keeping things simple. "They should be lifting off before too long."

"Good," the commander said. "The sooner they get here, the sooner we can get off this godforsaken island." He left the confines of the helicopter and jogged to another one twenty yards away.

There were five helicopters in total, all filled with fully armed combat soldiers. It was probably overkill, but the Black Vehm left nothing to chance. Taking control of the SANAE base was one more important step in achieving their grand goal.

Ivy watched from the front seat as the entire regiment began to gather. They would soon be advancing in force. She had hoped to stay behind on this mission, but the commander seemed intent on keeping her within reach. Though she never was told so, she knew they kept a close eye on her.

They had a strange relationship—she and the Black Vehm. Most of the time she hated them and all they represented. But she had to admit that there were parts of her job she enjoyed. One of her primary functions was to gather the historical details of the Nazi occupation in Antarctica. She was given special access to private libraries she never would have viewed otherwise. Through the research she learned a number of unusual facts, including the details of a cold war that had sprung up between the Americans and the Germans over the control of Antarctica.

She'd heard about the "war" before. She'd read about it in the bounty of conspiracy-based magazines that cropped up after the end of the Second World War. Most of the stories were incredibly fantastic—tales wrapped around descriptions of UFOs, called "foo fighters," and the Nazis' attempts to re-create the alien technology deep inside their Antarctic lairs. Other stories told of Hitler's fascination with religious relics, and his attempts to gather the most treasured ones and hide them, again, deep beneath the ice. All of it was fiction that should have been reserved for Hollywood screenplays. But the stories also bore fragments of truth—Ivy could feel it—and eventually she found the evidence that helped her to connect the dots. It all seemed to center on one critical event, something called Operation Highjump.

The venture was conducted by the United States military. It began in the late summer of 1946 and ended in failure sometime in the late spring of 1947. Organized by Rear Admiral Richard E. Byrd—famous both for being a direct descendant of Pocahontas and for being the first man to fly over the South Pole in 1929—the operation's stated goal was for the further exploration and understanding of Antarctica for American purposes. This is what the public believed, anyway.

The first diversion from this stated purpose had to do with Byrd himself. Ivy found that almost eight years before the advent of Operation Highjump, Byrd had been invited to Hamburg to discuss the possibility of helping the Germans with their own Antarctic mission. He met with them, but it was reported that he declined their offer. This wasn't surprising, given that the encounter took place on the historical eve of World War II. Despite Byrd's public disconnection from the Germans, Ivy suspected that he gleaned evidence from them regarding their eagerness to embrace the frozen wastelands of the Antarctic. This, she believed, was precisely why he was in charge of the American operation less than a decade later.

The true nature of Operation Highjump, and what Byrd had learned, came to light through a secret stash of letters Ivy uncovered at the Library of Congress.

Friday, November 8, 1946

Mom and Pops,

I'm writing to you from the South Pole. If you can believe it, they actually have a giant red-and-white-striped pole stuck in the ice beside the base. I'm told that the actual magnetic South Pole continues to drift away at the pace of about ten meters per year, but they don't change the placement of the pole outside.

It goes without saying that it's very cold here, colder than that night we had camping in northern Wisconsin. It's useless to try and stay warm, but we manage by staying active.

I'm sorry I missed Joan's wedding. Please tell my sister that I love her and I can't wait to see her and Harry when I get back. Mom, I know you'll be disappointed to hear this, but as long as I'm apologizing, I might as well tell you that I won't be back in time for Christmas. It sounds like we'll all be down here until sometime next spring. I'm sure we'll all look like human icicles by then.

I've been told that we will be exploring some nearby caves in just a few days. It should be exciting. One of my bunkmates said he thinks we're down here to find a hidden Nazi ice station, but I wouldn't worry because he's from New York and seems to have strange ideas about almost everything!

Your son,
Jack

Friday, December 6, 1946

Dear Folks,

Much has happened since I've written last. There are many things I will only be able to explain after I am home due to the secrecy of the information, but I can tell you that my bunkmate (the one I wrote about in my last letter) was more correct than I could have imagined.

Mom, you asked if I've made any new friends, and I have, though many of the guys don't seem to have what you might call a church background. About half of them were drunk last night, and even after I retreated to my bunk I could hear them carrying on for hours. I'm not sure what's gotten into them lately, but my bunkmate says he thinks it's because most of them think they're going to die down here. I wouldn't put much stock in those words, though, despite how right he's been about other things.

Dad, is it true that you caught that fish in the picture Mom sent? I'm impressed! Better than anything I ever caught, that's for sure! To answer your question, no, I haven't been ice fishing down here. The ice is too thick where we are right now. There has been talk about stuff other than fish under the ice, but I guess I'll have to wait until I'm home to tell you more about that!

Say hi to Joan! And don't forget to feed Tiger a raw hamburger every Sunday the same way I used to!

Your son,
Jack

Friday, December 13, 1946

My Dearest Folks,

The last week has been a disaster. I don't mean to worry you, but most of the men in my unit have perished. Please pray that I make it back home. I've heard that we won't be staying as long as originally planned, so maybe I'll be with you at Christmas after all.

I wrote before that I couldn't tell you about the things that have been going on down here, but I figure if they don't want you to know, then they won't let this letter get off the base. (They read all of our mail according to my bunkmate, who unfortunately died two days ago.)

On Monday, we ventured further than we'd ever gone before. We were exploring an area where a Nazi flag had been discovered in the ice. I saw the flag myself. The most interesting feature was the pole it was attached to. It was about five feet long and made of iron. On top of the pole was a swastika. My stomach did a back flip imagining that the Nazis could be here, but later they told me that the flag was one of many the Germans had dropped in the late 1930s during their New Swabia Expedition.

We stayed overnight in some tents made to withstand the cold. The wind whistled through the camp all night long, and I didn't sleep a wink. No one did. But I think it was more than just the wind that kept us awake. We were all afraid of what might be waiting for us outside.

Tuesday morning was beautiful. The wind had calmed down, and everyone was in good spirits. We drank coffee and laughed. Looking back, I think we were just fooling ourselves. The rest of the day was a nightmare.

Close to the place where the Nazi flag had been found there was a narrow opening in the ice. It revealed a manmade passageway, a tunnel that went straight down into the earth. A team of sixteen men was assigned the task of exploring the tunnel further. I was unlucky enough to be one of them.

We went down the tunnel one at a time, using a ladder that was fixed to the side. I was one of the last ones to go. We had battery-operated lights, but they didn't seem to do anything to fight against the darkness. The team leader called for the rest of us to stop when he reached the bottom. He asked for a rope. He said that below him was an underground hanger. He said there were Nazi emblems everywhere. I never saw it with my own eyes, but some of the other men did before they died.

Because I was the last one in the tunnel, it was my job to secure the rope to the top of the ladder. I triple-knotted the rope, just to be on the safe side, and one by one the men began to slide down into the chamber below. I can still remember the sound of their voices. Whatever they saw must have really amazed them.

I can't tell you how frightening it was to witness what happened next. The tunnel made a terrible groaning sound, and I saw a few bolts fall out from the sides. I quickly realized that the tunnel was going to collapse. I yelled to the men below, and they began to scramble back up. The tunnel began to fold in on itself. Voices above me told me to get out, but I didn't want to leave anyone behind. In the end, I'm sorry to say my fear got the best of me. I climbed up the ladder as fast as I could, barely making it out before the tunnel closed shut.

I'm alive and I'm okay, and that's the best I can tell you right now. Hopefully this letter makes it to you, and hopefully I'll be home again very soon. Please tell Joan that I love her and miss her. I love you both too.

Your son,

Jack

IVY COULD ONLY GUESS THAT JACK'S PARENTS NEVER READ ANY OF THE letters. She later learned that Jack died mysteriously only ten days after writing the final letter, right before he was scheduled to return to the United States. It was one circumstance among dozens that let her know that something sinister was going on under the Antarctic ice.

TWENTY-NINE

"We're ready."

Ivy heard the voice of the commander in her radio earpiece. She fixed her goggles into place and pulled down her hood. After grabbing her rifle, she jumped out the helicopter door, running to catch up with the brigade as they marched toward the SANAE base. Thirty minutes later they found themselves underneath the base, which was built up on stilts to accommodate the accumulation of snow.

"All teams ready," the commander said.

Ivy went with half the team to the left, while the others embarked to the right. She slid her gloved finger inside the trigger box, knowing that her services in the massacre were probably not needed.

"On my mark," the commander said. And then, "Go!"

The explosives performed their duty perfectly, the side door blowing out like a cork from a champagne bottle. Ivy watched as the soldiers climbed up and advanced through the smoking breach. Gunfire could be heard from the other end of the base and was quickly answered with shots from Ivy's side. If everything went as planned, it would be a rapid, mass execution.

"Hold your fire!" the commander said, his voice distorting on the radio.

Ivy felt a twinge of panic. Something was wrong.

The gunfire stopped. Ivy slowly approached the gash at the side of the base. A small fire still burned there, but through the smoke she could see the soldiers down the hall standing motionless, frozen. She got on the radio. "What's going on in there?"

It took a minute for a reply to come. "The base is empty."

"Empty? How is that possible?"

"I was about to ask you the same thing," the commander said. "From the look of things, they vacated the area hours ago, maybe days ago. You might want to come in here and take a look."

Ivy was about to reply when she heard a noise. She didn't recognize it at first—the muffled digital beeps. But she'd spent enough time in the trenches for recognition to ultimately ignite in her brain.

She hit the radio button.

"Get out of there!" she screamed. She turned and ran. Impaired by the thickness and weight of her ECWs, she felt like she was moving at a slug's pace, as though someone had hit the slow-motion button on her remote control.

Her radio earpiece cut in and out, hitting her with a constant rhythm of the soldiers struggling to escape their demise. She knew they didn't have enough time. The digital fuse was lit the moment they entered the base. The timing mechanism of the bomb would have ensured a sufficient duration to let everyone in, but no one back out.

Before Ivy heard the blast behind her, she felt it knock her to the ground with a wave of heat. She lay for a moment, stunned, then rolled over, hearing a hiss of steam as the fire on her back was extinguished. She coughed and choked at the air, gasping for breath, wondering if her lungs had been crushed by the impact. Turning her head to one side, she saw the burning wreckage of the base. It was clear there would be no survivors.

She propped herself up with her rifle and waited for the fog in her head to clear; then she forced herself to her feet and began the long walk back to the helicopters. She asked herself the same question again and again. *What just happened?*

Obviously it was a trap. But who had set them up? And why? She wondered where the occupants of the SANAE base had gone and how much they knew. She was glad they were still alive for the moment. If they knew the truth of the Black Vehm's plans, then no matter where they were hiding, their lives would be snuffed out.

After a torturous tour over the ice, Ivy returned to the helicopter she'd arrived in. She pulled out the sat-phone and dialed the number for the captain at Neumayer.

"Ms. Segur? I presume you're calling to tell us the mission was successful?"

"Go into a full lockdown!" Ivy said, not bothering with pleasantries. "Someone set us up. The entire company has been destroyed."

"Hold on. Repeat that?"

"They're all dead," Ivy said. "The base was empty and wired to detonate. The person responsible could be with you right now."

"I'm on it. Have you contacted anyone in New York yet?"

"No. And I'm not sure I should. One of them might have done this. If that's true, then that person thinks I'm also dead."

"Maybe that's what we should tell them," the captain said.

"Good thinking," Ivy said, starting up the helicopter. She was suddenly glad the Black Vehm had forced her to take some basic flight lessons. Though she'd never flown this particular aircraft, she felt confident that she could get the winged beast back to Neumayer in one piece.

"Ms. Segur?"

"Yes?"

"Just one more thing. What do you want us to do if we find the traitor?"

"Let me deal with it," Ivy said, throttling the engine for liftoff. "That's a death I don't want to miss."

THIRTY

August opened his eyes. Why was he still alive?

The thin man looked down at him. His expression shifted from infuriated to inquisitive. "Wait a second," he said, recognition blooming in his eyes. "Aren't you the guy that Lukas was supposed to take care of?"

"Lukas. You mean that knife-obsessed freak?"

"Yeah. That's him," the man said, as if the Black Vehm used the same label.

"I think he got stuck in traffic."

The man with the gun paused, staring across the room at the book lying next to the felled statue. He smiled, putting all the pieces of the puzzle together. "Lukas was supposed to get The Gospels of Henry the Lion from you. Guess he failed. Thanks for bringing it to us anyway."

August mentally slapped himself for leaving the book in a visible location. He really didn't have a choice, but he wondered if he could have been more resourceful. He tried to weasel his way out of the mistake. "It's just a replica. You think I'd be dragging the real one around like this?"

The thin man didn't seem to buy the act. "Why don't we go take a look?" he said, gesturing with his gun for August to accompany him.

They crossed the room in silence, surrounded by the hiss of the torches. As they passed the bloody sight of the thin man's bulldog partner, smashed beneath the statue, August tried to avert his eyes from the grisly display. The thug just laughed and shook his head, like he'd been warning his accomplice about the dangers of falling statues.

They stopped before the book.

"Pick it up," the thin man said.

August kneeled and placed his hands around The Gospels of Henry the Lion, wishing that what he'd said was true, that it was only a fake, that the real book was safe in some vault thousands of miles away. He rose, inspecting the center of the front cover.

"What is it?"

"I think it's broken."

The thug looked puzzled. "How do you break a book?"

"Nearly four hundred years after The Gospels of Henry the Lion was created, this binding was installed. The book was neglected during its tenure in Prague, so in 1594 this red silk cover was placed on it, along with all this intricate Bohemian renaissance metalwork." August pointed out the two flying cherubs that adorned the sides, along with the medals, inscriptions, crucifix, and multitude of other figures that ornamented the cover.

"What does it say at the top?"

"It says PATRONORUM, which is a form of the word *patronus*, meaning *protector*."

His captor snorted. "It's not doing much to protect you, is it?" He pointed to the middle of the book with his gun. "What's that?"

"That's where the book is broken," August said, referring to the cracked glass circle in the middle. He lifted out the pieces delicately, placing them in the pocket of his shirt. "Underneath are the relics of St. John and St. Sigismund."

The thin man leaned in closer. "What kind of relics? I don't see anything."

"They're wrapped in linen. I don't think anyone has ever taken them out."

"Then do it."

"Do what?"

"Take them out. I want to see the relics."

"I don't think that's a good idea," August said.

"I don't care what you think. Just do it."

August carefully removed one of the tightly bound bundles from the shallow hole. He began to unravel the package on top of the book, keeping his other arm under it for support. "It's probably just a tooth or a finger."

His captor's enthusiasm surged. "I heard someone say they were magical."

"Surely a smart guy like you—"

"Just show me!"

August obeyed, carefully peeling back the ancient, yellowed cloth. Inside was a thick collection of gray dust—ashes.

"That's it?" the thug said, not bothering to conceal his disappointment.

"No . . . there's something there . . ." August said, scrutinizing the pile more closely. "I think I see a bone fragment."

"Where?" He took another step forward.

"Right . . . *there*." And with that, August emptied his lungs, using the force of his breath to blow the ashes directly into his assailant's unsuspecting eyes.

The thin man yelped in pain and frantically rubbed away the stinging grit as August dove at him, striking him with The Gospels of Henry the Lion and knocking him backward into the edge of the fractured statue. The man growled in outrage as the gun flew out of his grip.

August lunged at his throat, wrestling with him across the floor, dangerously close to the narrow gorge where the statue once stood. At the edge of the chasm, he peered down and was stunned to see a long series of revolving cylinders, each bearing a spiraling set of articulated blades. It was instantly obvious that anything—or anyone—sent through the terrible machine would be chopped into a million pieces. The phrase *human confetti* came to mind as he envisioned himself falling through the carnivorous contraption.

August cried out as his rival's fingers dug into his neck. The man wrangled his way on top of August, pinning him down and pressing on his chest with his knees. August struggled for air. The thin man pushed him closer to the opening in the floor. As August's head floated out over the abyss, he heard the faintest whistling of wind cutting through the gnarled knives below.

"Stop!" someone roared from the other side of the room.

The Vehm assailant ignored the plea, his hands still clenched around August's neck, choking the life from him.

"I said *stop!*"

August knew the appeal was in vain. His body began to slip down, an inch at a time, toward a sickening fate. Suddenly, a deafening blast creased the air. The thin man's grip went slack, and his body toppled into the hole. August pulled himself up, trying desperately not to hear the spinning of the blades behind him. *He'll be a lot thinner now*, August thought, wishing the dark joke hadn't entered his mind.

He looked across the room to see who had delivered him.

It was Alex.

He was stationed in a wheelchair by the door, his expression shifting from grim determination to utter horror as he saw his future bride lying motionless on the ground. The gun dropped from his hand, and he climbed down to April's side.

"Is she okay?" August asked, racing across the room.

"I don't know," Alex said, laying her head in his lap. He pushed back her hair and kissed her forehead, saying something about never letting her out of his sight again. Her eyes fluttered open, and she wrapped her arms around his neck.

August stopped in his tracks. It was the first time he had seen the two of them *together*. "I'd love to leave the two of you alone," he said, "but we've got some serious problems to figure out."

"You're right," Alex said, giving April a hand as she stood. "We do."

April returned the favor by helping Alex back into his chair. "What is this place?" she asked, giving the strange room a good look for the first time.

"Why don't you ask your fiancé?" August said. "It seems like he may have most of the answers."

"I know what you're suggesting, but you're wrong."

"Am I?" August said. He pulled out the note from Dr. Rothschild.

"What's that?" April asked, stepping forward.

"You don't want this."

"Don't want what?"

"The truth."

April snatched the note away from him and brought it to Alex.

"What is this?" Alex asked, unfolding the paper.

August stood silent.

April looked worriedly at him. "What are you doing?"

"I'm giving you a chance to reconsider."

"Reconsider? August, I don't even know what that means."

"Enough!" Alex said. He glared at August. "If you have an accusation, make it. Otherwise, leave."

"I can't. None of us can until we figure this out." August motioned to the note. "Read it."

Alex smoothed out the page. "Slaughter the librarian's horrid myth?"

"It's an anagram," August said. "Given to me by Dr. Rothschild just before the Black Vehm shot and killed him."

April gasped. "That's awful. He was such a goodhearted man."

Alex read the page again. "What does this have to do with me?"

August explained. "Dr. Rothschild wrote the words, knowing I was trying to find the Stuhlherr, so I worked backwards from there. It took me awhile, but I finally figured it out."

"What is the answer?" April asked.

"Stuhlherr is hid at the Morgan Library," August said, aiming the words straight at Alex.

"It certainly sounds convincing," Alex said, "as we sit here in what appears to be a Vehmic court. But there are other possibilities."

"Like?"

Alex studied the words on the page. After a few moments, he looked up, amused. "The Stuhlherr mirth is a dragony lair, for example."

"Come on, that doesn't mean anything!"

"Exactly my point!" Alex said, raising a finger. "What kind of state was Dr. Rothschild in when he wrote this? Not a very good one, from the way you describe the scene. There are thousands of explanations for what he wrote. And this whole anagram idea . . . why, it's just like you to think that Dr. Rothschild wrote the note in some sort of riddle. 'Slaughter the librarian's horrid myth.' Maybe that's what he meant to say! Maybe he thought it would mean something to you. But you couldn't figure it out, so instead you concoct a way to make it point at me." He began clapping his hands. "Bravo, August! A marvelous performance!"

"Then how do you explain this?" August said, arms held out to the torch-infested cave.

"*This* has been here longer than either of us has been alive!" Alex countered. "I have no idea why it was originally constructed. But keep in mind, the model of the Vehmic court was used by most of the secret societies that came after them. This could have been the meeting place for members of the Freemasons or the Rosicrucians or the Illuminati or the hundreds of factions that sprang from them. This place proves nothing! You're on a witch hunt, August, and the only reason your search has ended here is because I'm marrying your wife."

The room fell into ear-shattering silence.

"*Ex*-wife," August corrected. He strode forward and plucked the note from Alex's hand. He read it over and over, hoping to find something new, a hidden clue, anything that would steer him in another direction from the one he chose before. "I don't know what to say. To either of you."

"Just say you're sorry," April said. "You're just like your father. So stubborn . . ."

August's face turned white.

"What is it?"

"Wait . . . don't say another word." He began mumbling.

"Is he okay?" Alex asked.

"Shhhhhh!" August said. He shook his head. "I can't believe it."

"Can't believe *what*?"

He smacked the note with the back of his hand. "April, you just gave me the clue I've been needing!"

"I did?"

"You mentioned my father. There was something he said earlier today. Something from my past. A name. Lord Imaginary Hart."

"Lord Imaginary Hart?" Alex asked.

April's jaw fell. "But that would mean . . . ?"

"I know. Lord Imaginary Hart is the Stuhlherr. That's the solution."

Alex slapped the arm of his wheelchair. "Would someone care to explain?"

"Lord Imaginary Hart comes from a book my father wrote for me. When I was a kid, he would occasionally call himself by that name. He did it today. Dr. Rothschild used to call him that too, but only when he wanted to ruffle his feathers."

"I didn't realize Dr. Rothschild and your father went back that far," Alex said.

"Since before I was born." August crushed the note and threw it at one of the torches, where it instantaneously turned to ash. "If anyone would have known some hidden secret of my father's, it would have been Dr. Rothschild. But it gets worse."

April put her hand over her mouth. "Charlie . . ." she whispered. "Is he with your father?"

"It's my fault," August said. "I thought Charlie would be safe with him. I can't believe how wrong I was."

"He wouldn't hurt Charlie . . . would he?"

"I don't think so," August said. "But I'm not going to sit here and wait to find out. Right now, he doesn't know what we know. There might still be a chance to catch him."

"How?"

"I know where he is. And he's waiting for me."

THIRTY-ONE

Cleveland glared at the man sitting across from him in the limo. "What's going on? This isn't what we agreed to."

"There's been a change of plans."

"Who are you?"

The man slowly articulated his left hand. The faint whir of tiny machines could be heard. The hand was mechanical but looked surprisingly real.

"My name is Conrad. The Stuhlherr has hired my services to help get things back on track."

"Where is my grandson?"

"He's in the car behind us. I've been asked to keep you two separated. Gives us bargaining power in case you try anything stupid."

Cleveland stared out the window. They were traveling over a bridge. "Where are you taking me?"

"For someone who's supposed to have all the answers, you sure have a lot of questions."

"I don't know what you're talking about."

"It's my understanding that you identified the connection between the book and the map."

Cleveland gave a short chuckle. "Whoever told you that was wrong."

"Apparently, *you* said it. In Germany. I've been given the audio recording, if you'd like to hear it."

"I lied. I was trying to keep them from killing me."

Though the limo was dark, Conrad wore thin, wire-rimmed sunglasses. A scar crept out from behind the left lens, hinting at a story with a violent ending. He wet his thumb with his tongue and wiped a smudge off the gun in his lap.

"Are you going to kill me?" Cleveland asked.

"You don't have the book. You don't have the map. And you're telling me you don't understand the connection between them anyway." He pulled off his sunglasses. The scar swept right through his eye, which had been replaced with a lifeless orb that currently peered out from the socket. "I'm running out of reasons to keep you alive."

"Then the Vehm has discovered the other relics as well?"

The dead-eyed man studied him. "Of course they have."

Cleveland smiled. "You have no idea what I'm talking about, do you?"

Conrad noticed another smudge on his gun and began working on it with the edge of his suit.

"The other relics are hidden in the pages of the book. I can show you."

"You're bluffing."

"If I am, you'll still have an opportunity to shoot me later. Kill me now and you'll never know."

An airplane passed over the limo. They were getting close to the airfield.

"I'll talk to the Stuhlherr about it."

"The Stuhlherr? I have business I need to discuss with him."

Conrad checked the clip in his gun, then returned his sunglasses to his face. "I'm sure you do. But you'll have to wait until you get to Antarctica to talk with him."

A chill ran down Cleveland's spine, as if the cold winds from the frozen continent had suddenly rushed inside the vehicle. "I'm going to Antarctica?"

"You're certainly not going to be left behind."

The driver presented his identification at the gate, and they pulled into the airfield.

"What about my grandson?"

"You never should have brought him."

"I didn't have a choice."

"If you're lying about the relics, then he'll share your fate."

"And what about August?"

The limo slowed to a stop.

"He'll be joining us soon."

"You caught him?"

"No," Conrad said. "He's coming to *us*. We were listening to you in the park. We know that he was supposed to meet you at that stone book. So we've left a little note for him . . ."

"He'll know it's a setup."

Conrad slid down the seat and opened the door to get out. "It doesn't matter. What choice will he have but to come?"

"He'll figure something out."

"He'd better. After all, he's taking on the Black Vehm all by himself."

Conrad stepped out the door. He left Cleveland with one more thought.

"It doesn't take a genius to know he doesn't stand a chance."

The limo door slammed shut.

Cleveland sat in silence, wishing the words didn't ring so true.

THIRTY-TWO

Nightfall had cleared most of the congestion from the streets, so the cab ride to Central Park didn't take long. During the ride Alex explained how he had been helped by two EMTs patrolling the streets. They brought him to a nearby hospital clinic, from which he escaped before the police could arrive to question him about the flaming SUV by the river. "I suppose it was wrong to steal one of the hospital's wheelchairs," he said. "But I left them a note promising to return it."

The three of them also compared notes about what they'd learned about The Gospels of Henry the Lion and the Nazi map. "There's obviously a connection between them," April said. "But right now we need to stay focused on saving Charlie."

The cab stopped, and they exited. August led them to Bethesda Terrace, where Charlie and Cleveland were supposed to be waiting.

"Are you sure Charlie wasn't confused about where to meet?" April asked.

"He knew this was the place," August said. "My father must have taken him somewhere." He put his hand on the stone book that marked the meeting place, recalling the make-believe tales that Charlie would pretend to read from its pages. Suddenly, he spied a note sticking out from behind it. He grabbed it and opened it.

"What does it say?"

"There's nothing written here but an address. I recognize it, though. It's for a small airfield just outside of town. I've been there before. It's where all the big shots in town keep their private planes."

"What should we do?"

"Do we have any choice but to go to the airfield? We still have the book and the map. Maybe they'll be willing to make a bargain."

"The Black Vehm doesn't seem to be much for deal making," Alex said. "I think we all can attest to that."

"Then what do you suggest? It's a gamble, but the alternative might be losing Charlie."

"He's your son too," Alex said, taking April's hand. "What do you want to do?"

She looked back and forth between the two men. "I think we have to go to the airfield," she said. "But I agree that the Black Vehm won't bargain with us."

"Not all of us," August said. "Just me."

"They'll kill you."

"Maybe. But if it's my life in exchange for Charlie's, then it's worth it. Now let's get out of here while we still have a bad option left."

THIRTY-THREE

Garrett sat huddled over his laptop in the backseat of the SUV, going over last-minute details. He was abruptly disturbed by a thick set of knuckles knocking on the window beside him. He rolled down the window, letting his face tell the story: *Leave me alone.*

"Sorry to bother you," the guard said. "I know you're busy."

"You have no idea," Garrett said, returning his attention to the screen. His fingers danced nimbly around the keyboard.

"There's someone here to see you."

"To see *me?*"

"He asked for whoever was in charge. I thought it would be best to bring him to you."

Garrett wondered for a moment who it might be. "Tell him I'm busy."

"His name is August Adams, and he said it's urgent."

"August Adams? Lukas was supposed to take care of him." What was he going to tell the Stuhlherr if he learned August was still alive? "Bring him here."

"Yes sir."

Garrett closed the lid on his laptop and awaited the arrival of the targeted man. He didn't have to wait long. The door on the other side of the SUV opened, and August climbed in.

"Has he been searched?" Garrett asked the guard holding the door.

"Yeah. He's clean."

"Totally clean," August said. "But thanks for the pat-down. Beats a massage any day."

The guard shut the door.

"Guess we're not going to exchange phone numbers," August said.

"Where's my brother?" Garrett asked. As he spoke he retrieved a gun from his jacket and placed it on the laptop, making clear the implications of not responding.

"Your brother? How would I know?"

"My name is Garrett Daraul. My brother is Lukas Daraul. He was supposed to kill you. But I gather from your presence here that he didn't complete that task."

"I get the feeling he's an underachiever. Am I right?"

Garrett said nothing. He tapped an eager finger on the gun.

August cleared his throat. "The last time I saw him was in the Lincoln Tunnel. He mentioned something about a career change. Roadwork, I think."

Garrett almost killed August on the spot. "If my brother is dead, this discussion is already over."

"Then he's alive."

"For your sake, as well as his, I hope you're right. In the meantime, why are you here?"

"I want to make a deal."

Garrett laughed. "You're obviously not familiar with the Black Vehm."

"I have the book."

Garrett's face became solemn. "I'm listening."

"I also have the map."

Garrett found it hard to conceal his displeasure at the news. He'd assumed both items were in the Black Vehm's possession. There would be no leaving New York without them, he was certain of that. "How do I know you have them?"

"I'm still alive. That should be all the proof you need."

"I'm not convinced," Garrett said. "But assuming you're telling the truth, what do you want in exchange?"

"My son."

Garrett nodded. "Agreed. Bring me the book and the map, and I'll give you your son."

"That's too easy."

"Is it?" Garrett asked. "We're both businessmen, Mr. Adams. We both know that if there's an easy deal to strike, it's worth doing. What use is your son to us? None, I can assure you. The book and the map are well worth the trade."

August stuck out his hand. "Then it's a deal?"

"I don't see why not," Garrett said, grinning. Before he could shake August's hand, there was a knock on the glass beside him. He rolled down the window. "This better be good."

"We just caught April Adams and Alex Pierson hiding in a hangar nearby," the guard said.

"What?"

"It gets better. They had the book and the map with them."

"Which means . . ."

August reached for the gun.

Garrett grabbed it first. He aimed the muzzle at August's forehead. "Don't move."

The door opened behind August, and two muscular arms dragged him from the vehicle.

"Give me back my son!" he yelled.

The guard pinned him to the ground. Two others slipped plastic ties around his ankles and wrists.

"What do you want us to do with him?"

Garrett opened his laptop. He'd dealt with enough foolishness. It was time to get back to work. "Kill him."

THIRTY-FOUR

Lukas blinked his eyes.

"He's awake."

Lukas fluttered his eyelids again. Where was he? He stared into a bright white light. He might have thought he'd died, but his head was killing him.

"Try not to move."

Lukas attempted to rotate his neck, but found himself fixed in place. He felt a nylon strap pressing against his forehead, then noticed the bindings restraining his arms and legs. "Where am I?" he mumbled.

"An ambulance. You were in a bad accident. We're taking you to the emergency room."

Emergency room? He didn't have time for that. He needed to report to Garrett and devise a new plan to catch August. He was still unsure how the book hunter had escaped him. Oh yeah. Maybe it was because he'd hit him in the face with a two-by-four.

"Sir, please don't move. Your neck may have been severely injured."

Lukas wiggled his fingers and toes. Would that be possible if his neck was broken? He didn't think so. He didn't need the emergency room, just a few Advil. Or some Percocet. Yeah. A bottle of whiskey and some Percocet would rock.

The ambulance hit a bump.

Lukas coughed and felt something wet on his lips.

"Get me a rag," said the paramedic. He wiped the blood away.

"Just let me out of here."

"Sir—"

"Let me out!"

Lukas felt a sharp pain in his neck. A needle. The white light faded away.

Silence.

Then, a quiet noise.

The rushing of air.

Voices.

Lukas pried his eyes open. He was in a surgery room. There were people—doctors, nurses, all wearing white—standing around him. None of them noticed that he was awake. They were busy getting ready. But for what? To sew him back up?

Next to him was a silver tray, laden with instruments, most of them variations on a particular theme. Scalpels. The sight made him wonder if his own precious blades were still in his possession.

The straps that held him earlier were absent. With a great deal of agony, he leaned his head forward. Good. His coat was still on. Better yet, he spied his knives bulging from underneath the thick black fabric.

One of the nurses turned to him, and he snapped his eyes shut.

"Dr. Richards, we're ready to begin," said the nurse.

"Then let's get started," the doctor said. "Does anyone know this guy's name?"

"There's nothing listed on the chart."

"Didn't anyone ID him?"

"The paramedics are slammed right now. He might have a wallet . . . I can check."

Lukas heard the nurse take a step closer. Panic gripped him.

"Don't worry about it," Dr. Richards said. "The front desk can figure it out after we stitch him back together."

Lukas relaxed for a second, then felt another surge of adrenaline as a mask covered his face.

"They gave him a pretty strong sedative on the ride here. But we don't need him waking up in the middle of surgery."

Everyone in the room laughed.

Lukas balled his hands, tightened his fists. He kept himself from breathing, from falling victim to the sandman.

"Nurse, could you cut away his coat?"

"We'll need to maneuver him carefully. Could I get some help?"

Four pairs of hands slipped under Lukas's torso.

"On the count of three, okay? One . . . two . . ."

Lukas sat bolt upright and tore the mask away.

The nurse screamed.

The doctor yelled for help.

Lukas yanked free the IV, too hard, and a small geyser of blood sprayed from his arm. He grabbed a gauze sponge from the tray next to him and squeezed it in his arm. The bleeding stopped. "I just want to get out of here," he said, his head spinning.

"Security!"

"Would you stop yelling?" Lukas asked. He slipped off the operating table and seized one of the scalpels. It felt puny. He threw it to the floor, replacing it with the Microtech Nemesis from his coat.

Dr. Richards gasped. "Is that a switchblade?"

"Technically, no," Lukas said, snapping out the knife. "It's front loading. Switchblades are side loading. Here, let me show you the difference."

Dr. Richards held up his hands, backing into the wall. Lukas was on him instantly, pressing the knife against the soft spot under his chin.

"Please, please . . ."

"Shut up."

The nurses scrambled for the exit.

Lukas walked Dr. Richards to the door. "I've always dreamed of being a surgeon," he said, allowing the blade to draw a drop of blood. "Maybe today would be a good day to start."

"I'll do anything. Just don't kill me."

Lukas kicked the door open, finding two security guards waiting on the other side. They pulled their guns.

"Let him go," said the guard on the right.

"He's guilty of malpractice! I'm taking him to court."

The guards looked at each other, puzzled.

"Is that a joke?" one of them asked.

"Yeah, but I'm not much of a comedian." He shoved Dr. Richards toward them, slicing the side of his neck as he fell. The security guards both reached out to catch his fall, giving Lukas a chance to escape. He darted for the door.

"Don't let him get away!" said one of the guards, holding his hands over the gash on the doctor's neck. His partner ran after Lukas.

The outside was only a few yards away. An old man in a wheelchair rolled in front of Lukas, who stumbled over him, then gave a kick that launched the unwitting patient at the security guard. The guard dropped his weapon to stop the man.

"Stop!"

Lukas sprinted out the door. An ambulance screeched to a halt, almost running him down.

The driver jumped out, furious. "I could have killed you, man!"

Lukas flashed his knife, and the driver backed away slowly.

"Whoa, man, seriously . . . I just wanted to make sure you were okay."

Lukas hopped into the driver's seat and threw the ambulance into drive. He punched the ignition, listening to the tires squeal as he peeled away from the hospital. In the rearview mirror, he saw the security guard running after him. He pressed the pedal all the way to the floor and flew through the parking lot. After a few near misses he crashed through the front gate and sped out onto the road.

Soon he'd trade the ambulance for something less conspicuous. But not before depleting the storage bins of any painkillers. And definitely not before having a little fun.

He searched the front panel of the vehicle for the emergency lights and switched them on. A smile curled his crooked mouth as the siren blared over his head—a warning to all that death was on its way.

THIRTY-FIVE

Charlie peeled back his eyelids, but the world remained dark. He tried to sit up, but his head hit the roof of his cage, or whatever it was—a wooden crate or an upright freezer or the trunk of a car.

He placed his ear against the floor but failed to hear the rumbling of an engine or the kneading of tire rubber against pavement. This ruled out the trunk idea. And it wasn't cold enough to be an upright freezer— a notion that popped into his mind because of a horror movie he'd seen at a friend's house. This left the wooden crate, which still didn't tell him where he actually *was*.

He heard voices behind him. The quarters were so tight it took him a few minutes just to turn around. Now facing the opposite way, he saw a hole, a tiny one, in the wall of the box. A pencil-thin beam of light streamed in, collecting like a white diamond on his shirt. He pressed his eye to the hole and looked out. The voices belonged to two men in black suits. Charlie presumed they were Vehm mercenaries, given they looked exactly like the men chasing him earlier. He put his ear to the opening, hoping to hear what they were saying. Unfortunately, the only parts of their conversation that entered his eardrum were an odd assortment of *s*'s and *t*'s, broken with a stuttered series of muted vowels.

He again turned his eye to the hole, straining for an angle to determine the area outside his box. He saw a wall to the left, long and curved, like the wall of . . . an airplane? *No*, thought Charlie. *That can't be right. Can it?*

He fought through the swirling mist in his brain, trying to recall the events since leaving Bethesda Terrace. He remembered following his grandfather to the edge of Central Park and standing with him on the sidewalk, hands held out, trying to hail a cab. He remembered being surprised when a limousine pulled up, and even more surprised when the door opened and a voice asked them to come inside. And then he remembered . . . actually, that was all he remembered. At that point, a hand covered his face with a thick rag—doused with some sweet-smelling, sleep-causing agent—and he was out cold.

I bet it was chloroform, thought Charlie. He'd heard about that sort of thing from the friend who let him watch the horror movie.

He slumped back, not sure what to do next. He pushed at the boards with his legs, but it was no use. He wasn't the strongest kid. This was probably taken into account when he was shut in the box. There was no getting out. He wondered if there were other boxes near him, and if one of them held Grandpa Adams. Or his dad. And maybe his mom too. Things were getting bleaker by the minute.

He heard the voices again, this time sounding more agitated. Charlie hurriedly put his eye to the hole and saw that the two mercenaries had someone new with them—a captive, bound at both his arms and his legs.

His head was suddenly yanked back into the light, and Charlie saw who it was. His father.

At that point Charlie's last sliver of hope vanished. It was bad enough thinking his dad might be stuffed inside a box, but this was much worse. He'd heard plenty of stories about his father getting out of sticky situations, but this particular circumstance was more than just sticky. It was unquestionably doomed.

Defeated, Charlie curled up in a ball. He felt something poke him in the leg. He reached down and discovered the source of the pain—his father's cell phone, which he'd placed in his pocket earlier. He flipped it open. It had a charge, which was good. It had no signal, which was bad.

Charlie's fingers jogged around the keypad, thinking of a new plan for the phone. He sprinted through the menus, finally finding the screen he wanted. VOICE MEMO, the small glowing device read. A month earlier, while looking for video games on the phone, he had discovered the digital reserve and spent more than an hour listening to it. He was amazed at how much his dad recorded. Apparently he never deleted anything. There were all kinds of memos. Grocery lists. Ideas for books and screenplays. Song titles that needed matching with a band name. There were private things too. Things he knew he never should have heard. Things about being lonely. About missing his family. About how he'd messed everything up. Charlie wondered why his father would record such personal messages, but he was never brave enough to ask.

He pressed PLAY on a particularly long message—the most recent one—recorded the night before.

"Reasons I hate Alex Pierson . . ." he heard his father's voice say through the phone's speaker.

For a second Charlie thought about switching to another message, but he knew there wasn't time to waste. He rapidly tapped the UP button on the phone, raising the level of the output until the speaker was distorting. It masked the words only minimally, and Charlie cringed at some of the terrible things his dad said about his mom's new fiancé.

He directed the verbal assault out the box's tiny porthole. He only had to wait a few moments before he heard footsteps clomping toward him. There was a bang against the side of the box, a steel toe checking for signs of life, Charlie imagined.

"You sure the kid's in here? Cause I'm hearing some weird computer voice. Did he have a laptop with him or something?"

Charlie heard a second set of feet march toward the box.

"A laptop? Are you crazy?"

"Listen! You hear that?"

"Yeah. I think I do."

The side of the box received another swift kick. "You in there, kid?"

Charlie kept quiet, still holding the phone's speaker up to the hole.

"It's coming from the front," the mercenary said.

Charlie pulled back the phone, just enough to see out. An eye came into view.

"I think I see something glowing in there," the mercenary said. "Kind of looks like—"

With as much force as he could muster, Charlie shot a finger directly into the eye. The mercenary screamed violently. Charlie pressed himself back as far as he could in the box. He put his hands over his head, already regretting his action.

THIRTY-SIX

"I'm gonna kill you!"

The mercenary's words came only seconds before a crowbar crashed through the top of the box. It missed crushing Charlie's leg by a fraction of an inch. He scrambled to get out of the way before the bar came smashing down again.

He waited for an explosion of pain. But there was nothing.

He gazed up and saw the crowbar-wielding mercenary being held back by his partner, who was trying unsuccessfully to calm him down. Charlie used the opportunity to break free of his confines. He ran toward the back of the airplane, where the rear cargo ramp lay open to the outside. His legs picked up speed, sensing that freedom was not far away.

A thunderous racket grew behind him. Charlie glanced over his shoulder and saw that the raging mercenary had thrown aside his partner and was now only a couple of yards away. One of his hands held the crowbar, while the other covered his bleeding eye socket. His face was twisted in a magnificently hostile display, and Charlie had no doubt that if he were caught, he would be bludgeoned to death without hesitation.

Charlie listened as his feet jangled the ramp, banging its steel slats like a hammer against a bell. Disembarking from the plane, he remembered his father and hoped that his distraction had given him a chance to make a getaway. Maybe the two of them could meet up, and maybe they could find his mom and his grandfather and maybe, just maybe, they would all make it out of this thing alive.

That's a whole lot of maybes, thought Charlie. But at the moment, maybes were all he had.

Hidden by the night, he darted toward a nearby hangar, whose colossal doors were split apart just wide enough for him to squeeze through. He entered the bright cathedral and saw that the entire space was packed with vehicles exhibiting enormous footlike treads and entwined hoses and bucketed claws—the scene looked like a museum filled with the skeletons of a thousand mechanical dinosaurs.

Behind him, he heard the mercenary push his way into the hangar. Charlie sped toward the back, where he decided to take his chances climbing a ladder up to a ledge that overlooked the space. He peeked down from his lofty vantage point at the madman chasing him.

"I know you're in here," the mercenary called out, his words echoing, eyes darting. Occasionally he swung at apparitions in the air, figments Charlie could only guess were caused by the damage inflicted to his eye.

Charlie stayed as still as a corpse, trying not to alert the mercenary to his presence. He glanced forward just in time to see a loose bolt slip out of place and roll toward the edge. Before it plunged from the elevated position, he grasped it in his hand. *That was close*, he thought, only an instant before watching a second bolt come loose and fall.

The tiny silver fastener dropped at an impossibly slow speed through the air, falling at the rate of one inch for every million years. It plummeted like a satellite that had broken free of its heavenly course, snailing its way downward through the atmosphere in a fiery trail only Charlie could see. He closed his eyes and covered his ears in anticipation of the bolt's triumphant finale—clattering around the bed of a gigantic truck.

The mercenary turned. Charlie froze, hoping that his body would be mistaken for a large toolbox if the one-eyed assailant happened to look up.

Which he did. "Gotcha!" he yelled.

Charlie leapt to his feet, but there was nowhere to go. The only way down was the same way up, a path now impeded by a livid maniac with a crowbar. He scanned the area for another route, coming up with only one viable option, if it were an option at all—a steel beam that connected the ledge to the opposite wall. The thought of walking out on its slim surface made Charlie's stomach do a back flip. But there really wasn't any other choice, and he figured falling to his death would be better than whatever the mercenary had in mind.

"Go ahead," the mercenary said, reaching the top of the ladder. "You wanna save me the job of killing you, feel free."

"I'm just a kid!" Charlie said, placing a wobbly foot on the beam. "Don't you know it's not cool to kill kids?"

"You should have thought of that before you butchered my eye!" the mercenary said, strolling along the ledge, thumping the crowbar in his hand like a baseball bat.

Charlie took another step out. He tried to keep his eyes facing forward, but he couldn't help but glance down. *Big mistake*, he thought, snapping his head up again. Carefully he put one foot in front of the other, pretending he was a gymnast, an Olympian, the world's best, on his way to claiming yet another gold medal.

Clang!

Charlie felt the beam wiggle under his feet. The mercenary was punishing it ruthlessly with his crowbar.

Clang!

The vibration wasn't severe, but it was enough to rattle Charlie's nerves. And that was enough, he knew, to send him tumbling to the floor below.

Clang!

Keep your vision fixed on a point in the distance, Charlie heard his father say in his head. He had been explaining how to drive a car, which was funny given that Charlie was only six at the time. *If you watch the road right in front of you, you'll make too many tiny corrections and swerve left and right. But if you look way out there to the place you're headed, then you'll keep a straight line.*

Clang!

Charlie found the point and focused on it. *Steady. Steady. Just walk forward. Don't look down. Don't think about the crazy man behind you who wants you dead. Just walk forward.*

The clanging stopped.

Charlie couldn't look back, but he knew that the mercenary must have given up the old routine and was trying out a new trick.

"Thought you could get away?"

The mercenary had followed him out onto the beam. And from his voice Charlie could tell the man was gaining on him. "As soon as I'm done with you, I'm going to go back and take care of Daddy. Like father, like son, huh? How do you like that?"

Charlie reached the wall. He couldn't believe he'd made it. Not that it mattered. The accomplishment of the goal seemed microscopic in contrast to the enormity of his looming death.

"You could always jump and save me the trouble."

Charlie slowly turned and placed his back against the wall. He watched helplessly as the mercenary approached him. Time was running out, like water through his hands. *His hands.* He opened his right hand and was stunned to see the bolt he had caught still lying in his palm. He had been clutching it tightly the whole time, its white image still marked on his reddened skin like a ghost. He steadied himself in place.

"What ya got there, kid?"

"Nothing much," Charlie heard himself say. He reared back his hand and threw the bolt. It soared through the air in a perfectly angled trajectory. Charlie's eyes widened as the gleaming projectile bulleted toward its intended target. Then missed the mercenary entirely.

The mercenary laughed.

Charlie's face fell, dejected, until he saw that the beam was quaking ever so subtly beneath him. He looked up again, just in time to see the mercenary wavering in space. And then, gripped in a guise of disbelief, the mercenary fell from the beam, far, far below to the unforgiving floor of the hangar. His body landed with a sickening thud, like a sack of melons dropped to the ground.

"Yes!" Charlie cried out triumphantly. His joy turned quickly to repulsion as he witnessed the growing pool of blood surrounding the mercenary's crumpled form. He felt a wave of guilt sweep over him, even though his attacker deserved to die. He closed his eyes and shook off the feeling. Crying would have to be saved for later.

The whir of a giant engine suddenly jolted him. He listened as the doors of the hangar rumbled, then watched as they separated. A man walked in, gun in hand. He walked directly to the place the mercenary had crash-landed.

"Such a shame," he said, turning his attention to Charlie. "But I'm honestly glad he didn't catch you."

Charlie shuddered, seeing who it was.

"After all," Lukas said, pulling black gloves over his hands. "If anyone is going to kill you, it should be me."

Charlie covered his face, anticipating the bullet that would end his life.

"Don't worry," Lukas said, his voice calm and reassuring. "I'm not going to do it now. I want to stuff you inside of a snowman first."

Charlie wasn't sure what the crazy words meant, but he knew he didn't want to find out.

THIRTY-SEVEN

The Starlifter's engines roared as the men scaled it shut. Soon the craft would be on its way to the bottom of the world, a place more alien than the dark side of the moon.

"We don't have meal service, so I hope you like duct tape," Lukas said, peeling a strip off the roll he held in his hand.

"It's an acquired taste," August replied, "but I've learned to appreciate it."

Lukas stretched the silver ribbon across August's face. "Good for you," he said. "I hope you have an equal appreciation for the cold, because soon you're going to feel it in a whole new way."

Mmmph mmmph mmmph, August said.

"What was that?" Lukas asked. He tore back the tape.

August howled. "Beats the heat," he repeated. A single tear ran down his cheek, now conspicuously absent of the stubble that was there a moment earlier.

Lukas stuck the tape back in place, securing it with a second, and then a third completely unnecessary piece. He rose to inspect the entire scene, and found that he couldn't help but smile at his handiwork. August, April, and Charlie all sat neatly in a row, stacked against each other like dolls. They were compelled to stay in position, held by a complex web of cords and wires, which he had checked and rechecked a dozen times. Their mouths were shut fast, and he looked forward to the task of taunting each of them during the long flight ahead. It would at least give him something to do besides argue with his older brother.

"How are things back here?"

"Speak of the devil," Lukas said, turning to meet Garrett.

"Do you mean me? Have you seen a mirror lately? You look like something from *Night of the Living Dead.*"

"Which is why I want to be the one to tear these three limb from limb," he said. He wasn't joking.

"Get in line," Garrett said. "I almost executed August myself earlier. But he and the others are needed by the Stuhlherr first."

"Just let me know when he's done with them," Lukas said. "I have many unpleasant plans prepared."

"Whatever makes you happy, little brother," Garrett said, patting him on the shoulder. "Just make sure the needs of the Black Vehm get taken care of first."

Lukas watched his brother leave. He hated the way Garrett treated him like an errand boy. Even worse, he hated that he'd failed the biggest errand he'd been assigned—reclaiming The Gospels of Henry the Lion. He sat down on the floor, glaring at the three frightened figures before him.

We got what we needed anyway, he told himself, trying to soothe his conscience. But he knew that Garrett had probably spared his life. No one failed the Black Vehm and got away with it.

His eyes danced from face to face, from Charlie to April to August and back again. He wondered why the Stuhlherr hadn't already disposed of them. "You must be pretty special," he said to the muted group.

A Vehm guard stepped through the door. "The Stuhlherr wants to speak with you," he said.

Lukas rose and followed the guard into a small chamber stationed between the rear cargo area and the front of the plane. The guard left him with the Stuhlherr, who was waiting for him.

"Sir?" Lukas said, lowering his gaze in respect.

"My dear Frohnboten," the Stuhlherr said, his voice quiet and smooth. "Do you plan on spending all your time with the prisoners?"

"No, sir," Lukas replied. "Soon it will be too cold. But I plan to visit them during the trip."

"So long as your 'visits' leave them alive," the Stuhlherr said. "Your brother fears that you may not be able to control your emotions."

"My brother is wrong."

"That would be a first."

Lukas didn't respond.

"You'll have your chance with them," the Stuhlherr said. "But you'll have to be patient."

"Patience is something I don't have," Lukas said, almost bragging.

"I thought you might say that," the Stuhlherr said, his voice filled with compassion and understanding. And then, without warning, he raised a cruel, crooked blade and slit Lukas across the throat.

THIRTY-EIGHT

Endless hours passed. August hadn't seen any sign of Lukas, which was the first good thing that had happened all day. *Probably too busy sharpening his knives,* he thought. The idea of why he might be occupying his time with such an endeavor made him quake. He pushed the gruesome mental picture out of his mind and tried to focus on his current situation.

Charlie and April lay slumped against him, one on each of his shoulders, fast asleep. Except for the heavy bindings, the tape across their faces, and the impending sense of death, it felt like old times. August tried to arch his back, to stretch his body, to fight off the numbing effects of his trammels, but it was no use. He was stuck in place indefinitely. Or maybe not quite indefinitely. At least until they reached Ushuaia.

He'd overheard one of the Vehm guards going over the details of the flight earlier. The only stop during their flight to Antarctica would be for a quick refueling in the Argentinean town of Ushuaia, called the

Southernmost City. Although it was a place he had never visited, August felt somewhat familiar with it, as well as with the Tierra del Fuego that surrounded it, because of a book called *The Uttermost Part of the Earth* by an adventurer named Lucas Bridges. August remembered the book as a fascinating account of the natives who lived there, a population that was slowly pushed into extinction. August wondered whether the extinction of his own "tribe" would come at Ushuaia, or whether it would be saved for the chilling world that lay beyond in Antarctica.

Why their journey was to end there was still a mystery to him. He knew the answer resided with the strange map April had discovered. He'd only had a glance at it, but the tiny Nazi flags that dotted its landscape were enough to dismay him. Something mysterious awaited them under the ice, and he wasn't anxious to find out what it was.

His father had hinted earlier that it had something to do with the infamous Spear of Destiny. But August couldn't figure out why the ancient relic would cause such a ruckus, especially since its very existence was still in question. There had to be more to the story.

August longed for a pen and paper to scrawl out his thoughts, but he made do with the paper and pen of his mind. In hopes that some semblance of order would strike him, he laid out the pieces of the puzzle in his head.

THE SPEAR OF DESTINY. *The relic that Hitler claimed to have found. He hid the legendary weapon in . . .*

NEW SWABIA. *A section of Antarctica claimed by the Nazis during the late 1930s. New Swabia was a reference to the Germanic territory known as Swabia, whose greatest duke was . . .*

BARBAROSSA. *Crowned Holy Roman Emperor. His cousin and bitterest rival was . . .*

HENRY THE LION. *The Duke of Saxony and Bavaria. Known for his famous gospel book, which included an illustration of . . .*

The Spear of Destiny.

It was an endless circle, a circuitous network of fact and fiction. He couldn't tell where reality trailed off and legend began. To make matters worse, even if he cracked the code he was bound to die. It was a sad state of affairs. But there was something even more troublesome to August. A greater mystery than the lost relics and ancient riddles that plagued him . . .

April.

With bound lips, he kissed the top of her head. She stirred, but didn't wake. It was for the best. There was nothing he could do now. He couldn't tell her what a fool he'd been. He couldn't ask her if she could find it in her heart to forgive him, to take him back, to try and start over. He couldn't find out if she still loved him. He'd wasted every opportunity he'd been granted, and now it was simply too late.

August closed his eyes and asked for one more chance. Then he fell asleep, joining his family in his dreams.

THIRTY-NINE

August was jolted wide awake. The airplane banked hard to the right, then took a steep nosedive. He glanced to either side to see if April and Charlie were okay. They were also shaken from their slumber and nodded their heads to acknowledge that they were all right. The plane veered to the left, and August was yanked by gravity against his restraints. It felt as if his arms were going to break behind his back. He strained with his legs to hold himself up in front of April and Charlie. Suddenly the plane leveled out, and they listened as the pitch of the engines began to drift lower. A few moments later August heard the plane's tires squeal on the ground. They had landed in Ushuaia.

The door opened, and Garrett Daraul walked in. He strolled over to August and bent down, ripping the tape from his face.

"That's the second time!" August yelled. He stretched out his jaw and batted the tears out of his eyes with his lashes. "You're just like your brother."

Garrett slapped him with the back of his hand and pointed a finger in his face. "Don't ever mention my brother again. You hear me?"

"Yeah," August said, more curious than scared. "I hear you."

"Good."

Garrett leaned him forward and began disconnecting him and his family from the wall of the plane.

"What's going on?" August asked.

"Not that I'm obligated to tell you, but we're changing planes. The local authorities have already inspected the other Starlifter, so we're moving you there while they inspect this one."

"Oh." August wondered if it was the truth, or if they were simply being led to their graves.

"Get up. All of you."

"Aren't you going to take off these bindings?"

"The bindings stay. The authorities believe you're criminals being transported. Now, get up before I find someone to force you up."

August pushed against the floor, his legs feeling like jelly underneath him. April and Charlie rose as well, dangling off him like ornaments.

"Before we go another step," Garrett said, "I want you to promise me that you're not going to try anything stupid."

August nodded.

"I want to hear you say it."

"I promise."

"One wrong move, and I kill the others," Garrett whispered to August. He walked toward the back of the plane and pressed a button on the wall, which lowered the rear cargo ramp. "Follow me."

August shuffled ahead, the bindings around his ankles only allowing him to move each foot a few inches at a time. April and Charlie fell in closely behind him, their own restraints offering hardly enough room to maneuver. August envisioned the three of them falling over each other, a bubbling nightmare that would probably not amuse even the most lighthearted members of the Black Vehm.

Garrett steadied them as they stumbled down the ramp. Although it was overcast, August squinted in the light. He gazed at their surroundings—a simple airfield, barely big enough to accommodate the gigantic Starlifters. In the distance he saw snowcapped mountains that reminded him of a stunted version of the Colorado Rockies. Though he guessed the temperature wasn't much below fifty, he shivered. It was half as hot as New York, and he welcomed the change.

"It's going to get a lot colder than this," Garrett said, noticing the effects of the climate on his guests. "Hope you brought something warm."

August stepped onto the tarmac, dragging his family behind him. Further down the tarmac he saw a refueling vehicle pulling away from the other Starlifter. Garrett pointed at it, tugging August to hustle the group forward.

After a difficult and somewhat humiliating journey, they reached the other plane. August still hadn't seen signs of anyone else and wondered especially about his father and Alex. Their fate was something he couldn't determine—as much a mystery as their trip to Antarctica.

The ramp yawned open, and Garrett shuttled them inside. August turned and watched as a group of armed men boarded the plane they left behind.

"Hurry," Garrett said, sounding worried.

Charlie slipped, and August nearly toppled onto him.

Garrett pulled the boy up by his shirt and violently shoved him up the ramp. "Get in the plane now!" he said.

"Don't talk to my son that way," August said, wishing he had a free hand to plant on Garrett's face.

"Just get inside!"

August was wondering why they were in such an incredible rush, when an intense blast of heat hit the side of his face. He fell down on the ramp, along with April and Charlie, who had no choice but to follow. Garrett ran into the plane and pushed the button to close the ramp. It lifted immediately and, after achieving an acute angle, spilled its occupants onto the floor of the plane.

"I'll be back later," Garrett said. He dashed toward the front of the Starlifter through a door and slammed it behind him.

August lay facedown, listening to the sounds of his family trying to recover their breath. The other plane—the one they had just been on—had just been transformed into a massive fireball. Who was responsible?

An alarm sounded, and the floor shook. The Starlifter's engines roared and the plane lurched ahead, sending August, April, and Charlie skidding back toward the cargo ramp. August felt a rush of air. He craned his neck around and saw that the ramp was slowly coming undone. The plane throttled its way into the air, and the ramp dropped open further. Scraps of plastic and paper twirled around August like a tornado, and he knew that in only a matter of seconds they would be dropping toward the earth without a prayer or a parachute.

The door burst open, and Garrett stepped in. He raced to the ramp and hit the button to close it. The wind quickly died down.

"Sorry about that, folks," he said dryly, helping August and the others to their feet. "Just blame it on the turbulence. That's what the pilots always do."

He situated them against the wall, then secured them in place.

"This leg of the flight won't be as long," he said. He grabbed a blanket from a storage bin and threw it over them. "I think you're going to need this."

August sighed. April and Charlie gathered in closer.

Next stop, Antarctica.

FORTY

Frost. It was everywhere. August knew he shouldn't be seeing it on the inside of the aircraft. He heard a faint whistle coming from the cargo ramp and saw that it was damaged, allowing the bitter cold to creep in.

He sent two jets of steam out from his nose, the only activity he'd engaged in since leaving Ushuaia. Looking down at the blanket draped over his lap, he wished his arms were loose so he could curl it around himself, along with April and Charlie. He heard the chatter of teeth and looked down beside him at his son. The poor boy's face bore a blue tinge. August felt a fire develop inside him, an intense flame fueled by his growing hatred for the Black Vehm.

The temperature in the cargo hold continued to drop, and August imagined a giant thermometer being drained of its blood. He wondered how much longer they had before becoming dreadfully ill. They hadn't eaten since leaving New York, and Garrett had only given them a few drips of water every so often, administering the liquid like a human IV, intending to keep them alive, but only barely so.

The Starlifter began its descent, the drone of the engines quieting as the aircraft cast itself from the heavens. August's heartbeat quickened as he realized they were approaching their final destination. As much as he wanted answers, he didn't want them at the cost of his life, or his family's. As the long journey to the ground began, he tried to remember the last time they all had been together and genuinely happy. Maybe it was the cold that helped, or seeing the icicles collecting on the ceiling, but suddenly a picture came to mind.

Christmas.

Four years ago.

Charlie was missing his two front teeth. August remembered teasing him mercilessly as they sat around the tree, waiting to open their gifts.

"Say thistle."

"Fissle," Charlie said, giggling.

"Say Theodore."

"Like the Chipmunks?"

"Just say Theodore."

"But I want to know if you mean the one in the Chipmunks or not."

"Um . . . sure . . . the one in the Chipmunks. Alvin, Simon . . . *Theodore*!"

"Feeodore!"

The two of them laughed.

"You're going to give him a complex," April said, grinning as she entered the room. She handed August a cup of hot chocolate, then gave one to Charlie.

"I think you gave him more marshmallows," August said.

"That's because he's six."

"But I *act* like I'm six."

"I wouldn't brag about that," April said, snuggling in beside him on the couch.

"Charlie. Say marshmallow."

"Marshmallow."

"Weird. It doesn't sound any different."

"Yeah, I guess not. Maybe we'll have to try somefing else."

"Wait! Did you hear that?"

"What?"

"Say *something*."

"Somefing!"

The two of them laughed, and August spilled hot chocolate on his shirt. "Sorry, " he said, getting up and going to the kitchen for a towel.

April followed him. "So . . ." she said. "Do you think we should tell him?"

August blotted the giant brown stain on his chest. "I think I'm just making it worse," he said.

April wrapped her arms around his neck and kissed him. "Should we tell him?" she asked again.

"Should we tell him what?"

April took the towel from his hands and put it in the sink. "You're right," she said. "You just made it worse."

"I know. It's like my special gift in life."

"I think we should tell him."

"Wait," August said. "I'm lost. What are we talking about?"

She took his hand and placed it on her stomach. "You know."

August *did* know. It had been the only thing on his mind since April had told him the news. He still couldn't believe he was going to be a father for a second time. "We can't tell him. Not yet. It's too early."

"I know," April said. "But it's Christmas."

August began unbuttoning his shirt. "I just . . . I don't know."

"We should wait."

"Are you changing your mind?" he asked.

"Maybe. You don't seem too enthusiastic."

August peeled the wet shirt off and threw it over the back of a chair. "I *am* enthusiastic. I just want to be careful. But if you want to tell him, that's okay with me."

April bit her lip. "Now I'm not sure."

"Then we should wait. He's going to be more excited about the new game system anyway."

"I'm getting a new game system?"

They turned to find Charlie standing in the doorway.

"How long have you been standing there?" April asked.

"Long enough to find out I have a new game system!" he said, his eyes brighter than the Christmas tree lights behind him. "Which box is it in?"

August turned his son back toward the other room. "Not so fast, mister. You're going to have to open the presents from Grandma Rose first."

"Awwwww, Dad. Sweaters and socks?"

"And maybe a tie. If you're lucky."

The rest of the day was a blur of wrapping paper and mistletoe. They decided not to tell Charlie the news about April's pregnancy, thinking they would have a chance to tell him after April saw the doctor. Unfortunately, on New Year's Eve, only days before her scheduled appointment, she lost the baby.

They never told Charlie.

It was tragic in more ways than one. August realized now that the loss marked the beginning of the end of their relationship. He began taking more out-of-town trips, spending more time with clients, and obsessing over the priceless rare books he hunted. He hated himself for it, but he couldn't seem to stop. It was a personal quicksand, and he quickly sank in it up to his neck. It wasn't long before he disappeared altogether.

"We're here."

August heard the words but couldn't see who was talking. He'd fallen asleep, and his eyelids had frozen shut.

"You don't look so good."

August felt a gloved hand wipe the crystals from his face. His eyes fluttered open, and he saw Garrett standing over him.

"Hoping for someone else?" his captor said.

"The cold got me thinking about Santa," August said. "But then I remembered, he's at the other pole."

"Plus," Garrett whispered, "he's not real."

"Neither is your Spear of Destiny," August replied, mimicking his tone. "But you still dragged us all the way down here to find it."

Garrett shook his head. "You really have no idea what you've gotten yourself into, do you?" He produced a wicked-looking knife.

"Go ahead," August said, readying himself for the blade. "I won't feel it. I'm frozen solid."

Garrett reached down and sliced the cords around August's feet. He did the same for April and Charlie, then cut away the rest of the bindings as well. "You're free," he announced. "Well, not really free. Just a little more free than you were before."

August shared a short embrace with April and Charlie, then helped them remove the duct tape from their faces. The cold diminished the effects of the tape, and it came off easily.

"I can't believe that," August said. "You guys got it so easy. Mine felt like a bikini wax on my face."

"What's a bikini wax?" Charlie asked, the pink beginning to return to his cheeks.

"Nothing you need to know about," April said, shooting a look at August.

Sorry, he mouthed.

Garrett cut open a large box in the corner. "Your ECWs are in here," he said. "That's Antarctic slang for 'clothes that'll keep you warm.'"

August hobbled over to the box, feeling like a walking ice sculpture, and dug inside. He pulled out three huge orange parkas. "Have these been here the whole time?"

"Yeah," Garrett said. "But they're so uncomfortable." He put away the knife and pulled out a gun. *No funny business*, it said.

August acknowledged the weapon and handed the appropriately sized gear to April and Charlie. Hats. Boots. Gloves. Goggles. Everything they needed. They all suited up, then stood and stared at the strange sight of one another.

"Ready?" Garrett said.

"As ready as we'll ever be," August said, speaking for them all.

Garrett pressed the button for the ramp. Slowly it lowered, and the luminous landscape of the Antarctic stretched out before them, lit by the bright lights of an ice base in the distance.

"Wow," Charlie said, the ground before him sparkling like diamonds.

"Wait until you see it in the daylight," Garrett said. "If you make it that long. Come on. Time to meet everyone."

August took the lead, sliding down the ramp to the ground. He held out his hands, expecting to catch snow, but there was none. Then he remembered one of the odd little facts he'd read a long time ago: Antarctica had almost no precipitation. So little, in fact, that it was considered the world's largest desert. *That's some bizarre desert*, thought August, as April and Charlie joined him at his side.

Garrett led them to the Neumayer base, which appeared to August like a giant white cigarette lighter propped up on stilts. It certainly didn't look like any building he'd ever seen. The structure was entirely born from function, yet its aesthetic was distinctly futuristic. August wondered if the science-fiction writers from the fifties might have had it right after all.

They entered the base, and Garrett brought them to a small, colorless room.

"You can take off your gear," he said.

They shed their thick, orange skins, keeping on their inner layer of protection. They were still frozen from the trip.

"What now?" August asked.

"You wait," Garrett said.

"Wait for what?"

Garrett walked to the door and entered a code into the touch panel next to it. He stepped out into the hallway, answering August's question before the door closed.

"There's someone I want you to meet . . ."

FORTY-ONE

"Ivy?"

She put her hand on the radio, but didn't answer. Not yet.

"Ivy? Can you hear me?"

She pressed the button, then let it go, still unsure. The commander had warned her that Garrett might not be trustworthy. One of the Starlifters had been destroyed in Ushuaia, and the perpetrator was still unknown. Ivy recognized the names of some of the people who had been killed in the blast. Their deaths weren't surprising—it was just a day-to-day reality of working in the Black Vehm. But that the most recent evidence alluded to a conspiracy within the organization—that was enough to make Ivy paranoid about everyone, including Garrett.

"Ivy? If you can hear me, I need you to meet me in the tower right away."

She picked up the radio. "I hear you. Be there in ten minutes."

She exited the Piston Bully and tromped over to the tower, a hastily constructed test site for the drilling rig. Light shone down from the top of the tower, showing off its circuslike exterior. The base of the structure was built from two rectangular huts, connected by a tall, white tent that curved as it rose from the steel substratum to a zenith three stories above.

The tower wasn't fully insulated, but it was warm enough for Ivy to shed the outermost layers of her ensemble. She debated what she would say to Garrett when he arrived. A part of her trusted him, or at least wanted to. She'd already confided so many of her secrets to him. But another part of her—the part that shielded her from ever getting too close to anyone—knew that something was wrong. Whether her distrust stemmed from the way he was flexing his authority over her or simply the flattened tone of his voice, she couldn't be certain. If it were anybody else, she would have already killed him by now.

"Ivy?"

She jumped an inch, startled.

"Sorry," Garrett said. He took off his heavy jacket and walked over to her. "Should have given you a better warning."

"I should have been more aware," she said, wondering if they were talking about more than his stealthy entrance.

"August Adams is here. Along with his ex-wife and their son."

"All of them?"

"It wasn't the original plan. But rolling with the punches is something I've become accustomed to." He paused. "Lukas is dead."

Ivy put her hand in his. "What happened?"

"No one will confirm it for me, but I know the Stuhlherr killed him. It was right before we left New York."

"Why would he do that?"

"Lukas was supposed to get The Gospels of Henry the Lion. He failed. But we still got the book." Garrett squeezed her hand. "I wouldn't say this to anyone else, but sometimes the Stuhlherr worries me. He acts without thinking."

"You don't trust him?"

Garrett looked alarmed at her wording. "I would never say that. If I didn't trust him, I wouldn't be here right now. But that doesn't mean I don't think he's a little bit—"

"Crazy?"

"Eccentric."

"That's just rich talk for crazy."

"Maybe. But there's no turning back now."

Ivy looked into his eyes. The insecurities she'd felt earlier seemed to vanish. She pulled him closer. "What about us? What happens after all this is over?"

"I don't know exactly," he said. "We do a good job here, and maybe we'll get to spend more time together. If you decide to stick around, that is."

Ivy winced. She regretted having told him that she was only working for the Black Vehm in exchange for the names of her long-lost family. "I might think about it," she said. "If I have a reason to."

"Let's take it one step at a time," Garrett said. "Making it through the next twenty-four hours alive is enough to think about right now."

"Especially with a traitor in our midst," Ivy said.

"What?"

"I heard about the Starlifter being destroyed," she said. "It sounds like someone inside the Black Vehm caused the explosion. And that's not all. The mission to the SANAE base went haywire. Everyone got killed except me."

"What? You weren't supposed to be on the mission."

Ivy took a step back. "What do you mean?"

"I mean that I asked specifically for you to be taken off that mission."

"Why?"

Garrett ran his fingers through his hair nervously. "Can I trust you?" he asked.

"I . . . I don't know . . ."

He grabbed her arms tightly. "There are some of us who are trying to install a new Stuhlherr. A *better* Stuhlherr. Someone who has a bigger plan than the Stuhlherr we have now."

"But that's mutiny," Ivy said, uncomfortable in Garrett's grip.

"Keep your voice down," he said.

"Why? Are there other people listening?"

"I'm not sure. But they've been watching me closely."

Ivy stood silent for a moment. But the only thing she heard was the familiar rush of the Antarctic wind.

"Are you with me?" Garrett asked.

"I don't know," Ivy said, shaking her head. "I can't lose the only chance I have to learn who my father is."

Garrett's hand crept into his side pocket. "Then what are you going to do? Are you going to turn me in?"

Ivy tried to calm him down. "I'm sure there's a way to work this out."

"No," Garrett said. "You're either in or you're out. Which is it?"

"I don't know."

He pulled out a gun.

"What are you doing?"

"I'm sorry. I really didn't want to have to do this."

"Garrett . . . please . . ."

"I've put everything on the line," he said. "I've lost my brother over this. Are you telling me it's too much to lose a father you've never even met?"

"That's not fair," she said. "You know how much I've sacrificed to get this far."

"We've all sacrificed," he said. He pulled the trigger. The gun jammed.

Ivy turned and ran to the only escape route in sight—the ladder leading up the side of the drilling rig. She rapidly began to climb, with Garrett close behind.

"Wait!"

Ivy looked down. Garrett had stopped halfway up the ladder.

"What if I told you I know who your father is?"

Ivy almost lost her grip. "You're lying."

"I'm not," Garrett said. "I overhead a conversation the Stuhlherr was having with one of the men in New York."

"I don't believe you."

Garrett slowly crept up the ladder. "I should have told you earlier, but I wasn't sure where things stood between us."

"Don't come any closer," Ivy said, her eyes beginning to swell with tears.

Garrett continued to climb. "Just give me a chance. This can all work out for both of us."

"I said, don't come any closer!"

Garrett was only a few rungs below her. "Please, Ivy. Do you really think I'd lie to you?"

"A minute ago you tried to shoot me!"

"You made me do that," he said calmly. "I thought you were going to turn me in."

Ivy wrapped her arm tightly around the top rung. She could feel the tower swaying ever so slightly, bending back and forth like a tall, slender tree. "I am going to turn you in," she said. "Just as soon as I get down from here."

Garrett's face contorted, twisting into a glowering snarl. "Let me help you with that," he said, surging forward with arm extended.

Ivy screamed, hanging on for dear life as Garrett grappled at her body, yanking at her with brutal force. Helpless to stop him, she felt her arm—her anchor—slip precariously away from the ladder. In one last attempt to stop him, she wildly swung her leg, grazing the underside of his chin with her boot.

Garrett seemed to hang in the air, dazed, his innocence returning for a fleeting moment. Then Ivy watched in mute shock as his body writhed and fell, landing directly on a pipe that pierced him through the middle.

Trembling, she stumbled down the ladder. Tears streamed down her cheeks as she put her hands on Garrett's lifeless form. He was her best friend during her tenure with the Black Vehm, and now, suddenly, he was gone.

She mopped the saltwater from her face and took a deep breath. It was only a matter of time before someone would come to see where they were. The body needed to be hidden, and fast. Luckily, there was already a suitable grave nearby.

Ivy climbed up into the seat of the drilling rig and fired up the engine. She knew the disturbance would be heard, but with everything that was going on, it wouldn't stir enough interest before her foul deed was done. She pulled back on the drill's lever and withdrew the gyrating blade from the ice. A deep hole remained where the drill had been, just wide enough to fit a man, namely her ex-lover, her traitor with a heart of gold—Garrett Daraul.

Ivy departed from the lurid spectacle undetected. She stole over to the main base and entered to find that the Black Vehm had taken over the space. The commander shut the lid of his laptop and rose to meet her.

"Garrett's looking for you," he said.

"Really? I didn't see him. He told me I was supposed to meet him here."

The commander shot her a probing gaze and pulled her to the side. "Is everything all right?" he asked.

"Everything's fine," Ivy said. She considered telling him what had happened with Garrett, but she was unsure where his allegiance fell. "I told you. I didn't see him."

The commander warily backed off, changing subjects. "You're supposed to see what information you can get out of the detainees," he said. "You remember what we discussed earlier?"

"Yes."

"Good. They're in room three."

"Okay," Ivy said, nervously tucking her hair back behind her ear. She couldn't tell if it was guilt or fear she felt. Probably both. If Garrett's body were discovered, she would be forced to confess. And no matter which party was in power, his death would be swiftly complemented with her own.

The commander went back to his task, leaving Ivy to take care of hers. She found the room where the detainees were being held, punched in the code for the door, and entered, not sure what to expect. She was surprised to find that the three people inside—August, April, and Charlie—were seated around a small round table, laughing at something one of them had just said.

"I hate to break up the party," Ivy said, "but I believe we've got some work in front of us."

The laughter died down.

"We were hoping you were the pizza delivery boy," August said. "Boy, were we wrong."

Ivy closed the door. "We need your help," she said, skipping the small talk. "As you're well aware, we've got the map and the book. But we're still not sure how they work together. Cleveland led the Vehm to believe he knew the answer. But one of our operatives has discovered otherwise."

"So you're clueless," August said.

"The Vehm is never clueless," Ivy corrected. "Just misinformed."

"Why are you so certain that they *should* work together?" April asked.

"To answer that would be to explain my entire history with the Black Vehm," Ivy said. "We don't have time for that now, so you're just going to have to trust me."

"I don't know if that's good enough," August said.

"If you don't trust me, then you'll just have to trust Hitler. His journal is what confirmed the link between the map and the book."

August, April, and Charlie were all speechless.

There was a knock at the door. Ivy opened it.

"They're ready for you in the conference room," a Vehm guard said.

Ivy turned to her captives. "You heard him," she said. "Let's go. No pressure, but if you fail in there, the consequences won't be pretty."

"Thanks for the vote of confidence," August said.

"I didn't want to say this," she said to him. "But to be quite honest, if there's anyone in the world who can crack this code, it's you."

FORTY-TWO

Two armed guards met them outside the door, and the group moved down the hallway to the large conference room. The chairs were stacked in the corner, and a long black table was pushed against the wall. On top of the table were the two objects everyone had been waiting to see—the Nazi map and The Gospels of Henry the Lion.

August still wondered where his father and Alex were. Perhaps they'd been on the other plane in Ushuaia and had died in the firestorm. Or maybe they were involved in the Black Vehm's plot and were waiting for the right moment to unveil their deception. It was just another layer to the mystery, but August was determined to figure it out.

The guards posted themselves at the door, and August walked with April and Charlie over to the table. "Where should we start?" he asked them.

"I think the map," Charlie said.

"Why is that?" August asked his son. Charlie had a keen eye for detail and a knack for spotting hidden clues.

"I just think maps are cool."

August reconsidered Charlie's position on the team. "Any other reasons?"

"Yeah," he said. "It's a *map*. Maps give directions. So if we can figure out what directions the map is giving us—"

"—then we'll know where to go. Good work, Son."

Charlie smiled.

August spread out the map in front of them. "Where did you say this came from?" he asked April.

"The Complete Traveler. Oh, did I forget to tell you? It turns out that Bernie was working for the Black Vehm."

"The little weasel . . ." August said, remembering the many times the two of them had haggled over the price of a rare book.

April's attention returned to the map. "Look at this," she said. "There are two different sets of flags here. Ones with poles, and ones without."

"What did you say?" Ivy asked, approaching the table.

"With and without poles."

"That's interesting," Ivy said. "Because I've read many accounts of the flags the Nazis dropped over Antarctica. They all had poles."

"That's a clue!" Charlie said.

"Thank you, tiny Sherlock," August said. "You're right. That would most definitely be a clue. But what does it mean?"

"That the flags without poles might not be flags at all," April said. "Maybe they mark something else."

August began counting the differing icons on the map. "There are three flags with poles—which we're setting aside for right now—and thirteen flags without."

"That's half the alphabet," Charlie said.

"Yes . . . but that probably doesn't mean anything."

"Ummmm . . . lemme think . . . thirteen is an unlucky number."

"Again, interesting, but not helpful."

"It's . . . it's . . ."

August patted him on the shoulder. "You just keep thinking about that for a second. I'm going to work on some other ideas. Okay?"

Charlie was lost in thought, his mind a blank slate waiting to be filled.

"Hey, buddy, you hear me?" August said, waving a hand in front of Charlie's face.

"Just let him be," April said. "I've seen him do this before. But it's usually while he's playing video games."

"Video games? I thought you didn't let him play video games."

"Only thirty minutes a day. And he has to earn it."

"Good for you," August said. "I think that's great."

"Letting him destroy his mind?"

"Think of it as training for better hand-eye coordination."

"You've got a spin for everything, don't you?"

"Almost everything," August said, smirking. "Okay, focus. Focus! What are some other possibilities here? Thirteen flags to represent . . . what?"

Charlie suddenly snapped out of his haze. "Mom said it!"

"Mom said what?"

"That the flags might mark something else. So what if they do? What if they mark something *off* the map?"

"Off the map?"

Charlie placed the map next to The Gospels of Henry the Lion. "The flags might mark something in the book!"

August shook his head in amazement. "Why didn't I notice this before? The book and the map are almost exactly the same size."

"I thought the map looked small," April said.

Charlie grinned. "I thought that book looked big!"

August held his hands out toward Ivy. "Paper? Pencil?"

"Get them yourself," she said, directing August to a cabinet in the corner. "Paper and pencil are kind of old-school, don't you think?"

"But they work in a blackout," he said.

"True," she said, unable to argue his point.

August sketched out some columns on the paper. "April, starting at the west, tell me the coordinates for each of the flags."

"Why west to east?"

"Just like reading," he said. "Left to right. It may not work, but we've got to start somewhere."

April traced the positions of the flags with her fingers, aligning each of them with the latitude and longitude markers that framed the map. "Did you get all those?"

He read them back to her.

"Sounds good. Now what?"

"Now, we transfer the coordinates to use on the book." He ran to the cabinet and fished out a pair of scissors.

"You're not going to cut The Gospels of Henry the Lion, are you?" Ivy asked.

"No!" August said. "But I am going to cut the map."

"You shouldn't do that," Charlie said.

"I know it's a priceless map," August said. "But it's also a priceless Nazi map, so don't feel too bad about it."

Ivy looked over at the guards, who seemed uncomfortable with the situation. "I really hope you know what you're doing, because this could get me in a lot of trouble."

"I know," August said, stabbing into the map. He cut out a rectangle, separating the longitude and latitude markers around the outside from the rendering of Antarctica within.

April stared at his handiwork. "Given that this idea works—and there's no way to know if it will or not—which pages do we use the coordinates on? And what should they point to?"

"I have a test," August said. He turned the pages of the book until he reached the miniature known as *The Scourging of Christ*. "This is the only place that the Spear of Destiny is shown. If the map coordinates turn up some information here, then hopefully it will work in other places in the book too."

He laid the latitude-longitude frame on the picture and handed the writing tools to April. "I'll read the coordinates to you," he said, "and you write down what they correspond to on the page."

"Got it."

He carefully read each set of numbers, starting with the information gained from the western flag and moving steadily east.

April frowned. "I've got good news and bad news."

"I don't understand."

"Give me the rest of the coordinates first. Then I'll show you."

August finished his reporting, the last few numbers rattling off his tongue so fast April could barely keep up. "What have you got?" he asked.

She showed him the list of thirteen letters:

uysykqmqprjza

"I was excited at first," she said, "because every coordinate you gave me lined up perfectly with a letter on the page. But the more letters I wrote down, the more discouraged I got. They don't look like anything, do they?"

August studied the letters. "I see what you mean. Looks pretty random."

"It's a mess," Charlie said, taking a peek.

August drummed his fingers on the table.

"Uh-oh," April said. "He's thinking."

"There's just something about it," August said, beginning to pace the room in circles. "Charlie was right. It's a mess. A perfect mess." He snapped his fingers. "Maybe *too* perfect a mess."

"It's encrypted!" April said.

August grabbed the page of random letters and showed them to Ivy. "Was there anything like this in Hitler's journal?"

"No. Every word was in German, not gibberish."

"What about any decoding information . . . a deciphering wheel, something like that?"

"Deciphering wheel?"

"Work with me here! Think! Were there any lists of codes?"

"Actually . . . now that you mention it . . . hold on a second." Ivy left the room. She returned a few minutes later with a laptop in her hands.

"I thought you were coming back with a gun," August said.

"If you could be that lucky . . ." Ivy said, switching on her computer and turning it to face the others. "This is a list of settings we found in the front of Hitler's journal."

"Settings?" August asked. "For what?"

"An Enigma machine."

August nodded, as if some of the puzzle pieces had suddenly slipped into place.

"What's an Enigma machine?" Charlie asked.

"A cipher device used by the Nazis," August explained. "It used a series of rotors to encrypt and decrypt messages. Both the sender and the receiver of the message needed to know the precise settings for the Enigma machine, or the result was gibberish. It was highly effective, until the code breakers at Bletchley Park figured the machine out."

"I want to be a code breaker some day."

"You're helping to be a code breaker right now," August reminded him.

"Oh, yeah. Cool."

Ivy continued. "The Enigma machine used to be a secretive device. But these days there are dozens of emulators you can run on a computer to duplicate its effects."

"Do you have one?"

"I do now. Just downloaded it. It's www.TheNaziCode.com."

"You have Internet?" Charlie asked, impressed.

"Do you have any idea how many hours I've wasted watching YouTube?" Ivy fired up the Enigma program on her computer, making sure the settings were correct. "All right . . . I'm ready to punch in the code."

August read the letters off the page. "U-Y-S-Y-K-Q-M-Q-P-R-J-Z-A."

Ivy typed. "Huh," she said. "That's not good."

"Didn't work?"

"Not even close," Ivy said. "Unless *Znvpxngesxgac* is a word."

"I think that might be a Pokemon name," Charlie said. "But I could be wrong."

"Even if you're right, that's not going to help us," August said.

"Of course, if it was a Pokemon name in Japanese, you'd have to read the letters backwards."

"Backwards!" August said, hugging his son. "That's it! I was assuming the map coordinates read from west to east. But maybe they read the other way. Ivy, try typing in the letters like this: A-Z-J-R-P-Q-M-Q-K-Y-S-Y-U."

She punched the characters into the Enigma emulator. "Hey," she said excitedly. "This might be it."

They all surrounded the laptop. The screen read:

berlin germany

"I did it, Dad!" Charlie said. "I helped solve the puzzle!"

August high-fived him. "Great job, kid. But we've still got work ahead of us. We need to find out what other codes are in The Gospels of Henry the Lion."

They worked their way through each of the miniatures, coming up with four more codes.

1. *The Dedication* produced the code IHYQZRJVGKKUC.
2. *The Annunciation* produced the code HIWSBQLOIFSYS.
3. *The Raising of Lazarus* produced the code XAKGMOFKMVBYC.
4. *The Coronation* produced the code THVTPQMWZKHCC.

"Let's put the codes into Enigma and see what we get," August said, handing the information to Ivy. It didn't take long before they were marveling at the results.

The First Code: IHYQZRJVGKKUC

Solution: *CALCUTTA INDIA*

The Second Code: HIWSBQLOIFSYS

Solution: *LONDON ENGLAND*

The Third Code: XAKGMOFKMVBYC

Solution: *SHANGHAI CHINA*

The Fourth Code: THVTPQMWZKHCC

Solution: *WASHINGTON USA*

"That's all of them," April said, looking through her notes.

"Hmmmm. A list of cities." August mulled the options. "These were all extremely influential places during Hitler's time. But I don't understand their connection to Antarctica. Could the Black Vehm have it wrong? Could the Spear of Destiny be hidden in one of these cities instead?"

Ivy shook her head. "No. I've read personal accounts from people who have seen it. There's no question that it's in Antarctica. We just don't know where."

"Do you have a globe?" April asked.

"In the library. Why?"

"I have an idea."

"Hang on." Ivy departed, and returned a short time later with the familiar blue orb.

"If you don't mind . . ." April said, taking it from her. "Do you have any masking tape?"

"We've got everything," Ivy said, retrieving a roll from the same cabinet as the other supplies. "Shipments don't make it down here often, so we stock up."

April took the tape and peeled off a few long pieces, sticking them on the edge of the table. "It just hit me how the list of cities could link with Antarctica," she said. She took a strand of tape and pressed one end down on the globe where Berlin would be. She then circled the globe with the tape, keeping it even with the longitude markers. She repeated the process with the other cities, creating a web that surrounded the globe.

"What is it?" Charlie asked.

April flipped the globe over and revealed that all five pieces of tape overlapped each other in the same place—right over the icy white plains of Antarctica.

FORTY-THREE

The morning sun arrived, adorned with a solar halo, a luminous circle caused by the ice crystals hanging in the air. Sun dogs pulled at each side of the halo, like wild animals trying to rip the sky in two. It was an ominous sign, August knew, and though he wasn't the superstitious type, he tried to blot the heavenly omen from his vision.

"Get inside," the Vehm guard said to him, after binding his wrists together.

August climbed into the back of the Haaglund—a brawny, tracked vehicle used mostly for long-distance trips—and sat down next to April and Charlie. He hadn't seen them for the last few hours and was happy to be back in their presence, even if the circumstances were less than ideal.

"Get any sleep?"

"No," April said. "You?"

"No."

"Me neither," Charlie said.

The vehicle jerked forward, and they were off. August looked through the back window and saw four other Haaglunds trailing behind them. He wondered if one of them held his father—if he was still alive. There were other vehicles too, dozens of them, Nodwells and Sprites and Deltas, all packed with equipment and soldiers and who-knew-what-else. August imagined that from the sky the fleet of vehicles must look like an entire town on the move—desperate to get away, or desperate to find someplace new.

"Amazing," August said. "They forgot to put tape on our mouths."

They were alone in the car, which trailed after the squatty front tractor like a wolf pup biting its mother's tail.

"I guess they're not too afraid of our getting away," August said, seeing that the door wasn't locked.

"Where would we go?" April asked. "There's nothing out here. The entire landscape is perfectly white. I've never seen anything like it."

"And hopefully none of us ever will again," August said. He saw a sorrowful expression cross April's face. "What are you thinking about?"

She gave a cheerless smile. "Alex."

"Alex? Don't you think he might be behind all this?"

"I thought you let go of that idea at the Morgan."

"I did. But that was then. *This*," he said, holding out his bound arms, "is now."

"What about your father?"

"He may be innocent."

"He kidnapped Charlie!"

"We don't know that."

April turned to Charlie. "Did he?"

"I'm not sure," Charlie said.

"But you were with him, right?"

"Stop," August said, halting the inquiry. "Obviously he doesn't know."

"Why, all of a sudden, are you defending your father, a man you haven't even spoken to for twenty years?"

"Because he's my father," August countered. "Why are you defending Alex?"

"Because I'm engaged to him! Remember?"

August was about to reply when he saw a tear in Charlie's eye. "Sorry," he said quietly.

For the rest of the trip he sat in silence, his thoughts drowned out by the rumble of the Haaglund as the husky cart ventured toward the unknown. Neumayer became a dot on the horizon, then disappeared altogether. Hours passed, and August wondered how far they had traveled. There were no visible landmarks—only miles and miles of frosty tundra.

"Are we there yet?" Charlie asked.

As if on cue, the Haaglund suddenly halted.

Charlie looked out the window. "I don't see anything," he said. "Why are we stopping?"

"From what I understand," August said, "Hitler's chamber is *under* the ice. That must be why they have all the drilling equipment."

"I wish they'd tell us what's going on," April said.

"I guess we're not exactly part of the inner circle."

The back door of the Haaglund opened. "Come with me," the guard said.

August, April, and Charlie stepped into the howling winds of the great Antarctic. Snow, blown up from the ice, swirled around them like sparkling tornadoes. The beastly weather made it difficult to follow the guard, who led them toward one of the larger transports.

They climbed inside it and saw Ivy waiting for them. She put up her hand to say *hold on a second* and finished typing some information on her laptop.

"Are we at the right place?" August asked.

"I believe so," Ivy said. "I translated the information we uncovered back at the base to a 3-D computer model. It gave us a more precise position, and here we are."

"So now what?"

"We figure out the way inside," Ivy said. "Right now we're gathering seismographic and sonar information about the area directly below us. We should know soon if we're on the right track."

"What if we're on the wrong track?"

"Don't ask," Ivy warned.

There was a knock on the transport door and a guard entered, holding a stack of papers. "Ms. Segur, you're not going to believe this," he said.

She took the papers and swiftly read through them. "Are you sure this is right?" she asked.

"We ran the information through twice, just to make sure."

August felt his heart sink. He knew it. There was nothing out here but ice. A secret lair? A hidden relic? All just a fable. A myth. And now he'd be blamed for the mistake. But the failure would be more than just embarrassing. It would be fatal.

He turned to April and Charlie. "I'm sorry, guys. I was starting to believe it too. I really thought there might be something out here. But—"

"August?"

Ivy was directly behind him.

He slowly swiveled to meet her gaze. "I know what you're about to say, and I'll take the blame."

"Blame for what?"

"For all that stuff about the Enigma machine and the encrypted city names and . . . well, I could go on, but it really doesn't matter now."

"You're right," she said. "It doesn't matter now. Because we found it."

"Excuse me?"

Ivy handed him the stack of papers. "I don't know how much this data will mean to you, but it appears that the chamber is *huge*. Much bigger than we thought it would be. And there's no doubt about it, it is definitely man-made."

"So it's real?"

"It's real. But that doesn't mean what we've come for is down there."

A guard interrupted. "Ms. Segur, a scan of the chamber's layout has just been sent to your laptop."

"Thanks." She punched a few keys and viewed the image on the screen. "Are any of these vertical tunnels still open?" she asked the guard.

"The commander thinks tunnel three might still be accessible," he said. "The others appear to be collapsed."

"What about the side entrance?"

"Side entrance?" August inquired, barging into the conversation.

"We've been traveling on top of a wide ridge. We suspected that the ridge might contain a side entrance into the chamber in order to accommodate large equipment and vehicles, and it appears that we were right."

"That sounds like a better way in than one of the vertical tunnels."

"Not really. The side entrance is blocked with ice."

"Not for long," the guard said. "One of the helicopters was sent to inspect it. If it looks promising, we'll blast through it."

"Couldn't that cause the chamber underneath us to collapse?" Ivy asked.

"The charges would be targeted very precisely."

"Still . . ."

"Take it up with the commander, Ms. Segur."

"I'd rather not," she said, getting up. She donned her protective gear and walked to the transport's exit. "August, you and your family are coming with me."

"Where are we going?" he asked.

"Where do you think?" She smiled. "We're going in."

FORTY-FOUR

Cleveland wiped the steam of his breath from the helicopter window. He looked out and watched as the Black Vehm soldiers drilled holes in the ice wall that stood before them. Each cavity they made was filled with a charge, wired for remote detonation.

Cleveland turned to Alex Pierson, seated across from him. "If we're lucky, they'll blow themselves to hell, back where they came from."

Alex just shook his head. "Hell won't have them."

The two armed guards beside them didn't seem to mind the comment. One of them even grinned.

Cleveland tugged against the cords binding his wrists. "I can't believe they've kept us alive this long."

"Don't be grateful. They're saving us for the big show," Alex said, examining his matching restraints.

Cleveland guessed the "big show" wasn't as much fun as it sounded. "I'm guessing the Stuhlherr will be there?"

"I would presume so."

"Odd," Cleveland said. "I thought *you* might be the Stuhlherr."

"I thought the same about you," Alex responded. "Of course, you're not completely incorrect in your assessment of me."

Cleveland had heard talk in Germany of a traitor within the Vehm. "You were the one trying to stage a coup?"

"A change in leadership was needed. The old Vehm hides in the dark. The world needs to see exactly how powerful we are."

"Surely you didn't think you could make that happen on your own."

"There were others." Alex stared out the window blankly. "But most of them were terminated in Ushuaia."

Cleveland nodded. "The plane explosion."

"Yes. But I believe they've saved me for a more ceremonious execution."

"Consider it a privilege. Think of all the attention . . . just for you!"

Alex chuckled. "You always had a diabolical sense of humor."

"It's not humor . . . it's nerves," Cleveland said. "I'm worried, and for more than just my own life. I have no idea what they've done with August, April, and Charlie."

"I saw them from a distance back at the base."

"Alive, I hope?"

"Yes, but they didn't look good."

Cleveland stomped his foot in anger, causing the guards to bark at him. "This is all my fault," he said. "I should never have dragged them into this."

"It sounds like you didn't have a choice."

"I *did* have a choice. I could have given the Black Vehm what they wanted."

"I could have done the same. Been a dutiful soldier. Gone along with the cause. But I suppose that's what sets us apart, Cleveland. We're better than that!"

"Or maybe stupider."

"What is it Oscar Wilde said? 'Whenever a man does a thoroughly stupid thing, it is always from the noblest of motives.'"

Cleveland nodded. "True. But speaking of nobility, I question yours. August told me that you and April recently became engaged?"

"We did."

"Did you truly plan on marrying her?"

"Yes."

"And you were going to keep the Black Vehm a secret?"

"Maybe. Maybe not. I was going to test the waters."

"Test the waters?" Cleveland asked. He suppressed a laugh, coughing instead. "What were you going to tell her the first time you came home wearing a black cloak and holding a bloody noose?"

"That's a stereotype. The Vehm has come a long way since the time of Emperor Barbarossa."

"Oh, yes, you're right. They're certainly not the same murderous group they were hundreds of years ago!" Cleveland shook his shackles to the contrary.

Alex's face didn't give any indication of whether he agreed or not. "You know," he said, "if my plans had worked out, I was going to spare your life."

"Glad to hear it."

"Not that it matters now."

"No. But the thought. That counts for something."

"Does it?"

"No," Cleveland said. "I suppose it really doesn't."

The helicopter door opened.

"One minute and counting," shouted a guard. He slammed the door and ran to his post behind a blast shield.

"Better hang on to something," Alex said, bracing himself.

The guards kept their hands on their weapons.

Cleveland gripped his seat. He and Alex exchanged glances.

Everything grew quiet for a moment.

And then.

The boom was startling. The helicopter shook like a toy in the hands of an angry child. Chunks of ice pelted the side of the helicopter. One of the windows shattered. The guards, having dismissed Alex's advice, were dislodged violently from their seats.

"Don't let them get up!" shouted Alex. Though his hands were bound, he pinned one of the guards to the floor with his body.

Cleveland tumbled from his seat, pressing his back against the other guard. "Now what?"

"Just keep them down!"

The guards thrashed underneath them. Cleveland felt as if he were holding down a live shark.

A guard tore the door open. "Get up! Now!" He stepped in and yanked Alex up by his collar, thrusting him into his seat. Cleveland followed closely behind, climbing into his chair before the guard could do the job for him.

The guards rose from the floor. Both of their faces were bloody, their cheeks sparkling with tiny shards of embedded glass. "I'm going to kill you both," one of them said.

"Save your payback for the Court," the guard at the door said. "The blast was successful, so get cleaned up. We'll be going in soon."

Cleveland peered out of the helicopter. Thick black smoke still curled in the air, but as the wind carried it away, he spied a gargantuan set of metal doors. A swastika was emblazoned across the entryway, its red paint looking as if it had been freshly applied.

"It's real," Alex whispered. "Hitler's lair is *real*."

"You doubted?" Cleveland asked.

"Of course I did. It's the curiosity that drove me to such great lengths. And now, to see that the legends were *true* . . ." Alex sighed. "It makes it all the more disappointing that I won't have a chance to enjoy the riches of the discovery."

"A point we can agree on. Yes, I'm afraid the old Stuhlherr doesn't have a history of sharing. Especially with people who've betrayed him."

"Do you know who he is?"

"The Stuhlherr?" Cleveland frowned. "I don't."

Alex didn't seem convinced. "Do you?" he asked again.

Cleveland sighed and finally answered with a voice soaked in regret. "I might."

The guards seemed interested. Cleveland suddenly realized they didn't have any more of an idea than he did as to the Stuhlherr's identity. "We'll know the answer soon enough," he said, to the satisfaction of none.

Everyone exited the helicopter. Cleveland was led to a small transport vehicle. Alex was placed by two of the guards in the seat next to him. They rolled forward, joining the rest of the brigade marching toward the underground ice station. The doors were pulled open by two Piston Bully tractors, and the entire group—save for Cleveland and Alex—entered cheering.

They stared deep into the tunnel that lay before them. "Where does this lead?" one of the guards asked, waving for one of the others to bring him a map printout.

"Straight into the belly of the beast," Cleveland remarked, and promptly received a blow to the back with the butt of a rifle.

The guard who struck him chuckled. "Remember your place, old man."

Cleveland started to respond, but the roar of an engine masked his words.

The members of the Black Vehm immediately lined up in formation. *The Stuhlherr is here!* they murmured.

Tension among the ranks grew. After a pronounced delay, the door to the helicopter swung open, and the Stuhlherr stepped out. His boot crushed the snow, and the sound echoed through the silence of the troops.

"Is it who you thought it was?" Alex asked, his voice barely audible.

Cleveland felt his heart drop. "Unfortunately, yes."

FORTY-FIVE

On the topside of the cliff, the colossal drill carved into the ice, auguring its nose into the ground like a monstrous mosquito in search of blood.

"Stop!" the crew chief yelled. "Stop!"

August watched in fear and wonder as the drill lifted from the earth.

The crew chief ran over to the hole and peered inside. "That took care of it," he said. "You can send the exploratory team down."

"That means us," Ivy said, grabbing August by the arm and leading him to the hole. April and Charlie followed, each led by an armed guard.

"*We're* the exploratory team?" August asked.

"You should be thanking me," Ivy said. "They wanted to slit your throats. I told them you'd make an excellent way to test the structural integrity of the top passageway."

"You mean, because we're expendable."

"That's one way to put it."

"Well, then, thank you."

"You're welcome," Ivy said, pulling on her gear.

With the help of his men, the crew chief lowered a cable down into the hole. "Whoa! That's enough!" he called out. He turned to Ivy. "You going to be the first one?"

"No." She pointed to August. "He is."

"Thanks for giving me the honor," he said.

"Someone has to be the canary in the coal mine," she said.

Two guards began strapping a harness around August's torso. "You're going to have to take these off," he said, holding up his bound wrists.

"Sorry," Ivy said. "I've been specifically instructed to make sure those stay on."

"What if something happens down there?"

"I'm willing to gamble a little."

They connected the end of the cable to the harness.

"Climb in," the crew chief said.

August tugged at the cable until it was taut, then began to ease his way down into the hole. He felt like a giant piece of bait.

"Be careful," April said, as the guards began to attach her own harness.

"Don't worry, Dad," Charlie said as the guards tightened the straps around his waist. "Looks like we're coming right after you."

August's line of sight met the ground; then the rapid descent began. Not having much else he could do, he gripped the cable in front of him tightly, using his legs to bounce off the wall. Above him, the wind whistled across the tunnel entrance, engulfing him in a hollow howl.

"How's everything look?" Ivy called down, preparing to descend.

August stared down between his legs. "I can't see anything."

"What about the tunnel? Does it seem stable?"

For some reason—possibly denial—August hadn't considered the idea that the tunnel could be anything but stable. "Are you saying that the tunnel is going to collapse on me?"

"I'm not saying it *will*," Ivy said. "I'm saying it *might*. But if you think it looks okay, then I'm coming down."

"By all means, come down."

The cable continued to give, and August plunged further down the hole. Ivy was now in the vertical shaft, as were April and Charlie. Two guards followed them, making for a grand total of six snow-stiffened spelunkers. Their cleated boots reverberated throughout the cylindrical antechamber, and August couldn't help but think that they were announcing their impending arrival to whoever—or whatever—might be waiting below.

August reached the bottom of the tunnel. The other climbers absorbed most of the light shining from above, so it was hard for him to tell what type of space he was entering. He knew one thing, though, just from the sound of it. It was huge. He let out a holler, and listened as his bellow took an eternity to decay in the darkness.

"What was that?" Ivy asked.

"Just me," August said.

"Let's keep the yelling to a minimum," she said.

There was suddenly another noise—louder, deeper, and angrier.

"That wasn't you again, was it?" Ivy asked.

"No," August said, panicking. "That was something else. It sounded like—"

The screech of ripping metal stopped him short.

April's voice rang from high above. "The tunnel is collapsing!"

August heard the terrible words just as his feet hit the ground. "Everyone get down here now!" he said, pulling at the cable with the whole weight of his body.

He listened as the steel of the tunnel continued to give way. Then a new sound entered his ears—*screaming*. The cable rippled violently, and August knew that the tunnel was falling in on itself.

"Hit the release button on your harness!" Ivy called out. A second later she slid down to the floor beside August. She reached into her backpack and retrieved two flares, which she set instantly.

Parts of the tunnel—jagged pieces of rock and debris—began to fall. August covered his head and jumped out of the way of a metal shard, which stuck like an arrow into the ground beside him. He looked up at the crumbling tunnel, and his heart sank. April and Charlie were nowhere in sight.

"Are they okay?" he asked Ivy.

"I'm not sure," she said, talking loudly to be heard over the rumbling.

One of the flares sputtered out, and Ivy lit a replacement. As the first brilliant blaze filled the area with light, August saw Charlie slipping down from the ceiling. The boy crash-landed beside him.

"Where's your mom?" August asked.

Charlie was crying. He could barely get the words out. "She's still up there."

"Is she . . . alive?"

Charlie shook his head, unsure.

The rumbling abruptly stopped, leaving only the soft, shimmering sound of settling dust.

"Light another flare," August said, trying to see if April was still stuck in the tunnel.

"That was the last one."

"April!" he yelled, his voice bouncing around the room like a rifle shot.

Nothing.

"April!" he called again.

"Maybe she didn't make it."

"No," August said. "She's still alive. *April!*"

Rock rained down, sprinkling the area heavily in gray soot. And then, like a drop of water traveling down a spider's silver strand, April descended from the ceiling.

Charlie clapped his hands.

August breathed a huge sigh of relief.

She hit the ground, covered from head to toe in a thick blanket of dirt—her hair matted, her clothes torn, her cheeks blushed with streaks of blood.

"You look beautiful," August said, putting his bound arms around her neck. Without thinking, he kissed her.

April's eyes opened wide in surprise.

"I'm sorry . . . I just thought . . ." He awkwardly removed his embrace, letting Charlie have his moment with her.

"Men," Ivy said, coming to his side. "Your timing is always terrible."

"I was late for our wedding," he said, watching as April hugged Charlie tightly, tears streaming down her face. "It was only by a few minutes, but it was enough."

"You're a man in desperate need of prioritization," Ivy said.

A few feet away, the last flare sputtered, then flickered out. They were drowned in darkness.

August didn't waste a second. He leapt in the direction he remembered Ivy to be, crashing directly into her. The two of them toppled to the floor, and August managed to get behind her, using his restraints to choke her. She fought hard against him, but he held on tight.

"What are you doing?" Ivy screamed.

"Holding you hostage," August said. "We've been brought down here to be killed, haven't we?"

"I don't know," Ivy said. "I just follow orders."

"Why?"

"I have my reasons."

"I don't care about your reasons. All I care about is getting me and my family out of here."

Small shards of ice continued to rain down lightly around them, the shimmering effect sounding like a million tiny bells quivering in unison.

"There is no getting out," Ivy said. "The one way we had to escape has just been sealed shut."

"What about the other team? Obviously they just blasted their way in."

Ivy laughed. "Do you have any idea how many men must have been sent in by now? The Black Vehm will soon be swarming this place. There's no chance of getting out of here. At least not *alive*."

August relaxed his grip. He knew she was right.

His hesitation gave Ivy the opportunity she had been looking for. She shot an elbow into August's stomach, and he groaned in response, falling from his vantage point. She was on him in a heartbeat, her blade held against his throat. "Give me one good reason I shouldn't kill you right now!" she said.

Suddenly, fire exploded from the walls of the cavern. August saw for the first time the vastness of the space, the grandeur of its design. He recognized immediately what it was, having seen a similar—although considerably smaller—version of it earlier at the Morgan Library. It was a Vehm Court, but on a massive scale, like a Roman stadium sunken into the earth. Enormous stone steps lined the room in long rows, providing seating enough for thousands. And at the head of the court, lit by the torches that lined the macabre cathedral, was a towering golden Virgin Mary, her gaze heavy with grief for those upon whom she was forced to pass judgment.

A man, bound at the wrists, entered through an arched doorway at the back of the room. Ten heavily armed Vehm guards flanked his sides.

"I'll give you a reason," the man said to Ivy. "He's your brother."

"Dad?" August said.

Ivy stood up. "Dr. Adams?"

"What are you talking about?" August asked.

"I don't know which of you this will be bigger news for," Cleveland said, as one of the guards brought him forward. The rest of the Vehm soldiers positioned themselves around the perimeter of the room.

"You're my father?" Ivy asked, stunned. "Did you know about this back when we worked together?"

"No," Cleveland said. "I never knew the possibility even existed. I need to explain. August, I should warn you, this might be hard to hear."

"I think I can take it," he said, feeling the place on his throat where Ivy had almost slashed him.

The Vehm guard checked Cleveland's restraints, then stood watch with his gun in the ready position. He didn't seem to care if they talked. August guessed it was because he knew they'd all be dead soon.

"I was in college," Cleveland explained. "There was a young lady, a daughter of one of the professors. She was kind and gentle, the antithesis of her father, who was harsh and judgmental. I was working on a project in the school library. It was late, and I guess I lost track of the time, because before I knew it I was locked inside. I probably could have found a way out, but before I did, I met someone else who had gotten locked inside—the professor's daughter. As fate would have it, the project I was working on was for her father's class. We talked about him for hours . . . actually, *she* talked about him, and I listened. It was shocking, hearing such spiteful words spilling from the mouth of such a beautiful girl. All the talk about her father must have stirred up some deep-seated need for revenge, because the next thing I remember was her lips pressed against mine. I really don't need to tell you the rest, as the result of the encounter is standing before me."

"She got pregnant and you never knew?"

"Soon after our escapade in the library she left the school, never to be seen again. I overheard her father saying something about not trusting the men at the school with such a beautiful girl. I guess he was right."

"What was her name?"

"Elizabeth Worth."

Ivy held her hands up to her face as her body convulsed. She sobbed, overcome with emotion. "They lied to me," she said. "Everything they told me was a lie."

August wasn't sure what to do. A part of him felt like he needed to put his arm around Ivy and console her. She was his half sister, after all. But another part of him remembered that she almost sliced him in two. The decision was finally made for him by Cleveland, who walked over and—encumbered by his restraints—gave her an awkward embrace.

"So you have a sister?" April asked.

August looked to see that she and Charlie now flanked his sides. "Apparently," he said. "Kind of weird, actually. I always thought of myself as an only child. I gave myself a lot more leniency because of that."

"You mean for your megalomania?"

"I was going to say disposition to greatness, but I suppose your version works too."

"I'm not sure how to feel about all of this," Ivy said, backing away from Cleveland. "I've been waiting for this moment for so long, and now that it's here, it frightens me."

"It frightens me too, Ivy."

She spun around to see who was speaking. "Stuhlherr!"

"Tie them up," the Stuhlherr said.

The Vehm guards sprang into action.

Suddenly, the entirety of the Black Vehm army spilled into the arena. They flooded the room and filled the seats. Apparently they were here for a show. And August had a good idea who the star performers would be.

"Where did they come from?" he asked Cleveland.

"They blasted in through the side wall. I was with them. The unit you were with on the topside gave them detailed radar information, so it didn't take long for them to find everything they were hoping for in this godforsaken Nazi tomb."

"That's hardly a fitting title for this fascinating facility," the Stuhlherr said.

August grimaced as he and the others were shoved to the floor and bound together. "This is a death trap. You make it sound like a day spa."

"You're probably right. I doubt the festivities to come will seem like much of a vacation for you and your family."

"You're heartless."

"On the contrary. I must admit to you that I feel a warm pitter-patter in my chest, seeing your whole family brought together. Such a shame that the reunion will be so short-lived."

"I should have known it was you," August said.

The Stuhlherr smiled. "You couldn't have known. You thought I was dead."

FORTY-SIX

August hated surprises. He remembered coming home from school when he was young, when his mother was still alive, and walking through the front door to find that his home had been invaded.

"Surprise!" the people yelled.

He knew he was supposed to laugh with joy, or simply be amused that so many people would come to celebrate his birthday, but for some reason he did the opposite—he cried and ran out of the room. His parents consoled him, thinking that he was embarrassed by the event, and at the time, August agreed with them. It *was* embarrassing. But later in life, as his self-awareness grew, he looked back and realized that it wasn't embarrassment that caused him to fall apart. It was the loss of control.

The revelation of the Stuhlherr's identity had a similar effect, sending a strong message to August, one he couldn't escape: *You are not in control.* He had been tricked, duped, sent on a wild goose chase. He felt stupid for being such an easy target.

"Are you surprised to see me here?" Dr. Rothschild asked.

"I have to admit that I am. It's not every day that you get to see someone die twice."

"Twice?"

"Once back at the library," August said, "and once when I push you inside that vicious statue."

Dr. Rothschild seemed to enjoy the bravado. "And how do you plan to do that?"

"I haven't got that part figured out," August said. He and the others—April, Charlie, Cleveland, and Ivy—were all tied together in a circle on the floor. "But I'll get back to you once I do."

"Please let me know," Dr. Rothschild said. "In the meantime, the Black Vehm needs to deal with the first of the accused."

Two Vehm guards—the *Freischoffen*—entered, holding Alex Pierson between them. He was beaten and bloody and looked like he hadn't slept since leaving New York.

"Alex!" April cried out. She struggled against the ropes, then suddenly went silent.

"What's going on?" August asked. He didn't have to wonder long. The Freischoffen marched by with Alex wedged between them. But he wasn't in a wheelchair. He was walking.

"Wait!" Alex said, halting the procession. "Before the court declares its judgment, give me a chance to talk with April."

Dr. Rothschild considered Alex's proposition. "Go and get her," he said, motioning to the Freischoffen. They dutifully marched over and untied April.

She ran to Alex. Her mouth opened, but no words came out. "You can walk?" she finally whispered.

"I should have told you," Alex said, his voice soaked in regret. "About six months ago, during rehab, I began to feel pain in my legs. For most people that would be bad news, but for me, it was the first sign that I could possibly walk again. I wanted to tell you about it right away, but the doctor encouraged me not to."

"Why?"

"He had countless stories about people who thought they were recovering, only to suffer a major relapse after telling all of their friends and family. He convinced me that it was better to wait it out, to see if the effects were permanent. For better or worse, I took his advice. Things continued to improve. After only a few months of work, I was walking again."

"But why didn't you tell me then?"

"Because I had a plan," he said. "I wanted to wait until the wedding. I wanted to walk down the aisle and see your face light up. It was going to be my wedding present to you."

Tears formed in April's eyes. "Oh, Alex, you should have just told me."

"I know that now," he said.

"But there have been other lies too," April said.

"There have been things I held back," Alex said, clarifying. "I've been a part of the Black Vehm for a long time. But I didn't want to tell you about it until I was declared the new Stuhlherr."

Dr. Rothschild entered the conversation. "You see, April, your fiancé was trying to wrest control of the Black Vehm away from me. And he almost succeeded. First he shot my closest ally, Christopher Vallodrin. Then he killed his wife, also a dear friend. Next he undermined one of our operations here in Antarctica. And the story goes on. It will take us weeks to figure out the depths of his betrayal."

He turned to the golden statue of the Virgin Mary. "Fortunately, there is a stiff penalty for traitors. The others who were a part of this futile scheme have already seen judgment. But I wanted to save Alex's sentence for this marvelous court."

April grabbed Alex's hands. "Were you trying to kill me too?"

"Of course not," he said. "I was trying to save you."

"Save me? This is saving me?"

"I know it seems absurd, but I thought you'd come around to the idea, and even embrace it eventually," he said. "But maybe it was never going to work between us anyway."

"What do you mean?"

"You can't love two people at once," he said.

"Two people? What are you talking about? *August*?"

"Don't pretend you don't understand. Just listen to the way you talk about him sometimes. Or notice the amount of time you spend getting ready if he might stop by. You're still in love with him! I hoped your feelings for him would go away, but they haven't. And something tells me they never will."

April gripped his hands more tightly. "You're wrong," she said. "I might care for August, but I don't love him."

"It doesn't matter now," Alex said, as the Freischoffen wrenched him away from April.

"No!" she said.

Dr. Rothschild lifted his hands and turned to face the court. "The time has come for the Virgin to declare her judgment!"

The Freischoffen pushed Alex down to his knees. He kissed the Virgin's feet. The floor began to rumble. Then he raised his eyes and watched the statue break open, revealing its treacherous innards.

"Please!" April said. "You can't do this to him!"

Dr. Rothschild pointed to Alex. "He is a traitor, but he is also a true member of the Black Vehm. He takes his punishment willingly."

"Alex!" she screamed.

The Freischoffen pulled Alex to his feet. He seemed at peace with his inevitable future. He didn't even resist when they threw him into the horrible machine and shut the doors.

April fell to the ground.

"My brothers!" Dr. Rothschild said. "There was a dragon in our midst, but the Virgin has carried him away!"

The doors of the statue opened. Alex was gone. Only a crimson stain remained.

The Freischoffen crossed the room and began working on the cords that held Cleveland.

"Leave him," August said. "Take me next."

The Freischoffen ignored him.

"It's okay, Son," Cleveland said. "I made my bed. Now it's time for me to lie in it."

The Freischoffen took him away. All August could do was watch as they paraded his father toward the golden statue.

FORTY-SEVEN

Cleveland was forced to his knees.

"Kiss the Virgin's feet," Dr. Rothschild said.

Cleveland knew what was coming next. "Why would you do this to me?" he asked. "We've known each other for so many years."

"I have no choice. You placed yourself in harm's way."

"But doesn't our friendship mean more than the Black Vehm?"

"Friendship?" Dr. Rothschild said, spitting the word out. "The Black Vehm is *family*."

Cleveland looked back at August, April, Charlie, and Ivy. "No. It's not," he said. "I just wish I could have known that long ago."

The Freischoffen put their hands on him.

"Stuhlherr!"

Everyone turned to see who had suddenly barged in on the party.

"Stuhlherr!" said the Vehm guard standing in the archway. "We found the Spear!"

A gasp went out from the members of the Black Vehm.

"Is it the one and only true Spear?" Dr. Rothschild asked.

"Yes. There's no doubt."

"Then bring it here."

A murmur swept the crowd.

"Silence!" Dr. Rothschild said. He turned to Cleveland. "Your judgment will have to wait. But not for long."

The Freischoffen took Cleveland back to the place where the others, including April, were tied up, adding him to the pile like another log thrown on a fire.

A moment later four men entered, carrying a box that resembled a narrow coffin. The case was marked with a series of symbols, the most significant of which was the swastika placed in its center. They brought the package forward and laid it at the feet of Dr. Rothschild.

"Open it," he said.

AUGUST WATCHED AS TWO OF THE MEN SLOWLY BEGAN TO LIFT THE LID from the box. Inside, on a bed of red silk, lay a simple wooden spear tipped with a gray steel point.

"Hand it to me," Dr. Rothschild said.

The two guards glanced at each other, as if questioning the authority of the Stuhlherr.

"Hand it to me," Dr. Rothschild repeated, his voice thick with lust for the weapon.

The guards delicately placed their fingers beneath the spear and raised it from its grave. They placed it in the outstretched hand of Dr. Rothschild, who took the lance and held it over his head victoriously.

"For those of you who do not know the history of the Spear," he called out to the congregation, "it has marked the greatest leaders in our history. Hitler owned it, and before that, the Holy Roman Emperor Sigismund owned it. These were his words, spoken so long ago: 'It is the Will of God that the Imperial Crown, Orb, Scepter, Crosses, Sword, and Lance of the Holy Roman Empire must never leave the soil of the Fatherland.' As your Holy Judge, your chosen Stuhlherr, I plan on making good on his pledge. The Spear will soon be returned to its rightful place—in the land of the *New* Holy Roman Empire!"

The entire room stood to its feet, and the cries of the men consumed the silence that had endured since the beginning of the gathering.

Dr. Rothschild waited for their cheers to die down. "But a spear isn't enough. It's a powerful symbol, but in the world we live in, symbols aren't enough. There was a time when the SSGG, symbol of the Vehm, brought fear to those who saw it. And there was a time, much later, when the Nazi's adoption of the blessed runes—the SS—created a panic in men's hearts. Those days, I'm afraid, have passed. In their place is a quest for *real* power. And that, my brothers, is what this court truly represents.

"We stand at the center of Hitler's greatest achievement. Not only this hallowed chamber, but also this entire underground estate. It has stood here for decades—suspended, frozen—waiting for its mountain king to awaken and return. That time has come, and this underground empire has been reclaimed. It's even bigger than we imagined, and it hides the key to gaining control of the world economy.

"It's been called 'black gold'—a fitting description for the treasure of the Black Vehm. *Oil.* A resource that becomes scarcer every day. We stand over the final frontier—the last of the supergiant oil fields. Hitler planned on taking it for himself. But where he failed, we will succeed. Fifty billion barrels—literally trillions of dollars' worth of oil—lie under our feet. It is ours for the taking. By the time the world has figured out what we've done, it will be too late. There are no rules here. Antarctica has no government to protect it, no police to hold us back. The United States has no authority here, and I doubt they will have the blessing of the world if they try to throw us out. So rise, my brothers, rise! Rise and tell the world that this is our *destiny*!"

Once again, the men stood. The sound of their voices was deafening.

August shivered. The idea of the Black Vehm having a stranglehold on the world was terrifying. Their control of the oil in Antarctica was frightening enough, but there were other effects too, things that could prove to be even more damaging. Refining the oil would surely melt the ice of the southern pole, wreaking havoc on the coastlines of the world. Cities would be swept under the sea, and millions of people would lose their homes and businesses, and their lives as well. It would be like Katrina, only on a global scale.

Dr. Rothschild dropped the lance to his side, looking to August like some hideous form of Polykleitos's famous *Doryphoros*, the Spear Bearer. He was a fallen god, a distorted deity, a myth gone awry, and there was nothing that could stop him—nothing within a thousand miles of the forsaken acropolis.

It would only be a matter of minutes before they would heave his father at the mercy of the golden Virgin. And what then? Who would die next? Would it be him? April? Or even—God forbid—Charlie? And what about Ivy? She had been nearly wordless through the entire ordeal. He didn't find fault with her silence, though. She had obviously gone to great lengths to discover who her family was. And now that she had finally found them, they were being taken away.

Family. It meant something to Ivy. Did it mean something to him?

"April?"

"Yeah."

"We're not going to make it out of here."

"I know."

"I just . . . I thought I should probably tell you . . ."

"August."

"Yes?"

"You don't have to say it."

"But this is the only chance I'll have to tell you how I feel about you."

"I already know how you feel about me."

"You do?"

"Of course I do."

"Then is there anything left to say?"

"Not besides *good-bye.*"

"Then good-bye."

"Good-bye."

August sat there, tied up, pent up, wishing he could say more. Even if this was the end, he needed April to understand fully how he felt. He loved her. And he needed her to hear it, not just know it. He started to say something when one of the Freischoffen slapped a piece of tape across his mouth.

"The Stuhlherr doesn't want to hear your screams when you die," he said.

August could only nod in response.

Dr. Rothschild began another speech. He was a ranter, apparently, and wasted no breath on anything other than the future goals of the mighty Black Vehm. August's gaze moved to his father, who had been taken and placed between two guards to the side of the statue. He saw his father's mouth moving. He was saying something.

Tell me when he's in front of the statue.

August shot him a confused look. The tape prevented him from being able to ask any questions.

His father's lips moved again. *Tell me when Dr. Rothschild is in front of the statue.*

August understood the words, but not the meaning. Why did it matter? He looked closer at his father's position. Because of the statue's open doors, he didn't have a clear view of Dr. Rothschild. But, again, why did it matter? His father answered August's puzzled expression.

I'm untied.

August's expression changed to alarm.

Don't worry about me. Just tell me when.

August focused on Dr. Rothschild. He was in a fever pitch, delivering the speech of his life. The members of the Black Vehm digested every word like a ravenous pack of wolves.

August blinked his eyes rapidly, hoping his father would understand the signal. *Now! Now! Now! Now!*

Cleveland darted forward, the guards beside him too startled to stop him. He raced to the front of the statue, and just as Dr. Rothschild held the spear high, Cleveland shoved him into the murderous womb of the Virgin.

Dr. Rothschild shrieked in disbelief as the blades closed in around him. Cleveland shut the statue with a clang, the metal doors resounding like a cymbal crash. The Freischoffen were on him instantly, but it was too late. Dr. Rothschild—the Black Vehm's precious Stuhlherr—was dead.

FORTY-EIGHT

He would kill them all.

It was what Alex Pierson had asked him to do, if things went wrong. And they certainly had gone wrong.

Conrad felt bad for his felled employer. His intentions were good. Though he had been accused, tried, and killed as a traitor, he wasn't one. A traitor was someone willing to hand an institution into the hands of another. But Alex had believed that the current leadership was doing exactly that—and he intended to stop it. He wanted to make the Black Vehm stronger than they ever had been—a true Fourth Reich—a world power to be reckoned with.

He'd almost succeeded. But almost was never close enough, was it?

Instead, he paid the ultimate penalty.

He was a martyr, clearly. He perished willingly, an act to show the other members of the Black Vehm that he died for a noble cause. They could have responded by picking up his mantle and extinguishing the existing Stuhlherr. Instead, they did nothing but look on with glazed expressions. They were zombies, caught up in the excitement at having claimed the final stronghold of the Nazis.

Conrad hated mindless religious zealots like the Vehmites. It would be a joy to extinguish them.

Luckily, he had been on the Black Vehm's exploratory team earlier in the day. He had seen the layout of the compound, the digitally crafted blueprints of its myriad tunnels and chambers, drafted from radar information the topside team had gathered. He was amazed at the complexity, the far-reaching capacity of the structure. He wondered if someone had remained behind, a true Iceman, closed away from the world, waiting to be discovered.

But there was no one home. Every nook and cranny was searched and found empty, void of any sign of life. It was a vast Nazi ghost town, an undiscovered country waiting for its fruits to be plucked—the fruit, of course, being the hidden bounty of oil beneath the clandestine fortress.

The oil would now be his salvation, his way to rid the earth of the Black Vehm. He felt a little out of control, a little out of his mind. He wanted them all to suffer. He wanted them all to burn. It was funny, really, the idea of creating a literal hell beneath the ice.

He punched a few buttons, listening as the small motors in his artificial left hand whirred in response. The panel before him began to glow. He had been amazed, earlier, to find that the Nazis' underground refinery was still operational. There was even gas remaining in the tanks. And there were rows and rows of them, all perfectly preserved by the optimal conditions. There was practically no humidity, and the frigid climate kept everything in near suspended animation.

The switch house to control the tanks was one of the first discoveries after the Vehm soldiers had blasted their way inside. They were amazed at how simple it was to start the torches burning in the Virgin's chamber, which symbolically was the right thing to do. Now, Conrad knew firing up the *whole place* was the right thing to do.

Getting away would present a challenge. There was a great risk he wouldn't get out alive, but the constant threat of death was simply something that made life more interesting.

Not that it would matter if he disappeared from the earth. He wouldn't be missed. He didn't have a home. No family to speak of, and even fewer friends. The only people who would notice his absence would be the ones glad to see him gone.

He scanned the controls. In addition to six other languages he understood German, so the task of figuring out which levers to pull wasn't too difficult. It would only be a matter of minutes before the entire place was filled with the volatile vapors created by the refinery. He made sure to keep the excess gas flow away from the Virgin's chamber until the last possible moment. The torches there would be the final link in his plan, his mad method of complete destruction.

He sat back in the chair and waited for the gas to fill the multitude of chambers that comprised the Nazi ice station. The needles on the gauges pushed into the red, and he reached under the control desk and ripped out the wiring. He didn't need an alarm going off, alerting everyone of his actions.

He heard a wheezing sound from the vent above him and found that freezing air was rushing in from the outside. It was obviously some precautionary measure set up years ago to keep people like him from gassing the place.

How annoying.

He searched for an override control, then realized he was simply going to have to climb into the vent and take care of it himself.

He pushed a chair against the wall and shimmied his way into the air shaft. It wasn't long before he found the source of the problem—a folding metal gate that lay open, allowing the free flow of air from the outside. He climbed past it, then kicked the gate shut with his feet, sealing the chamber and the gas inside. He suddenly realized that in solving that problem, he'd also found a solution for getting out. All he had to do was crawl to freedom. But he knew he'd better act quickly. All too soon, the entire Nazi compound would be swallowed in flame and turned swiftly to brimstone.

FORTY-NINE

Chaos descended upon the Virgin's chamber. Cleveland struggled against the Freischoffen, who had pinned him to the ground. Another assemblage of guards circled August and the others, in case they tried to make an escape of their own. Things were looking grim. Then something strange happened.

It was the most unholy thing August had ever witnessed. A hissing sound emanated from the base of the statue. And then, like lightning striking the tallest tree in the forest, the fire from one of the torches leapt through the air toward the statue.

The Virgin began to burn.

And that was only the beginning of the inferno. Within seconds, the ceiling was a swirling mass of reds and oranges. The torches on the wall exploded with force, sending a spray of brimstone over the Vehm army. Soon the entire assembly was engulfed in flames.

The Freischoffen lost Cleveland in the confusion. He rushed to August and unbraided his ropes. The two of them quickly turned their attention to the others, who were soon also free.

Confusion climaxed in the room. The fire burned out of control. The members of the Black Vehm fought the fire, but it quickly raged out of control.

Ivy waved for the others to follow her. "This way!"

"Do we have any other choice?" August said, watching as the sea of flames swelled behind them.

"Over there," she said, pointing twenty yards ahead at a square grate set in the floor. A Vehm soldier came at them from the side. Ivy gave him a swift kick to the solar plexus, and he fell lifelessly to the floor.

"Hurry!" August yelled, hustling everyone forward. He lifted the grate, and one by one they slipped into the narrow expanse beneath it. August climbed in last. He was pulling the grate closed over him when a mangled hand grabbed him by the collar. He slammed the grate down hard on the hand and heard every finger bone crack in unison. The hand retreated, and August fell into nothingness.

The floor was only a few feet below him. He heard the others running forward, down the tunnel. He quickly followed, hoping they weren't headed toward a dead end.

"I spotted this shaft on the last data readout," Ivy said, somewhere ahead. "I think it was used to wash out waste."

"We're in a sewer duct?"

"Something like that. If I'm right, it should lead outside."

"And if you're wrong?"

She didn't answer.

As August advanced, he felt the shaft growing warmer and warmer. "Ivy!" he said.

"What?"

"Hurry up!"

The heat grew, and he heard a sound behind him like a tornado trapped in a tunnel.

"Ivy!"

"We're almost there! I can see it!"

There was a loud bang as she slammed her fists against the vent to the outside, followed by a crash as the vent fell to the ice. Everyone tumbled out. August trailed just in time to escape the geyser of fire that erupted from the shaft.

"Come on!" Ivy said, running to a black helicopter.

They were located outside the ridge where the second Black Vehm unit had blasted their way in. There were ice-equipped vehicles everywhere, all lying dormant, their owners dying a slow, hot death only a short distance away.

They climbed aboard the helicopter, and Ivy started up the engine. A massive explosion rocked the earth, and the helicopter shook.

"What was that?" April asked.

"I think Hitler's compound is about to disappear," August replied. "Let's just hope we don't vanish with it."

The helicopter's engine whined, and the rotor began to turn. Faster. And faster. The ground rumbled again, shaking the helicopter with earthquake force.

"There's not enough time," Ivy said.

"Don't give up now," Cleveland said, putting a hand on her shoulder.

She throttled the engine, and the helicopter whirred to full speed. She grabbed the stick and yanked the spinning bird skyward.

"Go faster! Go faster!" Charlie yelled, his face pressed against the glass, his eyes fixed on the increasingly volatile view below.

"I'm trying!"

The helicopter crept up further into the blue, but not far enough to evade the effects of the underground compound blowing up like an A-bomb. The chopper convulsed as it battled to stay upright in the heavens. Ivy waged war with the stick and miraculously kept them afloat.

The shaking subsided, and Ivy banked the craft to view the damage below. Where the underground compound had once been, there remained only a steaming chasm leading into the earth. It reminded August of a volcanic depression, an abyss on such a large scale that it was almost otherworldly, like looking at a crater on the moon.

"No one could have survived that," Ivy said. She wasn't saddened to say the words.

"The Black Vehm is gone," Cleveland said. "And with it go the Nazi map and The Gospels of Henry the Lion."

"And the Spear of Destiny," Charlie said. "Don't forget about that."

As they headed back to the Neumayer base, August watched the smoke curl up into the sky, highlighted by the radiance of the setting sun. Hundreds of lives were represented by the ashen pillar, including two individuals he had once considered friends—Dr. Rothschild and Alex Pierson. It was hard for him to imagine that they were both gone. It was even harder for him to believe that they had become so filled with evil. What happened to them? How had they fallen into such madness? August knew he would probably never have the answers.

An eternity passed before they reached the base. They didn't even consider staying the night, or even one more minute. They boarded the Starlifter they had arrived in, and with Ivy at the controls, they took off into the twilight with thoughts of home.

FIFTY

"Dad?"

"Yes?"

"I've got a few questions for you," August said. "Is that okay?"

Cleveland smiled. "Why not? We've only got about twenty-four hours of flying still ahead of us. I think I can spare the time."

"It's about The Gospels of Henry the Lion," August said.

Cleveland frowned. "What about it?"

"Where is the book?"

"Where is the book?" Cleveland repeated. "You know perfectly well where it is. It's smoldering in the ice with a pile of corpses."

"No, not the copy. I mean the real Gospels of Henry the Lion."

"My boy, what on earth are you talking about?"

August surveyed the cabin of the airplane. Besides Ivy, who sat in the captain's chair, everyone was fast asleep on the floor. He turned to face his father. "My first clue was that you sent me the book in the mail. I don't care how much duress you were in, I have a lot of trouble believing that you would send a book like that to me through the mail."

"I didn't have a choice! Sending you the book was the only way I could escape Germany."

"If that were my only clue, maybe I'd believe you."

"What other evidence do you have for this ludicrous charge?"

"I've handled a lot of old books in my time, just like you. And, also like you, I have an innate ability to guess how old a book is, no matter what I'm told by the book's owner. You know how it works. A person tries to sell a book to you claiming it's a hundred years old when it's really only half that age."

"It's happened to me many times, yes."

"But you never got fooled, did you?"

"Every once in a while, I suppose."

"When? Name me one time."

"Oh . . . I think there was one time in . . . hmmmm. I'm sure I could think of something if I really tried."

"No, you couldn't," August said. "You couldn't because it's never happened. I understand, because it's never happened to me either. The book you sent me was the most perfect clone of The Gospels of Henry the Lion that I've ever seen, but it was still a fake. There was just something about the feel of the paper. The tone of the inks. I couldn't figure it out exactly, but there was just something that told me it wasn't the real thing."

Cleveland huffed. "So you're basing all this on a gut reaction? I'm sorry, Son, but that's not enough rope to hang me by."

"No," August said. "It's not. But that's not where this ends. My final confirmation came at Neumayer, after we first landed in Antarctica. We had just figured out the connection between the map and the book, and were using the map's coordinates to decrypt the codes in the book."

"A brilliant idea, I should mention."

"Thanks. It was a team effort."

"Well, you know how—"

"Dad?"

"Yes."

"Quit trying to throw me off track."

"Fine."

"As I was saying, we were using the map coordinates. With it, we began to extract letters from the book. The first code was AZJRPQMQKYSYU. Does anything about that code seem wrong to you?"

"Not necessarily."

"Not necessarily?" August said. "What about the letter J?"

"Well . . . perhaps it was just a glyph variant. Did you think of that?"

"This wasn't a glyph variant," August said. "It was a J. I saw it myself. Right away I thought, *That's funny. I wonder what a post-Renaissance character is doing in a book dated from the twelfth century.* And then it hit me. The book wasn't from the twelfth century. It was from the twentieth century."

"Preposterous!"

"I think the Nazis created a perfect copy of The Gospels of Henry the Lion. Perfect except for one thing: They changed some of the characters to fit the map key. But they were careful. Only the closest of inspections would have uncovered the disparity."

"I guess I missed it."

"You missed it? You spent all that time in Germany studying the book, and you somehow overlooked that critical detail? Now, if you were inexperienced, I could see how the information could have slipped by you. But you're a pro. Maybe the world's best. Which means that right now, you know where the true Gospels of Henry the Lion is located."

"I don't know what you're talking about," Cleveland said.

But August caught a glimmer in his eye, a nearly undetectable glow that told a different story. Or maybe he was just imagining things. "Where is it?"

"If the alleged *real* Gospels of Henry the Lion existed, then I suppose it would be in a safe location, far out of the reach of the Black Vehm or anyone else who would try to lay hold of it." He stared deep into August's eyes. "That includes you, Son."

"Me?"

"Your track record isn't exactly spot free."

August nodded. "You don't have to worry about me. I've learned my lesson."

"You have? Then why are you questioning me about the book?"

August knew that this marked the end of the interview. "Am I ever going to know the truth?"

His father smiled. "Someday you will."

EPILOGUE

Three Months Later
New York, NY

"Happy birthday to me!" Charlie walked in the front door and shook the leaves from his shoes.

"Charlie! You know better than to do that!"

"Sorry, Grandma Rose."

"Don't worry about it," she said, ushering the boy in from the cold and closing the door behind him. "I can't stay too mad at the birthday boy! Just come into the kitchen for some hot cocoa."

"With extra marshmallows?"

"Sorry, ate 'em all," August said, entering.

"Dad! Did you really eat them all?"

"Just kidding."

"Marshmallows aren't something you should joke about, Dad."

August made a solemn face. "Yes. Very serious matter, marshmallows."

The two of them laughed as Grandma Rose handed them mugs of the rich liquid. They clinked them together and sipped deeply.

"Happy birthday, kid."

"Thanks, Dad."

"How old are you now? Five? Six?"

"Dad! You know how old I am!"

"Seven? Are you eight? I just can't keep up anymore."

Charlie just shook his head, exasperated.

The doorbell rang.

"I'll get it," August said. He opened the door and discovered his father, laden with gifts.

"Grandpa!" Charlie said, running toward Cleveland and wrapping his arms around him. His eyes registered the colorful stack next to him. "Oh, wow! What did you get me?"

"It's rude to ask someone that," August said, admonishing his son. He turned to his father. "So . . . you heard the boy. What did you get him? Did you get that new game system he's been asking for?"

"You mean that *you've* been asking for?"

"Shhhhh!"

Cleveland removed his jacket and hung it on the coatrack. "You'll just have to wait and see."

"Can I open a present now?" Charlie asked, practically salivating on the wrapping paper.

"You're supposed to wait till after dinner. But I suppose you can open one."

"Yes!"

"Just one!" August said, holding up his index finger to reinforce the point.

Cleveland tapped his chin thoughtfully. "If you can only open one, you might want to make sure it's *this* one."

Charlie began shredding the gift. "A new Nintendo! I can't believe it!"

"I can't believe it either!" August said. He cupped his hand to Cleveland's ear. "Thank you."

"It's for the boy, you know."

"Oh, yeah, of course. It's just that it would be a shame for that wonderful game system to sit idle while Charlie is sleeping."

Charlie ran into the kitchen to show Grandma Rose the game system. August knew she would try her hardest to act excited about it.

The doorbell rang again. August opened the door.

"I'm here!" April said, stepping in.

"I'll take those." August put down his mug and helped her with the bundles of groceries layered in her arms. He leaned in and kissed her on the cheek.

She grinned. "That was nice."

"There's more where that came from."

"I bet there is . . ."

August watched as she joined Grandma Rose and Charlie in the kitchen. He still couldn't believe things were going so well for the two of them. Not long after they returned from Antarctica, they had begun seeing each other on a regular basis. On a romantic basis, in fact. There were no drastic plans, but things were moving in the right direction. It was good for the two of them, and even better for Charlie. The boy beamed every time he saw them together. Sometimes he just put his arms around them and held on for dear life, as if he were physically gluing them together, never to be separated again.

Grandma Rose popped her head in. "It won't be too much longer and we'll start eating."

"I can't wait!" Cleveland said. "Whatever you're cooking smells amazing."

"What are we having?" August asked. "You didn't burn another lasagna, did you?"

"Stop teasing." Grandma Rose threw a dish towel at him. "I did that one time. You'll make Cleveland think I'm a terrible cook."

August leaned toward his father. "She's an amazing cook," he whispered. "But I don't want her to leave, so I keep making her think there's room for improvement."

"Oh, you're awful," Grandma Rose said, returning to her work in the kitchen.

August and Cleveland retired to the living room.

"Have you heard from Ivy?" August asked.

"Not for over a month. Apparently there are still some details she needs to sort out."

"Details. Yeah. I'm sure those 'details' include some things I don't need to know about."

"Give her a chance, August. She saved our lives."

"I know. But I still have a lot of questions."

"We all do. But there comes a time when you have to move on. Which reminds me . . ." Cleveland smiled. "I have some news!"

"News?"

"Yes. Dr. Rothschild's permanent sabbatical has left an opening at the New York Public Library."

"And you've taken the position?"

Cleveland spread his arms wide. "You're looking at the new head of the Rare Books Division!"

"That's great, Dad. Congrats. Really."

"You'll have to come visit me. They have a Gutenberg Bible that would blow your mind. You must come see it."

August nearly fell out of his chair. "Actually, I don't think they'll let me near that. But I'll definitely stop by."

Cleveland handed August a heavy, rectangular package. "Here. This is for you."

"A gift for me?"

"I know it's Charlie's birthday, but maybe you can think of this as an early birthday present for yourself. And for April. Hold on a minute." He left the room and returned a moment later with her. He seated her next to August and clapped his hands together. "This is for *both* of you."

August and April glanced at each other.

"Do you have any idea what this is?" August asked.

"No. Do you?"

August picked up the box and was about to shake it when Cleveland stopped him. "You won't want to do that," he said.

"Is it a bomb?"

No one laughed.

"Sorry," August said. "Bad joke for this family."

"Let's just open it," April said, beginning to tear the wrapping paper.

August joined her, removing the rest of the paper and lifting the lid from the gift box. April reached in and took hold of the item inside, which was swathed in bubble wrap. It was a book.

"What is it?" August asked, almost scared to uncover the sizeable tome.

"Go ahead," Cleveland said. "Take a look."

Slowly August unraveled the protective outer layer. He gasped. "Dad. How is this possible?"

Tears formed in the corners of April's eyes. "Is this really ours to have?"

"It is."

August stared at the magnificent work in his hands: The Book of Chronicles from the Beginning of the World. It was the book that brought his parents together. It was the book that brought him and April together.

But the book had a dark side too. It was the reason he and his father had been estranged for so many years. "I don't understand. How is this yours to give?"

"Think back in time. Do you remember the name of the man who purchased the book from you?"

"You mean after I stole it from you?"

Cleveland nodded.

"I could never forget. I believe he was Turkish. His name was Mr. Harold Yariganti."

Cleveland reached out his hand. "Lord Imaginary Hart, at your service! Very pleased to finally meet you in person."

"But . . . no . . . it can't be."

"You never knew?"

"Never," August said, holding the book in his hands as if it were the Holy Grail.

"You've always been obsessed with puzzles. I figured that you'd solve that anagram within seconds."

"Mr. Harold *Yariganti*? Why did I not suspect something?"

"Maybe it was the paycheck that distracted you."

August was suddenly appalled. "That had to have been your entire life's savings."

"And then some, actually."

"I feel horrible," August said. He held out the book to his father. "I can't accept this."

"It's called a gift, Son," Cleveland said, gently pushing the book away. "And besides, it's not just for you. It's for both of you. You'll have to share. Think you can learn to get along?"

August turned to April and smiled. "We can try."

FURTHER MYSTERIES

While writing my first novel, *Illuminated*, I discovered that the best mysteries were the real ones. The same holds true for *House of Wolves*. It's what got me interested in writing these books in the first place, and it's why I continue to dwell on them long after they've been committed forever to the page.

House of Wolves will probably haunt me for a very long time, because I was unable to crack its greatest secret. For an entire year I tracked down an endless trail of information, only to continually hit dead ends. The question: Who possessed The Gospels of Henry the Lion when Sotheby's sold it in 1983?

At first, I hoped that Sotheby's would provide me with the answer. I contacted their office in New York, as well as the one in London. Both locations were extremely helpful, but were unable to provide me with the information I wanted due to confidentiality.

Sotheby's was, however, kind enough to send me some documents to help shed some light on the situation. One was a partial copy of *Art at Auction: The Year at Sotheby's 1983–84*. On page 164, writer Christopher de Hamel elaborates on the mystery surrounding the Gospels of Henry the Lion:

> *... the manuscript created something of a sensation simply because it had been lost for nearly fifty years. It was bought from Prague Cathedral in 1861 by the last king of Hanover, and his descendants still owned it in 1933, when Sotheby's wrote to ask if there was any chance of the book being sold. After the Second World War it was offered for sale secretly (both the British Museum and the Pierpont Morgan Library turned it down) and acquired by a group who never declared their identity or its whereabouts. Part of the aura of the manuscript was certainly due to its blazing reappearance after half a century of darkness.*

Did you read that? The group never declared their identity! Another dead end. But wouldn't the group make itself known once the sale was completed? Read on, my friend, this time from page 165 of *Art at Auction*:

> *The bidding for lot 50 on 6 December opened at £1 million and went up in increments of £100,000 and £200,000 to £7,400,000. The sale lasted two and a quarter minutes. The great book was bought at last by a consortium on behalf of the West German government. On 11 January 1984 a camouflaged military aeroplane was sent from Berlin especially to collect it; at about three in the afternoon the manuscript arrived back in Lower Saxony, the dukedom of Henry the Lion.*

What? A camouflaged military aeroplane? The story just gets crazier and crazier. I'm sure someone out there knows who this clandestine group of sellers was. (Maybe *you* know, dear reader!) Some research suggests that the Nazis stole The Gospels of Henry the Lion from a bank vault during WWII. I used that "best guess" while plotting *House of Wolves,* as it played perfectly into the mystery surrounding Hitler and the secret Nazi lair hidden beneath the ice of Antarctica.

Secret lair? Surely that's made up, right? Once again, I must confess that I am not the originator of the idea. There are dozens of books and Web entries that attest to its existence. Though the notion that the Nazis were hiding UFO technology can't be upheld with evidence, there are plenty of documents that support the American belief that the Nazis had a stronghold there.

One such document is the October 1947 edition of *National Geographic.* Inside is an article by Rear Admiral Richard E. Byrd, titled "Our Navy Explores Antarctica." It is a fascinating account of the U.S. exploration of the frigid underworld, with diagrams of the Navy's plans as well as pictures of their exploits. The mission was called Operation Highjump, and if you Google the phrase you'll find enough speculative articles to rattle your brain for days. Conspiracy theorists suggest that the true nature of Operation Highjump was to search for concealed Nazi compounds. Were they right? Was there a U.S. cover-up? I'll leave that to you to decide.

But what about the Spear of Destiny? How does that tie in? There are many accounts of Hitler's quest for the lance, most promoting the idea that he found the lance (or an ancient copy of it) and hid it in Antarctica. For further reading, I would suggest *Adolf Hitler and the Secrets of the Holy Lance* by Col. Howard A. Buechner and Capt. Wilhelm Bernhart. It's a lot of fun, whether you believe that Hitler got his grubby mitts on the fabled spear or not. (And for comic book fans who want to learn more about the Holy Lance, try picking up a copy of the four-part series *Indiana Jones and the Spear of Destiny.*)

In *Illuminated* I shed some light on two secret societies—the Orphans and the Order of the Dragon. In *House of Wolves* I explored another ancient, yet equally real, secret society—the Holy Vehm. There aren't too many accounts of the brotherhood, but if you search long enough, you'll find plenty of troubling information. One book available in most bookstores is *Secret Societies: A History* by Arkon Daraul. (Did you notice that two of the characters in *House of Wolves* bear the same last name—Daraul? Now you know why!) The Vehmic oath, which Dr. Cleveland Adams spoke aloud in the novel, is as accurate as any of the recorded accounts I have uncovered. It's almost as chilling as the Iron Maiden statue of the Virgin, which is another thing taken from historical fact, not fiction. That they developed and built such a device of torture seems unthinkable. But I thank them for saving me the trouble of dreaming one up myself!

Do the Vehm still exist? They certainly existed within the ranks of the Nazis symbolically—research supports the idea that the Nazi *SS* resulted from the fear-inducing history of the Vehmic *SSGG*. But what about today? I read an account by a man named Philip Gardiner, who claimed to have met some of them in Berlin. I e-mailed him to validate the meeting. He e-mailed me back: *The tale was true*. Scary stuff.

As I hopefully have shown you by now, I'm not a wizard creating dragons from thin air. I'm a collector, much like August Adams, rummaging through forgotten shelves for lost treasure. But I suggest—or rather, I *dare* you—to find the real treasure for yourself. You'll be rewarded for the effort. And in any case, let me know what you find . . . it could be the inspiration for my next novel!

Peace.
Matt Bronleewe

ACKNOWLEDGMENTS

I'm writing these acknowledgments on New Year's Eve. It seems fitting. I started writing *House of Wolves* last January, and now here I sit, nearly a year later, looking at the (nearly) completed document lying next to me on the kitchen counter. (I wish this were cause to celebrate, but I am reminded that I need to start writing my next book right away!)

New Year's Eve is the perfect time to reflect, especially upon the many people who have contributed to the completion of this book. As I think about those I've met along the way, and all the suggestions and comments and clues and ideas that came as a result, I'm reminded of the legend of the Stone Soup. I started with a small pebble of a story. But you—my dear friends and family—provided the meat and potatoes (and carrots and cabbage too), and as a result, I ended up with something much richer and more flavorful than anything I could have dreamed up on my own. To all of you I owe my gratitude. We wrote this together.

Karin. My wife and best friend. You are more beautiful every day. Your love and dedication amaze me. Your willingness to let me ramble on and on about secret societies and hidden relics and all the crazy ideas that might connect them . . . well, I simply can't tell you how much it means to me. You are an absolute saint. I relish hearing your thoughts after you give every page its official first read. For this and a million other things—thank you!

George. Cole. Grace. My three fantastic little bundles of energy and joy. Nothing lights up my face like you do. You each own my heart. For each disappointment I face in life, you provide a multitude of replacements, those little magical moments that make each day special. This journey would be meaningless without you. May our adventures be many!

Tom and Bev (aka Mom and Dad). You are the authors of my life! Thank you for raising me in an environment filled with encouragement and love. I strive every day to emulate your patience, your principles, and your passion for life. I'm proud to be your son.

Bronleewes. Swansons. Stansburys. Pardys. Duvalls. Funks. Cassells. Dochertys. Eatons. Kaskiewiczs. Sheffs. Monahans. Rockefellers. Sanfords. Taylors. And more. To my family everywhere, far and wide, thank you so much. It's been humbling to hear such positive words from you all. You are the first line of soldiers, putting books in the hands of everyone you know. You make more fans for me than I could ever win for myself. It's so wonderful to be related to each and every one of you!

Mike Hyatt. You lead the charge at Thomas Nelson with such conviction and fervor. It's so inspiring to watch you forge ahead through uncharted waters while others struggle to keep up. Thanks for taking the time to encourage me. I look forward to the many books we'll team up for in the future!

Allen Arnold. I'm still scratching my head in wonderment over why you've allowed me this awesome opportunity. Thank you so much for your encouragement and enthusiasm. You're an endless source of out-of-the-box ideas. Just when I think I've got it all figured out, you push things to a new level. What fun we're having!

Amanda Bostic. I don't think I've ever seen you without a smile on your face. You take all my crazy ideas and—somehow—turn them into reality. Thanks for helping me become a better writer—one word at a time—and for patiently dealing with my multitude of missteps. I can't wait to get started on the next book!

Jennifer Deshler. We rival each other for the number of exclamation points we can fit in an e-mail . . . ha! You make the extra calls and spend the extra hours, and I'm the one who reaps the benefits. I'm indebted to you for the contribution you've made in putting my name on the author map (if such a thing exists). I look forward to watching you light the fuse on a thousand more book campaigns!

Katie Schroder. Welcome to the team! I'm excited to work more with you . . . and help get the word out about the new book. Your cheer is infectious!

Mark Ross. Thanks for including me in the process and letting me contribute in creative ways. You make these book covers rock!

Natalie Hanemann. Ami McConnell. Lisa Young. Becky Monds. Jocelyn Bailey. And everyone else at Thomas Nelson who makes these endeavors possible . . . thank you. It's been a joy to work with you all. You provide light to a dark world!

L. B. Norton. The editing stage is supposed to be nightmarish. So how is it that you've made it seem like a walk in the park? A wild park, for sure, filled with roller coasters and tilt-a-whirls . . . but what a great time we've had! I've enjoyed working with you immensely, and would jump at the chance to do so again. I'm a lesser writer without you. You're a coach, a cheerleader, and a star quarterback all wrapped up in one!

Charlie Peacock. You started this whole adventure. All I did was mention that I was "starting to do a little writing. . . ." You connected me with the people that turned my dreams into a reality, and for that I am forever grateful.

Don Pape. What can I say? You've been my champion since word one. You took my inklings, my tiny notions, and helped turn them into something meaningful. Through it all, I've gained more than a great person to work with . . . I've gained a lifelong friend.

Rick Christian. You provide vision to the visionaries. You lead Alive Communications with compassion and respect, and it shows in the lives of the people who surround you. Thanks for taking the time to impart some wisdom to me. I'm excited for the voyage ahead!

Lee Hough. Agent of the Year! You deserve it! I'm constantly impressed with your bounty of talents and your insight in dealing with the most precarious of situations. I've enjoyed our time together tremendously. Thanks so much for sharing your heart and soul, and for constantly putting everything on the line to move onward and upward!

Dave Steunebrink. When I think things are falling apart, you see opportunity. When I believe things are on the brink of disaster, you see another chance for success. And all while never cutting corners, never letting your integrity dip even an inch. You make optimists look like worrywarts. I'm lucky to have you as a manager, and even more fortunate to have you as a friend.

Lani Crump. What a year it's been! This book would have stalled at the gates without you involved. I throw a thousand new ideas at you every day, and somehow you find workable solutions. How do you do it? You jump back and forth from task to task, balancing and juggling and maneuvering all the little pieces until they fall neatly into place.

Lori Hughes. You tracked down people all over the world for me. Thanks for taking on some difficult tasks . . . and conquering them all! I really appreciate everything you did to help improve this novel.

Kami Rice. You tore through dozens of thick encyclopedias and dusty books and forgotten Web sites to dig up anything you could to make this book better. You were tireless in your researching efforts. And you chased every rabbit I sent your way! Thanks for lending your talents to this project.

To Everyone Else. Thanks to the librarians, the researchers, the historians, my author friends (Ted Dekker, Robert Liparulo, Eric Wilson, Chris Well, Allan Heinberg, Sigmund Brouwer, Reed Arvin, Xan Hood, Tom Davis, Robin Parrish, and Dan Haseltine, to name a few!), my studio friends (Jeremy Bose, Shane Wilson, Paul Evans, Sarah Deane, and all the interns too!), my friends on MySpace, Facebook, LinkedIn, and whatever other Web sites I've joined both purposefully and accidentally, and anyone else I've somehow failed to mention.

And finally, to a loving and inspiring heavenly Father, without whom nothing would be possible.

Thank you!
Thank you!
Thank you!

A prelude to Matt Bronleewe's next novel,

THE DEADLY HOURS

CONRAD EASED THE VEHICLE TO THE SIDE OF THE STREET AND watched as August Adams walked by his window. And what was this? A special surprise! April was with him. She was cute enough, but definitely not his type. Not that it mattered. He didn't have time for a relationship right now. Not while things in his life were so volatile.

He watched as August and April swung their grasped hands, strolling down the street without a care in the world. Conrad even thought he heard them laughing. But they wouldn't be laughing for long. Soon their lives would be a living hell.

Of course, providing such misery wouldn't be easy. It would require patience, persistence, and months of planning and preparation. The job before him made escaping Hitler's lair in Antarctica seem like a cakewalk in comparison.

But the effort would certainly be worth the prize waiting for him at the end. An unimaginable treasure. And a powerful secret that would shock the world.

Suddenly, August stopped in his tracks.

Conrad sank in his seat. Had he been spotted? Had August somehow sensed that he was being watched? He slowly reached over and retrieved his gun from the bag in the seat beside him. It was stupid to get so close this early in the game. He swore under his breath and promised himself to be more careful in the future.

August kissed April gingerly on the cheek.

Conrad smiled. How sweet! He genuinely felt sorry to cut such true affection short. But somehow he'd get over it. Being rich beyond belief would certainly help.

He watched the hapless couple wander into the distance until they were just a dot on the horizon. He'd see more of them soon. But not until the other pieces of the puzzle had been set firmly in place.

He put the car into drive and pulled away from the curb, departing for his destination on the north side of town—the Cloisters, a little-known reserve of ancient artifacts.

Someone was waiting for him there. Someone he didn't want to leave waiting long. The countdown had already begun, and there was still much to do before time ran out . . .

COMING AUGUST 2009